MINE TO TAKE

Mine to Take

Sofia Barnes

I've always loved to play dress-up.
Creating fake weddings was my childhood pastime.
Now it is my dream come true.

I've finally been handed my first client.
But nothing could prepare me for who greeted me when I walked in.

He was my first kiss, my first everything, including my first and only heartbreak.
Now I have to plan his wedding.

Matthew Petrov

My family is filled with hockey royalty.
From my grandfather to my uncle to my father.
Now it is my turn to work my way up the leaderboard.
I had everything I've ever wanted in my life.
Or so I thought.

Nothing could prepare me for coming face-to-face with Sofia.
I knew her inside and out.
She knew my inner secrets.
Two years ago, I let her go, and now she's planning my wedding to someone else.

They say time heals old wounds. They lied.
Maybe she is just mine to take.

BOOKS BY NATASHA MADISON

Southern Wedding Series
Mine To Kiss
Mine To Have
Mine To Cherish
Mine to Love
Mine To Take
Mine To Promise
Mine to Honor
Mine to Keep

The Only One Series
Only One Kiss
Only One Chance
Only One Night
Only One Touch
Only One Regret
Only One Mistake
Only One Love
Only One Forever

Southern Series
Southern Chance
Southern Comfort
Southern Storm
Southern Sunrise
Southern Heart
Southern Heat
Southern Secrets
Southern Sunshine

This Is
This is Crazy
This Is Wild
This Is Love
This Is Forever

Hollywood Royalty
Hollywood Playboy
Hollywood Princess
Hollywood Prince

Something So Series
Something Series
Something So Right
Something So Perfect
Something So Irresistible
Something So Unscripted
Something So BOX SET

Tempt Series
Tempt The Boss
Tempt The Playboy
Tempt The Ex
Tempt The Hookup
Heaven & Hell Series
Hell And Back
Pieces Of Heaven

Love Series
Perfect Love Story
Unexpected Love Story
Broken Love Story

Faux Pas
Mixed Up Love
Until Brandon

SOUTHERN WEDDING SERIES TREE

Mine To Have
Harlow Barnes & Travis Baker

Mine To Hold
Shelby Barker & Ace

Mine To Cherish
Clarabella & Luke

Mine To Love
Presley & Bennett

Southern Family tree
Billy and Charlotte
(Mother and father to Kallie and Casey)

Southern Chance
Kallie & Jacob McIntyre
Ethan McIntyre (Savannah Son)
Amelia
Travis

Southern Comfort
Olivia & Casey Barnes
Quinn (Southern Heat)
Reed (Southern Sunshine)
Harlow (Mine to Have)

Southern Storm
Savannah & Beau Huntington
Ethan McIntyre (Jacob's son)
Chelsea (Southern Heart)
Toby
Keith

Southern Sunrise
Emily & Ethan McIntyre
Gabriel
Aubrey

Southern Heart
Chelsea Huntington & Mayson Carey
Tucker

Southern Heat
Willow & Quinn Barnes

Southern Secrets
Amelia McIntyre & Asher

Southern Sunshine
Hazel & Reed Barnes
Sofia

Copyright © 2023 Natasha Madison. E-Book, Audio and Print Edition

All rights reserved. No part of this book may be reproduced or transmitted in any form or by any means, electronic or mechanical, including photocopying, recording, or by any information storage and retrieval system, without permission in writing.

This is a work of fiction. Names, characters, places and incidents are the product of the author's imagination or are used factiously, and any resemblance to any actual persons or living or dead, events or locals are entirely coincidental.

The author acknowledges the trademark status and trademark owners of various products referenced in this work of fiction, which have been used without permission. The publication/ Use of these trademarks is not authorized, associated with, or sponsored by the trademark owner.

All rights reserved

Cover Design: Jay Aheer

Editing done by Jenny Sims Editing4Indies

Editing done by Karen Hrdicka Barren Acres Editing

Proofing Julie Deaton by Deaton Author Services

Proofing by Judy's proofreading

Cover picture by: Britt & Bean Photography

Formatting by Christina Parker Smith

mine to TAKE

Southern Wedding Series

NATASHA MADISON

One

Sofia

I jump when the alarm starts blaring from the island behind me. The milk I was pouring into my coffee cup is spilled on the side. I put the frother down at the same time the blaring of the alarm gets louder and louder as the seconds tick by. "I'm coming, I'm coming!" I shout to the alarm, which at this point is so loud I'm about to cover my ears like my baby cousins do when I squeal out that I love them so much.

I press snooze by mistake. "Dammit," I say, grabbing my phone and walking back to the sink. Turning on the warm water, I wet a cloth before cleaning up the spilled milk. "I think this is good luck," I mumble to myself before rinsing the cloth off and returning back to the coffee. I grab the cup and bring it to my lips, smelling the aroma of coffee fill my nose makes me smile right before I take a sip. "That's like little pieces of heaven," I whisper before walking back up the stairs toward my bedroom.

When I get to the landing, I look over the railing that lets you see down into the great room. This house is massive, way too big for me, but try telling my grandfather that. The house was bought, and security was installed before I saw it. "Don't argue with me," he said softly, "I'm old." Which made me snort-laugh. My grandfather is a lot of things, but old and delicate aren't any of them. If you looked up Southern gentleman in the dictionary, there would be a picture of him.

I shake my head thinking of the last time we had the conversation, missing him just a touch more today. As I make my way toward my bedroom, I walk down the hallway. I look at all the pictures I lined up on the wall of my family. The middle picture on the wall is the whole family. It took some hours to rein everyone in, then about a hundred pictures to get the picture. My great-grandparents stand in the middle while everyone is around them. Around that picture is a picture of me with my parents taken at graduation day. My father with his arm around me, pulling me closer to him as he looks at my mother with all the love I've always seen in his eyes. It's right next to the first picture we ever took together. I'm sitting on the horse with him behind me, his shirt is off, and he's got his arms wrapped around me. From the story they told me, my parents shared one night together before my father joined the military. Wires got crossed, and he found out about me the first time we met. Even in the picture, we have the same smirk. From that day on, he made sure I knew how much he would have changed the past. I smile when I think about him, sending him a text.

Me: Just sending you a message to say I love you, Dad.

I walk into the two open French doors and go straight to the bed. Turning on the television that faces the bed, the soft light fills the darkened room as I watch the news before turning on the Investigative Discovery Channel. I'm in love with my bed, something my grandmother, Olivia, set up for me. The whole house actually has her stamp of approval. I want to say I helped pick the things in my house, but I didn't, she did it all. It's not because I didn't want to, it's more that I know how much she loves this stuff. Literally, the whole family just lets her do things because it makes her happy. My grandfather let her style one of their homes in all white. They even call it the White House, and no one wants to stay in it.

The phone rings, and I pick it up, smiling again when I see it's my dad. "Hello."

"Hello, Sunshine." He calls me by my nickname like he always does. "Why are you up so early?"

"It's not early." I look down and see that it's six ten. "Okay, fine, maybe it's a bit early." I bring the cup of coffee to my lips. "But the first day on the job is a big deal."

"It is," he agrees, and I hear the truck door close on

his side of the phone. "You've been dreaming about this since you were seven, and Grandma Olivia bought you a mini wedding dress."

"It was the best gift I ever got." I sigh, remembering all the time I spent in that dress. If I wasn't in school, I was in that dress. I prepared so many weddings with so many of my stuffed animals, it was crazy.

"I bought you a horse and Pops bought you a pink tractor," he points out the other two gifts that are also on the *best gift I ever got* list. To say I was spoiled was an understatement.

"Okay, fine," I huff, "you got me good gifts also."

"Good," he says, chuckling. "Okay, I'm heading into the gym."

"Have a great day, Dad. I love you."

"Love you more." He hangs up the phone, and I place mine beside me.

I take another sip of my coffee and press the button to open the shades, the sunshine coming straight in. Slipping off my bed, I walk over to the window, looking out at the trees that are all around me. This is definitely not where I thought I would end up. When I was in high school, I dreamed of going to Chicago, LA, or New York and planning events. I wanted to be in the glitz and glamor. To set up the best events I could, with a whole team under me. But instead, I came to visit my aunt, Harlow, and fell in love with this town. One weekend here and all my plans went out the window. Plus, Harlow's sisters-in-law owned their own event company. It's as if it was fate. I finish my coffee. "Time to meet my first ever client."

Three hours later, I'm walking up the steps of the little bungalow they built with five offices where the bedrooms would be. The living room and dining room are where the waiting area is, it's filled with pictures of past events they have done. I take a second to look at the side of the barn. Or at least what looks like a barn. Once you get inside, you'll find rustic wooden floors and exposed wooden beams that can be dressed up. It can fit up to five hundred and fifty people. Right behind the barn is a kitchen where the caterers can set up.

Taking a deep breath, I turn the handle on the door to start my very first day as part of the team. "Surprise!" is screamed by Clarabella, Shelby, and Presley.

I put a hand to my chest in shock. "What is this?" I ask them as I step into the cool room.

"Why did we think a surprise was a good thing?" Clarabella looks over at her sisters.

"I specially said that it was stupid, but no one listened to me," Shelby states, folding her arms over her head.

"I don't even think I was part of the conversation," Presley complains to them, and they glare at her. The three sisters have become my closest friends. I would do anything for them, and I know they have my back.

"Well, whatever it was," I say, smiling at them, "it's wonderful."

Shelby steps forward. "Are you ready?" she asks, and I just look at her confused.

"For today?" I say, putting my hand to my stomach. The nerves have been going since I opened my eyes at 5:00 a.m. "Not even a bit."

"What time is the appointment?" Clarabella asks.

"Ten," I reply, my fingers shaking a bit. "So I have an hour to get all my ducks in a row." Even though I went over the file three times already.

"Well, we will have drinks as soon as you land this client," Shelby announces, and I just hold up my hands in the air. I walk over to the side and step into my new office. It was an empty office before I came in, and slowly, when I was interning with them, it became mine.

The white L-shaped desk sits against the right side of the room. A vase of white peonies is at the corner of the desk with a gold card holder in front of it. Behind the desk is a chalkboard with the calendar on it. There are also frames about love and romance, as well as a couple of events I helped plan while I was still in school. My computer is set up on one side of the desk, right next to a white and gold lamp that is just for show. The pink chair faces the door, and two more pink chairs face the desk. I put my purse on one of the chairs before I walk over and sit down.

I turn on the computer to see if anything came in from when I left home until now. I pull up the email we got from Helena again. When it came in, Shelby came by and handed me the file and said, "Good luck."

I read the interest form she filled out on the website. It really doesn't tell me much. She left blank spaces everywhere. I put together a couple of pictures from past weddings that we have done to give her an idea of what we can do. It's an hour later when I push off from my desk and get up to take one look at myself before I make my way into the waiting room.

Standing in front of the long mirror, I look at myself, the baby-blue pants fit me tight around the hips but loose all the way down to my ankles. A matching thick belt around my waist is paired with a white, sleeveless bodysuit. A matching blue jacket completes the look with neutral, peep-toe Christian Louboutin shoes. My brown hair is parted down the middle and then tied at the nape of my neck in a ponytail. I twirl the end of the ponytail, placing it over my right shoulder. "It's showtime," I tell myself, grabbing the file and walking out of my office.

I take two steps out before I hear some commotion coming from the side. I peek my head in and see that kids have now joined the party. Everyone is sitting down and talking. "I'm going to go and wait for the couple in the front," I say, trying not to be nervous but probably failing miserably.

"You've got this," Clarabella reassures me from behind her desk.

"Just remember, none of us knew what the hell we were doing," Presley says as she nurses her son on the couch, while her other son is bouncing in the saucer right in front of her. Irish twins are what we call them. Shelby calls them a walking birth control sponsor.

"And if you need anything, we are here," Shelby reminds me, and all I can do is nod at her.

"I've got this." I try to sound more sure of myself than I really am, ignoring the way my hands shake just a bit and the fact that my stomach is rising all the way to my throat, making me feel like I'm going to throw up. "I've got this."

"Who runs the world?" Clarabella asks.

"Boys and girls, according to Violet," I joke with her.

"Get out of my office and go nail that couple." She points at the door and turns and walks out.

My stomach has been in knots since last week when they handed me this client. I know I can do it. I just have stage fright. "Here we go," I say, as I pull open the door to the room where the couple is standing with their backs to me.

I look down at my nude heels for a second, and when I look up, everything inside me stops. There, standing in front of me with a blond girl holding his hand, is my first love, Matthew Petrov.

Two

Matthew

They say in life there are moments you will always remember. Like the first time I scored a goal at seven, in overtime, in a hockey tournament. Or the time when I got drafted into the NHL. There is even the time when I suited up and scored my first goal as an NHL player. And then there will be this moment. Definitely this moment.

My hand is in Helena's as we look at a picture of an elaborate altar. She is going on and on about it and how she would have added color into the flowers. When I hear the sounds of heels clicking behind me, the sound coming closer and closer to us, I can see the woman approaching in my peripheral vision. The sun comes into the windows all around her. My head turns in slow motion or maybe that is just how I feel it happens. I blink once, twice, three times, wondering if my head is playing tricks on me.

My vision is almost blurry at this point, or at least that is how it feels, until the woman is standing closer to us. It can't be. Again, I blink my eyes, hoping to fucking God that this isn't happening to me right now. I even lift my free hand and rub my eyes to see if it's all in my head. Sadly, it is not.

My heart is beating so fast and so loud in my ears that all I hear is the thumping it makes. My hands are now getting sweaty, and the heat is rising to the back of my neck. She is looking down at her feet, and when she finally looks up, she spots me and we make eye contact. Full-on eye contact. There is no denying it's her and not some long-lost twin that everyone has. You know the one everyone is always telling you about but probably doesn't exist. Yeah, that one.

She stops mid step, and if you didn't know her, you wouldn't see the way her eyes light up for one second before the wall comes down, shutting it out. Her eyes go from mine to Helena and then down to our hands. My head is screaming at me while I keep asking myself the question over and over again. What the fuck is she doing here?

"Hello," Sofia greets when she is standing in front of us. "You must be Helena." She looks over at her and extends her hand to her. "I'm Sofia."

"It's so good to meet you," Helena says, "this is my fiancé." She hugs my arm with her hands and looks up at me. "Matthew Petrov. We call him Matty."

I look over at Sofia and see her blue eyes get a tad darker when she looks at me, everyone calls me Matty, except for Sofia. She always called me Matthew or MVP, but that was as a joke every time I won a game. "Matty." She extends her hand to mine as if she doesn't know me, as if we've never met. I don't know how I feel about this. On one hand, I should be happy I don't have to explain this to Helena, and on the other hand, I'm pissed. Which I shouldn't be, especially with the way things ended. "It's a pleasure to meet you." My hand moves up and clamps on to hers, and I swear to God it's like I'm being electrocuted or something. "Thank you so much for coming in today," she states, and I can't help but take her in. Her brown hair is pulled back in a ponytail, but I see the end of her hair is curled and drapes over her shoulder. Her smile is as fake as can be. Trust me, I spent two years knowing the ins and outs of Sofia. No one knew me better than she did. No one knows me better than she does, is more like it. Not even Helena, I don't know, and I can't even explain it. With Sofia it was just so easy, me being me never fazed her. "And congratulations on the engagement," she says, and I see her eyes looking straight down at the ring on Helena's finger.

"Thank you so much," Helena replies, and my tongue just keeps on getting bigger and bigger in my mouth. She picks her hand up to look at the diamond in front of her before she turns to smile at me. All I can do is smile back at her. "It was a special surprise."

I almost laugh because it was not a surprise at all. In

fact, she left me subtle messages since the second week we started dating. She was at the peak of her prime and wanted to get married when she would look amazing in her pictures. We've been together for nine months and this was the next step, so I thought why not. "That sounds very romantic," I hear Sofia say, shaking my head.

"Shall we sit down and go over a couple of things?" Sofia suggests, pointing at the round table to the side. "Would you care for anything to drink?" She looks at Helena first.

"I'll have a bottle of water," Helena says, "sparkling if you have it, if not still is good." She nods her head and then has to look over at me. I'm waiting for it, and when she does, I really wish that she hadn't. Her eyes pierce my soul and make my heart stop in my chest. "He usually has still water."

"Coming right up," Sofia declares, turning and walking away from us, disappearing around a wall. I swear, if I could, I would let out a deep sigh and hang my head. I really want to get the fuck out of here. Seeing her it's just, I don't even know what to say. I'm surprised. I'm shocked. I'm blown fucking away that she is here. Not only is she here but I'm also going to sit down and discuss my wedding with her. I close my eyes; not even sure I want to think about how things would be if the roles were reversed. I would not be okay with any of this. I guess I would be happy for her, maybe, not sure. My head is going around and around, I'm literally hanging on by a thread.

"What is wrong with you?" Helena hisses to me. "You

are acting so freaking weird."

"No, I'm not," I scoff at her, shaking my head while my whole body wants to pick up the chair and throw it across the room, right before I run out of here. "I'm fine," I confirm, walking over to the round table Sofia pointed at before walking out. I pull out a chair and sit down, my foot moving up and down, the nerves just radiating in my body. "Sit down." I pull the chair beside me out. "Before you agree to anything…" I want to tell her more, but I hear the clicks from Sofia's shoes coming again.

She holds a silver tray in her hand, coming into the room and spotting us sitting down. She walks over, placing the silver tray down on the table. "I didn't know if you wanted lemon or lime." She smiles at Helena as she puts two small plastic containers on the table, each with lemon and lime. "I also didn't know if you wanted it chilled or not, so I got you both," she goes on, putting the four bottles on the table, along with a crystal glass for each of us. She sits down in the chair facing us, and I grab the closest water bottle to me, not noticing if it's cold or hot or fizzy or not.

"Okay, before we start," Sofia says. She looks at Helena and then looks at me, and I think this is it. This is the moment she is going to say we dated. My heart speeds up even faster and my fingers squeeze the water bottle hard in my hand. She places her hands in front of her, crossing her hands together. Poised. Controlled. Classy. Unlike me, who is now starting to sweat and wondering how long this is going to be. "Why don't we see if we are compatible?"

Oh, you're compatible all right, my head screams, laughing.

"That sounds amazing," Helena says as she grabs a bottle of water, opening it. "As I mentioned to you before, my fiancé is Matthew Petrov." I close my eyes, knowing where this is headed, I think I even roll my eyes at her. "I'm not sure if you are familiar with his name?"

"No," Sofia answers, and my eyes snap back to her as she looks at Helena. "That name doesn't ring a bell." I want to pfft out and remind her of all the times she called my name while we were together. Dammit, now is not the time for this. I shouldn't be this affected by her. Not after all this time. I close my eyes to erase the memories that all of a sudden have come full force.

"He plays hockey for the Carolina Whalers," Helena announces proudly from beside me, and I look over to see her brown eyes shining. Her blond hair is neatly styled with a curl at the end, she is the picture of Southern beauty.

"I don't watch hockey," Sofia says and all I can do is look at her, waiting for her to look at me so I can silently call her a liar. "I prefer football instead." She smiles at Helena, who just smiles and shrugs her shoulders.

"Well, because of his schedule, we would have to be married in the summertime," Helena explains and all I can do is nod at that.

"Do you know what services you are looking for?" Sofia asks her and Helena just looks at her dumbfounded. "There are wedding planners and there are wedding coordinators." God, I missed her voice. "A wedding planner assists you in planning the entire wedding or specific wedding activities. What we do is provide you with a list of vendors for the wedding and you tell us if you have a specific vendor in mind, and we will handle all contracts on behalf of you." Helena looks over at me. "I will be there every single step of the way as soon as you sign the contract until the last guest has left your wedding reception."

"What does a coordinator do?" Helena asks, and I literally want to get the fuck out of here as fast and as soon as I can. My body feels like it's been asleep for the past two fucking years, and all of a sudden, every single sense in my body has been awoken.

"A coordinator is there for you for a specific period, be it a month before the wedding or even sometimes two weeks before the wedding. You provide the list of venues and then I make sure everyone shows up," Sofia says and then she starts talking about other things, but I can't even concentrate on what she is saying right now. The only thing I can do is beg for this to be over.

"That is something to discuss." I finally find my words and look over at Helena. "We should discuss things and then we can get back to you." I turn now to look at Sofia, seeing her smirk and then look down. Everything about her is polished, from the softness of her makeup to the way her nails are manicured. She was always so put together, except when we went riding horses. It was the only time she would let her hair down. It was one of her favorite things to do. I wonder if it still is.

"That is the best way to do it," she suggests and

pushes away from the table now. She stands up and Helena follows her. I put the bottle of water back down on the table, untouched except for the time when I was squeezing the shit out of it.

I stand as Helena walks in front of me to stand in front of Sofia. "If you have any questions," Sofia says as she walks out with us, "please give me a call. One of the team members will be happy to assist you in any way we can." She stops walking when we are in front of the door and my heart speeds up for a whole different reason. I'm leaving her and I'm not ready.

"Thank you so much," Helena replies, holding out her hand to shake Sofia's, "for taking the time to sit with us and discuss things with me."

"This is what I'm here for," she responds, extending her hand to shake Helena's. "Mr. Petrov," she says with a tight smile, "it was a pleasure meeting you."

My hand extends to shake hers, and unlike before, I squeeze her hand just a touch. "We will be in touch."

She lets go of my hand, but it feels like she's still holding it as my hand falls to my side. "Well, whatever it will be. Congratulations on the engagement and the best of luck for the wedding."

I nod at her and look at Helena, putting my hand at the base of her back and ushering her out of the place. The door closes behind me and it takes everything I have not to look back. "We aren't using her."

Three

Sofia

I wait for the door to close and then literally count to ten before I let out the huge breath I have been holding in. I look up to the ceiling, blinking as I breathe in and out to get my heart rate down. I'm surprised I didn't have a fucking heart attack. "What. The. Actual. Fuck," I curse out loud as the adrenaline I had running through me slowly leaves and the reality hits me. "This is not happening." I walk on shaky knees, looking in the offices and seeing no one is there. I hear chatter coming from the end of the hallway and walk into our makeshift conference room.

The three of them sit around the round table, each looking down at the paper in front of them. I walk in and place the manila folder on the table. "I quit," I declare to all of them, pulling out a chair and sitting in it because my knees are going to give out. I'm so filled with nerves I quickly get back up and start pacing the room. "I'm not doing that." I point at the file on the table and feel like it's a ticking time bomb before quickly exiting the room.

"Oh, shit," I hear Presley say from behind me as the sound of the three of them getting up fills the room.

"She needs some of the sweet tea," Clarabella says in a whisper but not really whispering.

"This does not bode well," Shelby says under her breath.

"That I do." I point at them. "That is exactly what I need." My feet make their way straight into my office and toward the bottle of sweet tea I keep hidden in the closet for emergency situations. Grabbing the bottle, I unscrew the gold cap before I take a swig of the liquid. It tastes sweet but it burns all the way down. I put the bottle on my desk and slip off my jacket when I feel suddenly hot.

"Oh, shit," I hear from behind me again when I see Presley walk into my office and going to sit down on one of the pink chairs facing my desk. She crosses her legs and just waits for me to say something.

"Is this code purple?" Shelby asks, not sure what to do as she comes into the room with her hands in front of her, wringing them together.

"Everyone needs to calm down," Clarabella says, her voice coming out smooth, as she walks over and turns one of the pink chairs around for me to sit. "Why don't you have a seat?" Clarabella is trying to remain calm, but from the way she is breathing heavily, she is not relaxed.

"Yes, let's sit down," Presley urges, patting the chair beside her. "Just so you know, you can't just quit." She laughs nervously, trying not to panic. I can tell all three of them are slowly starting to panic as they share a look with each other.

"I can't believe I'm going to say this," Clarabella says, "but Presley is right." She looks at Presley, who blows on her nails and wipes them on the white silk shirt she is wearing. "You can't just quit."

I wish it was that easy. I wish she was right. But fuck me, seeing Matthew again, after all this time, was a shock. It also felt like someone wound up and kicked me right in the vagina using a soccer cleat.

"Whatever happened," Shelby soothes in a soft motherly voice, "we can recover from it."

"I don't think so," I fire back, picking up the bottle and having another swig. This time the burn doesn't really get to me, which should be an indicator that I should not be drinking anything more.

"It's not as bad as you think it is," Clarabella says quietly, waiting for me. I put my head back and close my eyes, but then I just see Matthew's face again and no one needs that right now.

"It really is," I finally reply, looking at all three of them.

"I can assure you it's not." Shelby walks to me and puts her hands on my arms and smiles at me.

"I just met my ex-boyfriend and his fiancée." I say

the words out loud into the universe so now everyone fucking knows.

"Fuck," Clarabella blurts, "it is as bad as you think." If I wasn't in my own shoes, I would laugh at this whole thing.

Presley's and Shelby's heads whip toward Clarabella, who holds up her hands. "Don't shoot the messenger. I'm just stating the obvious."

"Okay," Shelby remarks, "this might be a little hiccup."

I laugh at her. "A minor issue." She looks around.

"A little bump in the road," Presley follows Shelby's lead.

I look at Clarabella, waiting for her words of encouragement, but instead she shakes her head. "This is like an asteroid coming to the earth."

"What is wrong with you?" Shelby hisses between clenched teeth at Clarabella. "This is not helping anyone."

"Fine." Clarabella rolls her eyes. "Why don't we start from the beginning?"

"Yes," Presley says, looking over at me, "define ex-boyfriend."

"Ohhh, good one." Clarabella nods her head. "Let's define what kind of ex-boyfriend."

"How long did you guys date?" Presley asks.

"Two years," I tell the group.

"How long ago did the breakup happen?" Shelby asks.

"Almost two years ago," I share, trying not to think of the day it all came to a screeching halt.

"Was he the best sex you ever had?" Clarabella

questions, while Presley and Shelby groan. "What? This is a great question. We need to know what level it was on." They just glare at her. "Okay, fine, we will table that question for after." She glares at her sisters. "On a scale of one to ten." She puts her hand on my desk and starts tapping her finger. "Ten being the highest, how much did you want to throat punch him when you saw him with his new girlfriend?"

"Fiancée," I correct her. "Not like we just ran into each other at a bar or in Walmart. He came here with his fiancée." Clarabella cringes at that statement and I swear if it wasn't happening to me, I might laugh at this whole situation. "I mean, what are the odds that your ex-boyfriend is going to walk into your place of employment on your first day on the job and you get to plan his wedding?" I mean, the irony behind it, I just can't even wrap my head around it. "But the answer is ten."

"Okay, I'm sorry," Shelby says. "But I have to ask, does the fiancée know?"

I shake my head and laugh. "I walked in there, and I swear to God, it was as if time was standing still and everything was in slow motion. I felt eyes on me, and then when I looked up, I saw him." I grab the bottle and take another swig of the sweet tea, wiping my mouth with the back of my hand. "We pretended we didn't know each other."

"What?" Clarabella shrieks out. "And what did you do?"

"I pretended I didn't know who he was," I say, folding

my arms over my chest. "I even pretended I didn't like hockey," I pfft out.

"He plays hockey?" Clarabella asks. "Like professionally?"

"Yes." I nod my head. "Even when we were in school, he was drafted when he was eighteen, but he wanted to get a degree before he played."

"Shut up," Clarabella squawks, taking out her phone. "What's his name?"

"Matthew Petrov," I reply as she opens Google and must type in his name.

Her eyes come to me. "Stop it."

"Let me see." Presley extends her hand for the phone. She gets it and I ignore the gasp from her and then glance away when she looks at me with her mouth hanging open, and then she closes it again as she hands the phone over to Shelby.

She grabs it, and I see her eyes go big. "He looks awful," she tries to say, and even I know she's lying.

"Maury said that's a lie," Clarabella jokes, shaking her head. "But did he look at you and was like, holy shit, what do we do?"

"I have no idea. I avoided him as much as I could. I directed my questions straight to Helena," I state, proud of myself. No matter how many times my eyes wanted to look over at him, I just stared straight ahead. I swear, I could feel his eyes on me the whole time, but I didn't look over at him. Not once. The only time I did was at the end and even that was too much for me.

"Did they have a date in mind?" Clarabella leans back

in her chair and I shake my head.

"No, obviously it has to be in the summer since he's off then," I share with them the only detail I really paid attention to. The whole exchange was also a touch weird and not just because it was with my ex, but she name-dropped who he was every chance she could.

"It'll probably be a big wedding," I fill in. "He has a big family."

"Define big." Shelby lifts her eyebrows at me.

"About as big as mine, if not bigger," I share and ignore the pull to take the phone from her now.

Shelby puts the phone down and I wonder what pictures they looked at. After we broke up, I blocked his name from my phone. I mean, not really, but I definitely didn't go on and google him. I mean, maybe I did just the one time, but that was after a long day of drinking and an unsuccessful date where I had to pleasure myself. It was a moment of weakness. "How did you leave it?" She taps her manicured finger on the phone.

"They would get back to me," I say and laugh, "as if I would even think about doing this." I roll my eyes.

"Okay, I have to ask, who broke up with who?" Clarabella finally asks the loaded question.

I shake my head and put my hand to my forehead. "He broke up with me." I thought I was over the pain from that day, but clearly, I am not. I'm far from over it. It's been two years. It should be dead and buried in my memories. Sadly, seeing him for even five minutes brought it all back.

"This is getting sad," Clarabella says, "so let's get

back to the questions about sex."

"Dear God," Shelby mutters. "Maybe there are some things she shouldn't share."

"Bite your tongue," Clarabella retorts, "I literally heard you and Ace going at it in a shed."

"It was in my backyard, my fenced backyard!" she shrieks, and I roll my lips. The three of them have caught each other in so many compromising positions, it's always a new story. I have even caught or heard one of them at times. I mean, if I was in a committed relationship like all of them, I guess I would be doing the same. Especially since Shelby and Clarabella were supposed to marry one person and then married someone else. Presley was so scared she fought really hard to push Bennett away, but he did not let her go. I would love to have a love like that. I thought I did have a love like that. Sadly, I was wrong.

"It was also one hundred and twenty degrees, I'm surprised you didn't faint," Presley reminds her. "You came out a sweaty mess."

"I'm surprised we didn't have to take you to the hospital for dehydration." Shelby shakes her head.

"Can we please focus on Sofia for once?" Shelby redirects.

"Yes, can we," Clarabella agrees. "Sex on a scale of one to ten?"

I look at the three of them, putting my hand to my stomach. "He was my first kiss," I admit, breathing out and looking at the ceiling to blink away the tears that have now crept up on me. "My first everything, really,"

I whisper as I walk around the desk, avoiding looking at them. I'm not sure I can stand them looking at me and seeing the pity in their eyes. "Needless to say, I'm not working with them." I finally look at all three of them and they just look at me and nod.

"If they call you back," Shelby says, getting up, "I'll take it."

"Do you really think that he would come back?" Clarabella questions me and all I can do is shrug my shoulders. "Okay, he came today but did he know he was meeting you?"

"I don't think so," I answer honestly. "They filled the doc out online and all correspondence was done through the main email address, so there isn't a fixed name on there," I say, putting my hand in front of me. "Either way, that was my one and only appointment I will do with him."

"Or," Clarabella suggests, "you show him that he means jack shit to you and plan him the best fucking wedding of his life."

"How is that going to help her?" Shelby asks the question I almost asked.

"Think about it." Clarabella smiles. "Every single time he thinks of his wedding, he is going to think of her." If I have to admit it, I think it's genius, but I won't put myself in that position. "It's up to you." She gets up. "And no more sweet tea, your face is already flushed."

I take a deep breath. "I guess we will see if they call or not."

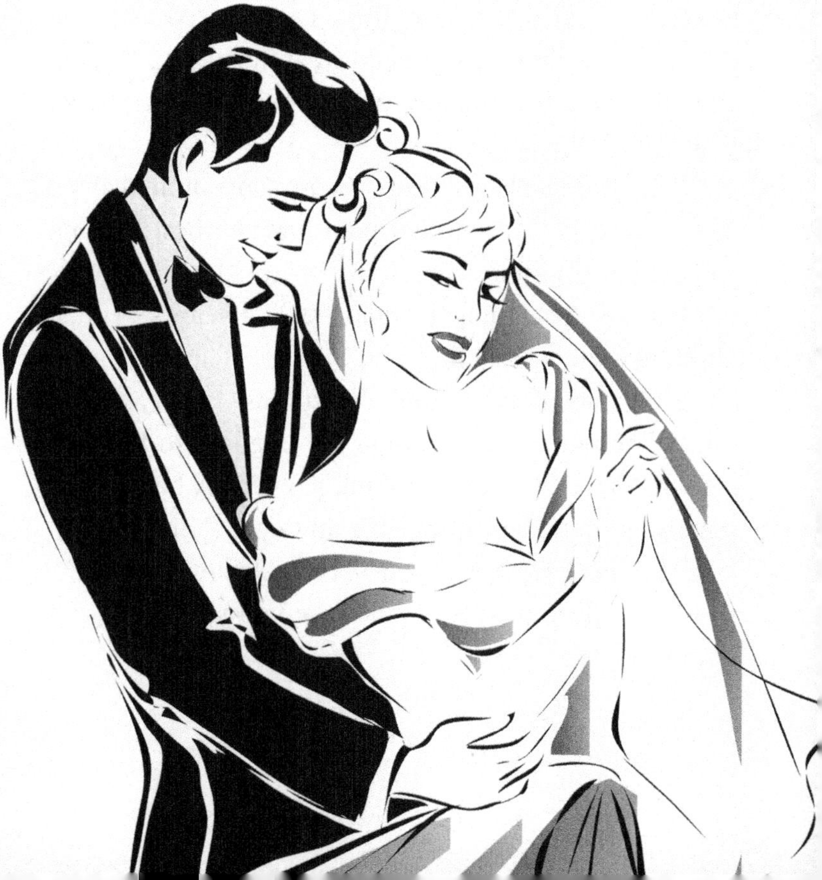

Four

Matthew

I huff as I skate off the ice, taking one of my gloves off while I unsnap my helmet. Making my way down the red hallway toward the locker room, I place my stick outside of the door along with all the other ones. Walking into the room, I pick up a bottle of Gatorade from the tray in the middle of the room before I head over to my spot on the big, long bench and place my gloves on the small square shelf above my name. "I was dragging my ass out there," I say, trying to get my breathing back as I sit down on the bench and unscrew the cap.

"I think we were all dragging out there," Jeff observes from beside me. He takes off the jersey he has on and tosses it in the big bin that is in the middle of the room, right beside the team logo on the carpet.

"Beginning of the season is always like this," I say to Jeff as the locker room fills up with the guys who have come off the ice. Everyone sits down at their place as they get their energy back. "At least we don't have a game tonight." I put the Gatorade beside me before leaning down and untying my skates.

I've been playing hockey since before I can remember. I think there is a picture in my parents' house of me on skates at a year old. I could barely walk but my father laced up my tiny skates and skated with me. I always knew I wanted to play hockey. I mean, coming from the family I came from, it was a given. My grandfather was a hockey god, to say the least. He literally still has records that no one has beaten. My father played hockey. My uncles and most of my cousins all play professional hockey, so it was no surprise that I wanted to do it also. I just did it a bit different from my cousins. I got drafted when I was eighteen. Not first like most of them, but it didn't matter to me, because no matter what number I went, I was going to finish school before playing. It was something my father and I decided together when I was thirteen. I would be drafted and then get a degree in business. I played hockey in college where I recorded twenty-two goals and nineteen assists in thirty-six games. I was at the top of the standings. When I came back the second year, I dominated even more, with thirty-two goals and fifty-seven points in thirty-one games.

Needless to say, when I finally got my degree and graduated, I went straight to the NHL. Luckily for me,

Carolina drafted me, so I didn't have to move far since I went to school here. In March before I graduated, I signed an entry-level contract and finally suited up in April for the farm team. I scored two goals and one assist in that game and quickly was called up to play my very first NHL game. It took me three games to get my groove and I finally scored my first ever NHL goal. I still remember to this day how it felt, like I made the family proud. It was so hard growing up and walking in everyone else's shadow, having to prove you belong there, and not that you were there because of the dynasty you grew up in. I slip on my slides and put my skates under the bench before fully undressing. I hear some conversation all around me, but now that I'm not on the ice, my mind wanders. It takes me right back to yesterday. Right back to seeing Sofia again.

The minute I got into the car with Helena, I told her we should check out other event planners. I knew we would never, ever use Sofia. Can you imagine? Even when I dropped Helena off at her place, she was still telling me how much she loved Sofia. I just needed to have my space to get everything in my head clear. News flash—it just made it worse. I swear it feels like the Pandora's box that was Sofia and me magically opened, and now the only thing I could think of is her.

I walk out of practice wearing my track suit and my baseball hat backward. My brown hair under it is still wet from the shower, as I shake my protein shake cup. I unlock my car door before sliding in and starting it. I pull away from the parking area and call my father. We speak daily, sometimes twice a day. He answers me right away. "Hey," he greets, and I hear he's in his car also.

"Hey there," I reply, smiling and then suddenly missing him. It's strange the way time works. When I was a teenager, I couldn't wait to be out from under their rules and now there is nothing that calms me down like talking to my father. "Whatcha doing?"

"Just left the rink," he says, and I laugh. He played for many years in the NHL. He actually got traded to New York while he was in rehab. My uncle Matthew took a chance on him. He met my mother, Zoe, who is Matthew's younger sister, when he was looking for a house.

"Who were you training with?" I ask as I make my way over to my house.

"Uncle Evan, Max, and Matthew," he says, "Grandpa Cooper came also." I smile thinking of my grandfather still lacing up. He may not have the speed he had before, but he's got the plays all in his head. "What are you doing?"

"Nothing much," I huff, "just got out of practice and I'm going to go home and get on the bike."

"What's the matter?" he asks right away. I knew if anyone could tell that something was bothering me, it would be my father. If I was in front of my mother, she would be able to tell right away. It's like they have this parent superpower.

"Nothing really," I lie to him but my father laughs.

"You sound like someone stole your favorite snack at school," he teases, and I can't help but chuckle. "How is it to be back on the ice?" He changes the subject, not pushing me, knowing that when I'm ready, I'll tell him what is bothering me.

"It's good, felt a little off today but…" My voice trails off and I wait for my father to say something, but he knows that I'm not done. "Can I ask you something?" The nerves start in my stomach and then spread right up my chest.

You can ask me anything," he assures me softly.

"How did you know Mom was the one?" I finally ask the big question I asked myself all night.

"Matty," he calls me by my nickname, his voice going soft, "I like Helena, she's a nice girl from what I can tell." I smile because even if he didn't like her, he wouldn't tell me, the whole family would be supportive of me no matter what. "But if you are thinking this now, how do you think it will be in the future?"

"What do you mean?" I ask, confusion running through me.

"You aren't supposed to think you found the one. You are supposed to know. If it's the one, there isn't that question," he explains. "There isn't any question, it just is. There is no second-guessing when you know it's the one."

"It's fine, Dad." I cover it up as much as I can to make him not worry. "I was just…"

"It's a big step, Matty. For both your sakes, if you aren't sure, don't rush into it," he advises, and I nod my head as I pull into my driveway.

"Thanks, Dad," I say, smiling before I turn the car

off and get out of it, grabbing the protein shake and the phone. "I'm going to head on to the bike, I'll call you later."

"Love you," he says, like he always does, right before we hang up. Every single time, even if we talk ten times a day.

"Love you, too, say hi to Mom for me," I reply right before we both hang up. I walk to the side of the house instead of going through the house. Making my way to the pool house I converted into a home gym, I enter the code on the lock pad and hear the lock turning to open the door. Once it's open, I walk right to the bike that sits in the corner next to the treadmill.

Once I get on the bike, I start slow and then work my speed up. I chuck off my jacket and then my T-shirt. Two hours later, I've finished off the water bottle I started thirty minutes ago as I sit on the weight bench and try to catch my breath. The sweat pours off me as my phone rings from beside the bike.

I get up and walk over to grab it, looking down and seeing it's Christopher calling me. "Yo," I say, walking out of the gym.

"Hey," he greets, and I can hear that he, too, is out of breath. "What's going on?"

"Nothing much, just finished the bike," I tell him, walking to the back door and putting in the code for it. I hear the sound of the lock turning, and then walk into the back door and straight into the kitchen. I walk over to the huge, stainless-steel double fridge, pulling it open and grabbing one of the prepared meals my cleaning lady puts in there every other day. "What about you?" Walking around the island to the eight-burner stove, with double ovens, I turn the red knob for the oven, placing the container on the pan that is already inside. I set the timer for thirty minutes before I make my way upstairs to my bedroom.

The shades are still closed, so the room is pitch black, but I walk toward my bathroom.

"I just finished the treadmill," he says, and I hear a door slam on his end. "What's new?"

"Not much," I tell him, putting the phone on speaker before I walk over to the shower. "Met my wedding planner," I say before I pull open the mirrored door, turning on the water.

"Oh, nice, I still can't believe you are actually getting married." He chuckles.

"It's Sofia." I cut to the chase and walk back over to the phone that is on the counter as I look down at it.

"Um, excuse me?" Christopher says in shock, and I swear I can hear him stop moving.

"Yeah," I huff, kicking off my shoes, "you heard me."

"What the fuck?" I can't help but shake my head.

"Yeah, that is what I said also," I admit to him.

"What the hell?" He continues being in shock.

"Yeah, I said that also." I peel off my socks and toss them into the laundry basket in the corner of my walk-in closet, adding my track pants to it.

"Jesus, how was it?"

"What the hell does that mean?" I ask.

"I mean, like what did you say? What did she say?"

He is asking all the questions I would ask if the roles were reversed.

"I didn't say anything and neither did she," I tell him. "She pretended she didn't know me."

"Oh, burn," he says, laughing and I roll my eyes.

"It wasn't a burn." My head screams out that it was, in fact, a burn. "It was."

"Did you tell Helena who she was?" he asks me, and I choke.

"Are you out of your mind? We both pretended that we didn't know each other. What did you want me to do? Get in the car and be like, 'hey, you know that hot girl we just met, we dated for two years before I—'" I stop talking when I think about it when I hear his question.

"Is she still hot?" he asks, and I groan.

"Out of everything I just told you, that is the only thing you caught?" I say between clenched teeth. Then I want to kick myself for even bringing up that she was hot in the first place.

He laughs. "Well, why would you notice she was hot if you were with Helena?" he asks. I open my mouth and then close it before opening it again, but nothing comes out. "What are you going to do?"

"What do you mean, what am I going to do?" I ask.

"Are you going to call her?" he asks me, and I just look down at the phone.

"Who?"

"Sofia?" He says her name.

"Absolutely not. Why the hell would I call her?" *It's*

two years too late for that, you asshole, my head screams to me.

"What are you going to do?" he asks. "Are you going to use her for your wedding?"

"Are you out of your mind?" I screech. "I'm never talking to her again."

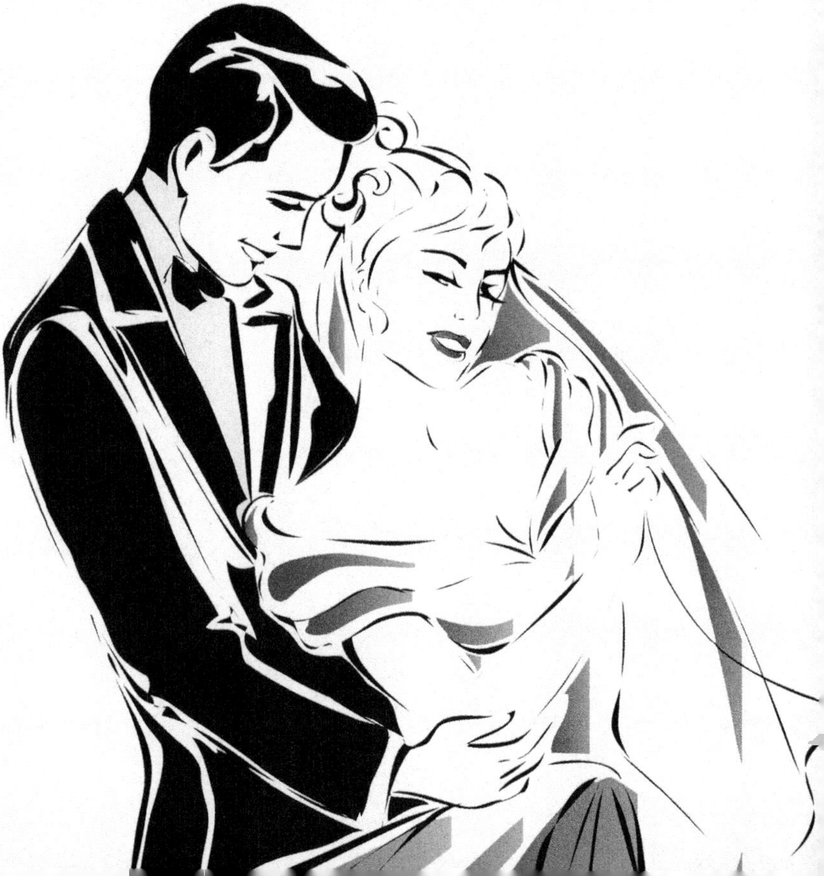

Five

Sofia

I put the car in park before pressing the engine button. Unbuckling my seat belt before I reach for the door handle, I open my door and kick it all the way open with my foot. I lean over, grabbing the carry-out tray holding the four cups of coffee I just picked up. I then grab my purse and my carry-on bag that holds my laptop.

I step out, closing the door with my hip before I make my way up the steps. The clicks of my heels fill the silent morning. The sun is already high in the sky, but luckily there is a little breeze in the air. My hair blows back as well as the white capri pants I'm wearing. The hair on my bare arms also starts to stand because of it. I even feel it go through the front of my crisscross satin shirt. I reach for the handle of the front door before walking inside. "You just made that look so effortless." I look over and see Presley walking out of the kitchen with a glass of water in her hand.

I chuckle at her. "Happy Friday," I greet, holding up the cups of coffee as I walk toward her.

"Where are we having our meeting?" I ask and she just points at the hallway and toward the conference room.

"Perfect." I walk back with the tray in my hand. Every single Friday we have a meeting on what we are working on. What we did this week. What we have coming up and, most importantly, if we have any issues that we need help with.

I place the coffee down on the round table before I turn and walk to my office. I take the sunglasses off as soon as I put my bags down. I grab my laptop from the bag and then the folder of notes I have. "Good morning," I hear Shelby say from the hallway as she walks toward her office followed by Clarabella, who also grumbles a *good morning*.

I walk out of my office and take myself toward the conference room where the three of them are. "I have to ask you," Clarabella starts, sitting in one of the chairs, then leaning over to grab one of the coffees from the tray. "How many times a week do you work out?" I look at her confused. "God, she doesn't even have to work out to have that body." She puts her head back and takes a sip of the coffee.

"I usually work out three to four times a week," I tell

them. "Not lately, but usually."

"I keep forgetting when I look at you that your grandmother was a Victoria's Secret model and that it's in your genes." Shelby looks at me and all I can do is shake my head.

"She is the most beautiful woman I've seen in my life," Clarabella says in awe, and I can't help but smile. She was a fashion model her whole life, but she is well known for being a Victoria's Secret angel. "I still remember when you moved here, and she sent clothes to you."

"I used to get boxes weekly," I reminisce, grabbing my own coffee, "but then I started running out of space, so she sends them to me monthly now."

"Well, not that I could ever fit into your clothes," Shelby pouts, "but if I could."

"My closet is open to all," I invite as I open my laptop. The three of them do the same as we start the meeting.

Shelby starts us off as always. "Okay, let's start. Any news from the um…"

"Ex-boyfriend," I finish for her, and she just nods. "Nope," I state with a smile on my face. "It's been a week, so I'm going to go out on a limb and say they are looking elsewhere."

"Wonderful," Shelby says, smiling at me and then turning to look at Presley.

It's been a week since I saw Matthew. I want to tell you that as soon as he walked out of here, that was the last time he came to my mind, but I would be lying. All I've done this week was think about him. I look out the window at the field in the distance. The colors of the trees are now in the middle of changing from green to orange. The wind makes the trees move side to side and now all I can think about is him. Especially the first time we met or, better yet, the first time we spoke to each other.

I walked into finance class and saw it was almost empty, except for two guys sitting in the second row. I kept my head down as I walked over and sat down in the row ahead of them. I heard the two guys talking behind me and I made the foolish mistake of looking back at them. My eyes found his dark blue ones right away. As soon as we locked eyes, he smirked at me and it was as if the earth shifted, which was the stupidest thing I'd ever heard in my life. I turned around just as quickly and looked straight ahead. I felt him staring at me the whole class, but I refused to turn around and look at him.

When the professor dismissed the class, I was the first one out of my seat and I rushed out of there like the building was on fire. I didn't give him another thought until I was at the bar on Saturday night. I sat down in the middle of the long bar as I sipped my beer and traded stories of the week with my best friend, Ella. I heard the chatter from people around me before I turned my head toward the door, wondering why everyone was suddenly hooting and hollering. There he was, the guy from my finance class. Except he wasn't wearing jeans and a shirt. No, he was wearing a suit. His hair was wet and he was walking in high-fiving everyone. "What the?" I mumbled, not sure what was happening.

I was about to turn my head around when his eyes

met mine. The smile he had on his face faded to a smirk. His eyes never left mine until he walked over to me. "It's you," he said as he pointed at me.

"Excuse me?" That was the only thing that came out of my mouth.

"You're the one from class who was eyeing me." He leaned against the bar and motioned to the bartender with his chin, and I had to wonder if it was a secret language I didn't know.

"You must have me mistaken with someone else," I said, annoyed. "I don't think I've ever seen you," I lied to him, and he just laughed.

"Finance class." He refreshed my memory, but truth be told, obviously I remembered it. "You turned around and we shared a moment."

"We shared a moment?" I repeated after him to see if I actually heard him right. He just nodded his head while the bartender came over and handed him a bottle of water. "It was a five-second look."

"A lot was said in that five-second look," he stated, and I grabbed my phone off the bar and opened the text app. "What are you doing?"

"Messaging my mailman," I told him, trying to hide the smile on my face. "I looked at him for seven seconds today, and I'm just wondering if that means marriage."

"You're funny," he pointed out, smiling and his eyes lit up.

"You're not," I retorted, and he just threw his head back and laughed even louder. Even though the bar was overwhelmed with noise, all I heard was his laugh.

"I'm Matthew." He extended his hand to me. "People call me Matty."

I thought about not answering him and ignoring him, but my hand moved before my head told it no. "I'm Sofia." I smiled. "People call me Princess Sofia." His hand enveloped mine and I felt the tingle go from the tips of my fingers toward the tip of my toes. That was the night I had my first ever kiss. It was also the same night I fell under the spell that was Matthew Petrov.

"Sofia." I hear Shelby calling my name and I blink twice. I turn back to look at the table instead of looking out the window at the vast countryside. "Are you okay?"

I tap my finger on the desk. "I think I should start dating again," I say to the three of them, and they all look at me with their eyes shining up.

"Um, yes, please," Clarabella agrees.

"I think that is a fantastic idea," Shelby says, clapping her hands in front of her.

Presley stands and reaches out, grabbing my phone. "No time like the present," she declares with a huge smile on her face. "Let's create a profile now."

"This is the best meeting I've been to in a while," Clarabella grabs the phone, making Shelby look over at her and glare. "Oh, please, Presley said it also."

"No, I didn't," Presley denies.

"I have it on text," Clarabella retorts, lifting her phone.

"Can we focus on Sofia?" Presley says. "What are you doing?"

"I'm filling out her name and stuff," Clarabella explains.

"Don't put her real name!" Shelby shouts.

"They only share her account name which is Sunshine45," Clarabella says. "Okay, what do you do at the end of the day?"

"Watch reality television," I answer and the three of them look at me.

"Curl up with a good book or watch an action movie," Clarabella redirects and I gasp.

"Why?"

"Well, a good book, you are going to get the studious guy, and an action movie, you get an adventurous guy." Clarabella looks at me.

"Oh, good idea," Presley concurs. "You should put hiking in there so you get the ones who like to do all that outdoorsy stuff."

"Yes." Shelby snaps her fingers. "Also loves going out." We all look over at her. "We don't want him to think that she stays inside with her eight cats."

"Oh, yes," Clarabella says and starts typing things. "Cat person or dog person?"

"I'm a horse girl," I state, and they all shake their heads. "What? I love my horse." I point at Clarabella. "Put that I prefer horses."

"Can you put save a horse, ride a cowboy?" Presley asks Clarabella, who just smirks.

"Do not put that," I grumble between clenched teeth.

The phone in her hand starts ringing and she hands it to me. I see that it's a number not stored in my phone, so I put it on speaker and answer, "Sofia Barnes."

"Sofia." I close my eyes when I hear the female voice.

"It's Helena." I open my eyes and look over toward the girls, whose eyes go big. "We met last week, my fiancé is Matthew Petrov."

Why does she always name-drop his name? I ask myself. "Yes, of course," I say, my finger tapping the desk. "How are you doing?"

"I'm doing amazing," she replies cheerfully. "I'm calling because we would like to come in and meet with you."

I look up to the sky, thinking this can't be happening. "That would be great," I say, and I hold up my hand to stop the girls from talking. They jump out of their chairs. "When would you be free?"

"How is next Tuesday?" she asks me, and I pull up my calendar.

"I have one o'clock on Tuesday, if that works for you," I tell her, and she squeals.

"I'll make it work. Worse case, Matty can meet me there," she says. "Thank you so, so much, Sofia."

"I'll see you then," I reply, and the phone disconnects.

"What the fuck are you doing?" Clarabella asks, putting her hands on her hips. It's the same question my head was screaming at me.

"I'm doing my job," I shoot back, pissed now. "Fuck him. If he doesn't care that I'll plan his wedding, why the hell should I?"

"That's the spirit," Clarabella says and my heart speeds up even more when it finally sinks in that he's coming in, and I have to plan his wedding.

I pick the phone up again. "What are you doing?"

Shelby asks.

"Calling my great-grandfather." I look at them. "If I'm going to be doing this, I'm going to need a case of sweet tea to get me through it."

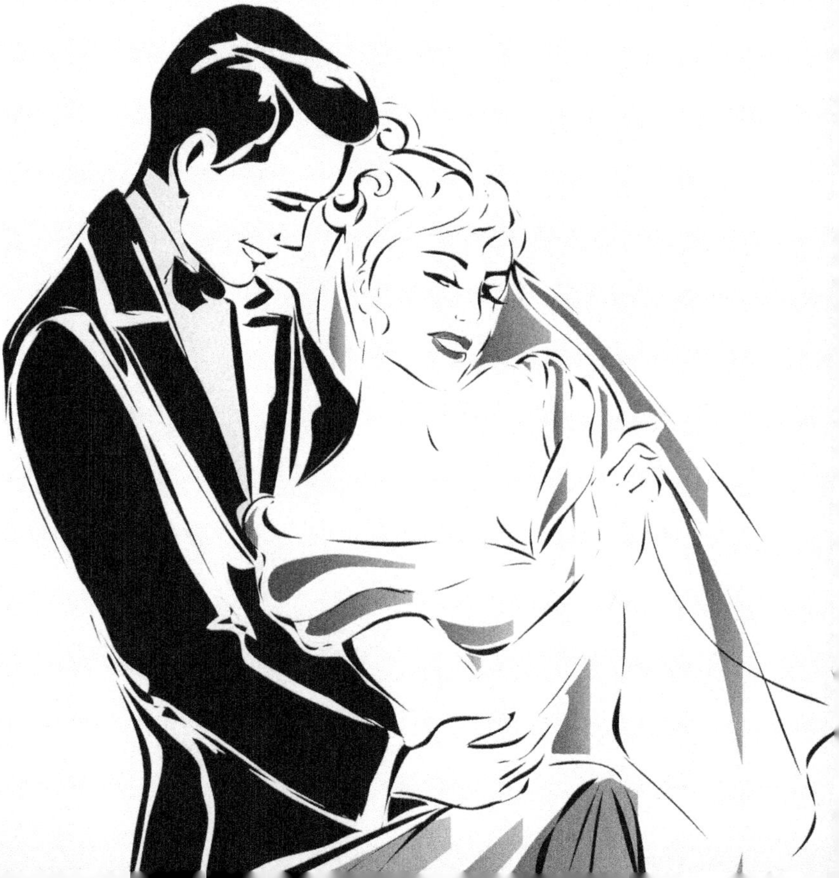

Six

Matthew

I walk off the plane and the cold air runs through me. Holding on to the metal stair handle with one hand while I hold my bag in the other, I make my way down the stairs. No one says anything as each of us makes our way over to our respective cars. I've just come back from a four-day road trip where we got our asses handed to us on a silver platter. There was nothing good that came out of this road trip, and I'm not the only one glad to be home.

"See you later, Petrov," I hear Brock, our captain, say as he gets into the truck beside me. I lift my hand as I unlock my doors. Pressing the trunk button, I also toss in my bag with my backpack. I get in the car and make my way over to my house, seeing Helena's car in the driveway when I get there. We've been together for a while and moving in would have been the obvious choice, but to be honest, I never asked her to move in. That and our busy schedule keeps us from even discussing it. She's also on the road with her pharmaceutical sales job. She works primarily with spas and salons for all cosmetic aspects.

I'm assuming, once we get married, she is going to be moving in, but she hasn't even brought it up. The only thing she really has at my house is a toothbrush and maybe some shampoo. Whenever she comes over, she always brings an overnight bag, and when she leaves, so does the bag.

I don't know why, but I'm irritated that she is here right now. After four days on the road, all I wanted was to unwind. I press the button to open the garage door, driving in and parking the car. Turning the car off, I get out and grab my stuff before walking over to the stairs leading to the mudroom. I press the garage door before I walk into the house. I see that Helena's shoes and purse sit on the gray bench. I kick off my dress shoes and put them to the side before walking into the kitchen.

Helena sits on one of the stools at the island and looks up when she hears me walk in. "Hi." She smiles at me, not getting up or coming to me.

"Hey," I greet, walking past her with my bags. "I didn't know you would be here."

She looks at me as I walk past her. "I was in the area and figured I'd come work here a bit."

"Cool," I say, and I don't know why it feels fucking

awkward. When did it start feeling awkward? Was it always like this? Did I always get irritated when she came over?

I walk past the family room and toward the stairs, making my way to my bedroom. I open one of the double doors before stepping inside and seeing the drapes are open. When I bought this house, it had five bedrooms and I didn't see the need for all the bedrooms, so I combined two bedrooms to make one massive one. There are six windows across the whole back wall with a sitting area right in front of it with a U-shaped couch I don't really use. It faces the brick wall that has a fireplace on the bottom and television on top of it. The king-size bed is against the back wall facing everything. Walking onto the plush carpet, I go to the end of the room where the walk-in closet is. I dump my bags there before I shrug off my suit jacket. Unbuttoning the white dress shirt, I pull it out of my pants. I quickly slip into basketball shorts before walking downstairs.

I can hear Helena's voice as I make my way into the kitchen, going straight over to the fridge. "Tuesday would be amazing," she says and then I look over as I open a bottle of Gatorade, leaning on the counter behind me. A soon as she puts her phone down, the doorbell rings.

"The food is here." She gets off the stool and walks over to the front door. She is wearing tight black jeans and a knitted shirt, and I wait for my dick to wake up, but nothing happens. *I must be really fucking tired,* I think to myself at the same time that my head laughs at me.

She walks back in with two brown carry-out bags. "I ordered you a couple of things since I didn't know how hungry you were," she explains, putting the bags on the island as she takes out the black to-go containers. "I got you chicken and also steak," she says, and I turn to grab two forks and knives before walking over beside her. "I got you a baked potato and also some asparagus."

"Thank you." I stand beside her and look at her smiling. She grabs her two black containers as she walks over to where she was sitting, pushing her computer to the side. I pull the stool out beside her, sitting down, and opening my own containers.

"So how was the flight?" she asks as I cut a piece of steak.

"Short, thank God," I answer, looking over at her. It dawns on me that she didn't kiss me hello, but then I didn't kiss her hello either. Have we gone into a room before without kissing each other?

"So I have some news," she declares, and I look over as she grabs her grilled salmon and pops some into her mouth. "I called Sofia."

The minute she says her name, everything inside me tingles away. "What?" I say, looking up at her, trying to calm my body down. But it's as if my body is getting ready to go to war with a hurricane.

Helena doesn't even catch the change in the room as she continues to eat her salmon, like she didn't just drop a bomb on me. "I checked your schedule," she continues slowly, and I want to yell at her to hurry up, but all my words are stuck in the back of my throat. The food I ate starts to come back up. "And I know you have Tuesday off, so we are meeting her at her office." She smiles at me.

I can't do anything but blink at her. "Why?" I ask the stupid question. Obviously, I know why.

"Because she is the only one I connected with," she clarifies. "I met with four other planners since her, and she is the only one who knew what she was doing."

I look back at my food and wonder if I should tell her who Sofia is. But then, something stops me. "We should go over a couple of things." I push the food around the containers, thinking about the things we should go over.

"That is why we are meeting with Sofia," she says, "she is going to help us every step of the way."

"Have you thought about not having a wedding planner?" I ask. "My aunts and mother are pretty much all party planners at this point."

"Absolutely not," she declares, shaking her head. "I've met them maybe three times. They don't know my style, nor do I want to spend that much time with them."

"What?" I ask, shocked. "My family is a big part of my life."

"And you can have that part of your life and I'll be there when I have to be, but they are just—what is the word I'm thinking of?"

"Amazing," I say, annoyed with her even more than I ever was.

"Pushy," she replies. "Wait, that isn't a good word. Overbearing." She points her fork at me. "That's an accurate account of them."

"You don't even know them," I say, getting defensive. "You spent what… an hour with them?"

"I spent the whole Sunday with them at the Sunday lunch." She shakes her head. "Everyone is in everyone's business. They ask questions that they shouldn't."

"Like what?" I'm shocked and pissed. Can my family be overbearing? One thousand and one million percent, but I wouldn't want anyone else on my side. They are all ride or die. It's just like, known. You have a problem, you make one phone call, and you have the support of everyone. It's what I thought every family was until I met Helena's family, and they didn't ask me one question about myself. They were prim and proper and the opposite of what my family was like. I knew it then, but I had no idea she felt like this.

"I don't know, it was just intrusive. Maybe if I knew them better, but it was the second time we met." She shrugs her shoulders. "I'll still play nice." She pushes away from the counter and places the covers on her takeout containers. "I have to go. The girls are having a mini get-together at Sierra's house." She puts her stuff in a takeout bag before grabbing it and her computer. She comes by the side of my stool. "I'll call you later." She kisses my cheek before she walks to the mudroom.

I look down at my plate, my stomach suddenly sick, and I have to wonder why it's sick. Is it because we are going to meet Sofia, or is it because she hates my family? "Don't forget Tuesday," she calls out right before I hear the door to the garage slam shut behind her.

"Yeah," I say to the empty room. I don't bother eating

another bite. Instead, I get up and pack everything back up, putting it in the fridge. I look over and see that it's just after six, but instead of getting comfy on the couch, I walk back to my bedroom.

Sliding onto the bed, I grab the remote and turn on the television. My head is spinning around and around like a hamster on a wheel. I flip the channels, but my head goes back to my first date with Sofia.

After we met at the bar, I walked her home. She let me kiss her, and I swear to God, it felt like I was floating on air. She walked into her apartment, and I walked away, only to go back and ring the bell again. She came out, her face still flustered from when I kissed her. "Are you okay?" she asked me, and all I did was smile at her.

"Yeah," I said. "Go out with me?"

"Now?" She just tilted her head to the side, and all I could think at that moment was she was the most beautiful woman I'd ever laid eyes on. I spotted her right away when she walked into class. I stared at the back of her head and hoped she would turn and look my way. When she did, I swear I heard my jaw hit the floor. Her blue eyes mesmerized me; all I wanted to do was ask her name. I figured I would be able to after class, but nope, she snuck out. When I walked into the bar that night after the game, I never thought I would see her, and when I did, I knew I had to take my shot with her. I thought I was slick. I wasn't. She let me know right away, and it intrigued me even more.

"Tomorrow." I said the words even though I would have said yes to them right then.

"I guess so." She smirked. "We did have a ten-second look, so I'm assuming we have no choice at this point." I couldn't stop myself, even if I wanted to, and took a step forward. I wrapped one arm around her waist as I pulled her to me.

"Thank you," I said right before I took another kiss from her. This one was soft and slow. Her tongue quickly slid into my mouth. Her hands rested on my chest. I would have spent the night kissing her, but I slowly let her go. "Good night," I said before I stepped down the stairs and walked away from her. "See you tomorrow at five, Princess Sofia."

I rub my hands over my face to stop thinking about the past. "It's over," I tell myself, just like I've been telling myself this since I've seen her again. "But fuck, is she beautiful."

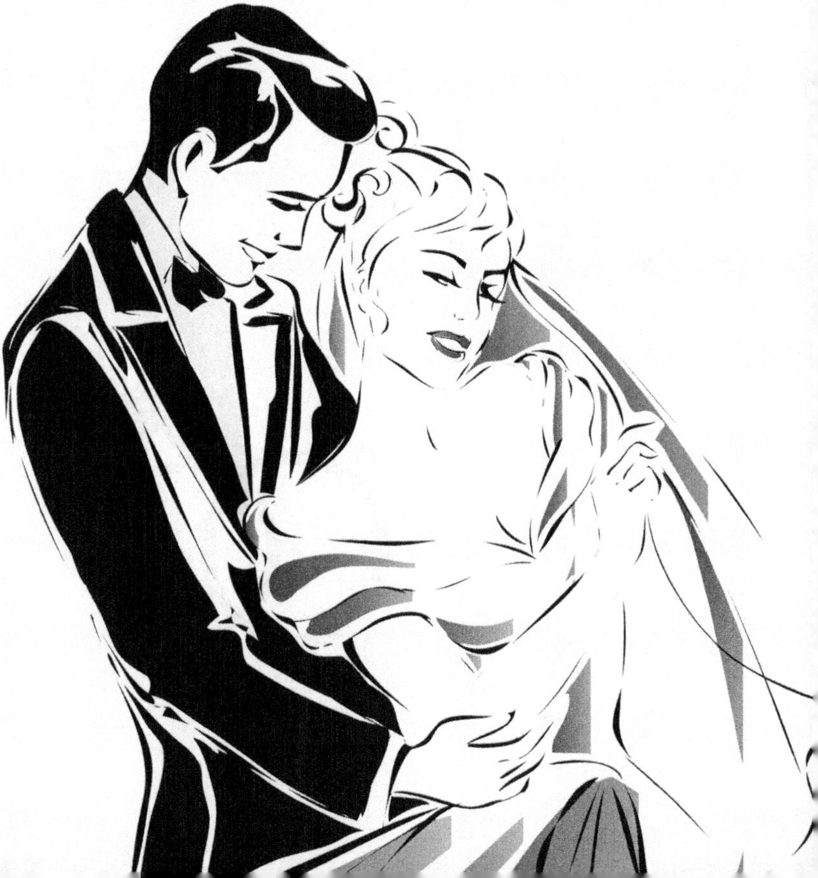

Seven

Sofia

I get out of my car and try not to pay attention to the butterflies in my stomach. But I'm a lost cause. The last four days I've been on edge, to say the very least. Not only that, now when I go out, I look around for him, which is the stupidest fucking thing I could ever do. Like he's going to be randomly at the grocery store or at the bakery.

I barely slept last night, knowing I would be seeing him today. I'm going to pretend that it's because I'm nervous and not because my ex is coming in with his fiancée for me to plan their wedding. As soon as I saw the clock hit 5:00 a.m., I got out of bed, putting gold under-eye patches on. My great-grandmother would have probably given me tea bags if I was still at home.

I took extra care with my outfit today. Choosing one that looks elegant and sexy in an eat-your-heart-out kind of way. The champagne-and-black checkered skirt hits mid calf, which molds my hips and makes my ass look perfect. The long-sleeved, champagne-colored silk, V-neck, button-down shirt molds my breasts. The sleeves tie tightly around my wrists, making it sleek and elegant. I couldn't not wear the sky-high black shoes because I knew he loved them, and I also knew it drove him crazy when I wore them. This time, I wear my hair loose with thick curls, knowing again that he loved how long and lush my hair was. So I guess you could say I dressed for Matthew today but not because I wanted to. It was more of a *go fuck yourself and I hope you suffer from erectile dysfunction.*

Pulling open the door, the cold air hits me right away. "Morning!" I shout out so whoever is here hears me.

"My, my, my," Shelby says, coming out of the kitchen with a cup of coffee in her hand, "I believe someone is coming to slay."

I can't help but chuckle. "I don't know what you mean," I deflect, turning to walk to my office, my feet already informing me that these shoes will not last long. Walking into my office, I take off said shoes and slip my feet into my Ugg slippers. Dumping my bag on the chair, I make my way back out and to the kitchen to grab myself a cup of coffee.

"That didn't last long." Shelby notices when I walk past her in the hallway. "Those shoes are sexy as hell but only good to sit in or have sex in."

"I know," I concur, turning and trying not to think of the time I wore them for our date, and he refused to let me take them off when we got home. "He's engaged," I remind myself as I grab a mug and place it underneath the spout before grabbing a coffee pod and putting it in. I press the button before walking to the fridge to grab the milk.

I'm pouring some into my cup of coffee when I hear my phone ringing from my office. Rushing back to my office to answer the phone, I pray it's Helena deciding that she has changed her mind, but instead, I look down and see it's my father.

"Hello," I huff as I walk back to the kitchen.

"You sound out of breath," he says. "Are you working out?"

"I'm at the office, Dad, and don't even pretend you don't know that." I grab my cup of coffee from the kitchen and walk back. "You don't think I know you put my location on the last time we were together?"

"What?" He tries to act like he's surprised. "I don't know what you mean."

"Dad." I chuckle. "You know it says I'm sharing my location, right?"

"I thought I deleted it," he says, not even trying to pretend anymore. I walk around my desk, placing the cup down on the coaster before grabbing my laptop.

"You did, but I have my iPad and my computer all logged into my Apple ID so…" I sit down in my chair. "You got caught."

"Duly noted," he says. "Now, what is this I hear that you are on a dating app?"

I put my head back and groan. "I am never telling Mom anything again."

"Your mother knew?" he shouts, and I roll my lips. "Hazel!" he yells her name. "Why didn't you tell me Sofia was on a dating app?"

"Who told you?" I hear my mother ask, and then I sit up.

"Is my phone tapped?" I ask, shocked that I never even thought about it.

"You tapped her phone?" my mother yells.

"Goodbye," I say, disconnecting the call and then calling the one person I know made it happen.

"If it isn't my favorite first grandchild," he greets, and I can even picture him smiling. I press the camera button, and his face fills the screen a couple of seconds later.

"Hey there, gorgeous." He smiles at the phone. I know he's in the war room when I see all the screens behind him.

"Oh, don't you gorgeous me." I glare at the phone, and he leans back in his chair. "I'm going to ask you something, Pops." I say the nickname I gave him when I was seven. "Did you or did you not put a tracker on my phone?"

I stare into his eyes, and I don't know why I'm surprised that he gives away nothing. This is the same guy who trained with the Navy SEALs for fun. "I think I'm going to need a little bit more context than that."

"Don't you even try to lie about it. Dad just got

caught," I inform him, my eyebrows rising.

"I'm not confirming nor denying anything," he deflects, picking up his cup of coffee. "The question is, why the hell do you think you need to be on a dating app?"

"Pops!" I shout and smack my desk. "This is the biggest invasion of privacy." He rolls his eyes. "What if I was sending nudes to a man, and you had one of your men going through my stuff?"

It's his turn to glare at me. "Once those pictures are in the universe, it's forever."

"Take it off my phone now," I threaten between clenched teeth, "or I'm telling Grandma Olivia."

He stares at me, wondering if I'm bluffing. "Good, then that means you are going to come home for a visit because she will force you."

"And Grandma Charlotte." I play my last card, and he just glares at me. "I'm not kidding. I swear this feels like I'm in college all over again when you put all those trackers in my purse without me knowing."

"Sofia," he murmurs my name softly, "how was I supposed to know that you wouldn't be sex trafficked or kidnapped?"

"Three hundred and forty-seven trackers!" I shout. "I'm surprised I wasn't followed by the FBI."

He laughs. "Please, my guys are way better than the FBI."

"Okay, I'm going to go now and get myself a new phone and not give you the number," I tell him. "Then I'm going to go on ten blind dates, and you'll never know."

"Okay, okay, fine," he concedes, holding up his hand and then turning to click two things on his keyboard. "There, done." He looks at me. "Now, when are you coming home?"

"Never." I side-eye him, trying to ignore him.

"Your horse misses you," he says softly. He knows that I'll do anything for Peaches.

"I'll come home sometime next week, but it'll probably be just a day trip," I inform him. "Now, I have to go. I love you even though you are you."

He laughs. "I love you more, Sunshine." He uses my nickname, and I suddenly miss home.

"Bye." I reach out to press the red button, not waiting for him to say goodbye.

I turn my computer on, checking the emails. I reply to the ones I can respond to and then send the ones that need to be looked at to Shelby.

"Are you ready for today?" Clarabella walks into my office a couple of hours later. She is wearing slacks and a sleeveless shirt with sneakers. She sits in one of the chairs.

I look up from the notes I made yesterday with another couple. "No," I immediately tell her, leaning back in my chair.

"What are you two discussing?" Presley asks, walking into the room with the baby in her baby Bjorn strapped to her chest.

"If she is ready for today," Clarabella replies and Presley just raises her eyebrows.

"What are you wearing?" Presley asks, and I stand and walk around the desk.

"Damn, girl, look at that ass," Clarabella declares. "That is the best revenge outfit I ever saw."

"It's not a revenge outfit," I try to tell them. "It's more of an *I am doing fine without you*."

"Well, whatever it is, it's working," Clarabella says.

"And," I tell them, walking back around my desk, "I have a date."

They gasp at me, the baby jumps in front of Presley, so she moves side to side to not wake her. "What do you mean?" she asks in a whisper.

"It means that I connected with someone on the app," I tell them of the date that I made while I was three glasses into my white wine the other day.

"Let's see his picture," Presley says. I grab my phone, pulling up the app, and turning to show her the picture.

"He looks cute," Clarabella states and I look at the phone when she gives it back to me. I look at the man who is dressed in a polo shirt. He has curly black hair and wears glasses—not someone I would typically go out with, but this is about changing things up.

"He likes walks in the forest," I tell them as I look at them and Clarabella grimaces. "What?" I ask.

"That sounds like, sketchy to me," she warns. "Walks in the forest. You better bring mace with you."

"And a Taser for sure," Presley adds, still moving from side to side. "You are going to have to share your location with us."

I'm about to tell them something when the bell rings,

alerting us someone has come in. "Shit, is that them?" I look at my watch to see they are five minutes early.

"Oh my God." Clarabella jumps out of her chair and rushes out of the door. "Dibs."

"Wait until I call you," Presley says in a whisper as I see Shelby rush down the hall also.

"Is this show-and-tell?" I whisper-hiss.

"If it's show-and-tell," Presley teases, "how big is the eggplant?"

"Go away." I walk over to my heels and slip my feet inside them. I can secretly hear them weep as I walk over to the desk and grab my phone and the manila folder that is the couple's. I sit down in the chair trying to steady the way my heart is speeding up, knowing he's out there.

"You can do this," I say to myself, "it's going to be fine. You are going to go out there and you are going to give them the best service you can."

I hear the speaker turn on. "Sofia." Clarabella's voice now fills my office. "Your…" I close my eyes hoping to hell she doesn't say your ex-love is here. "…appointment is here."

"Showtime," I say, getting up and stopping by the mirror before I go out. I smooth down the skirt a bit before walking out.

The hallway seems to be shorter than it's ever been, and right before I walk into the open area, I put on my game face. I smile as soon as I walk into the room.

My eyes find his staring at me, making me hate that the first thing I looked at was him. His blue eyes look straight at me, and I can see the vein in his jaw pulse as he bites down hard. My eyes quickly look away, going to Helena. "Helena," I greet her first, "so nice to see you again." I hold out my hand to shake hers.

"Sofia," she says my name and I look to see she is wearing pants and a button-down shirt with heels. Her hand is holding her black Chanel while the other hand holds on to Matthew. "You remember my fiancé, Matthew Petrov."

"I do." I turn my focus to Matthew and see that he's dressed up today, minus the jacket. "Matty, nice to meet you again." I use the nickname everyone calls him, everyone but me that is. I regret reaching for his hand the minute it slips into mine. I swear to God a tingle runs right through me like an electric shock. Pushing it away quickly, I pull my hand out of his. "Shall we get started?"

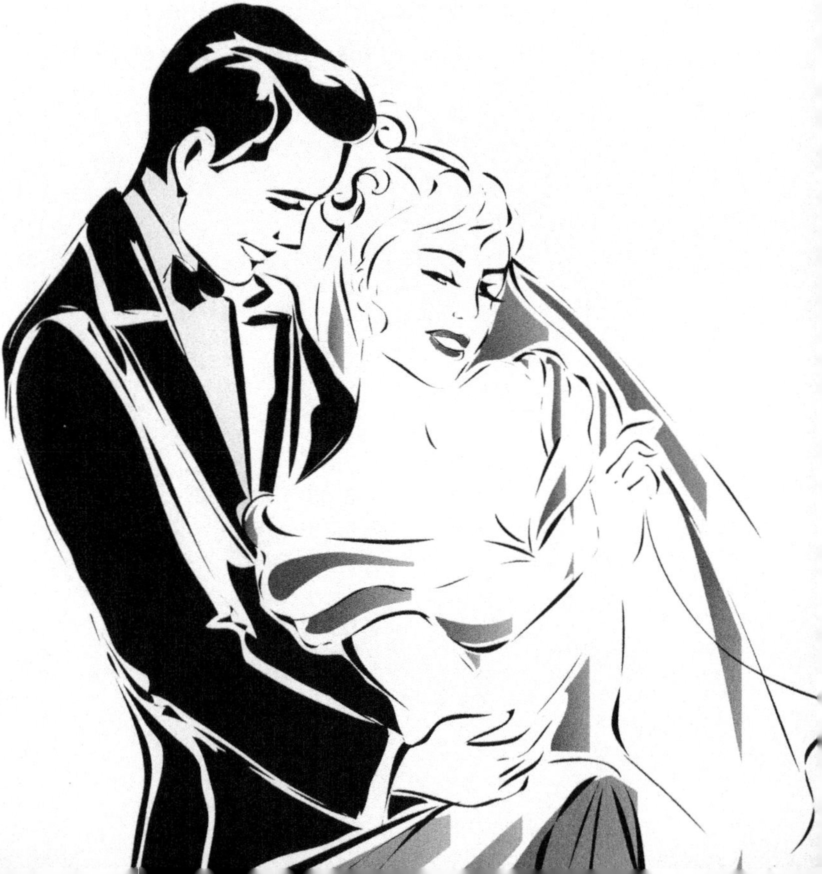

Eight

Matthew

I put my hand in my pocket the minute she lets it go for two reasons. One, it literally tingles, and, two, my cock who has been in hibernation is suddenly peeking its head out. The whole thing puts me in a foul mood, that, and the fact she is still calling me Matty. "Shall we get started?"

Oh, I'll get started all right, my head screams. I make the mistake of looking at her again and I hate that my body is reacting to her the way it is. She's just my ex-girlfriend, so what if I want her again. So what, that one look at her dressed in those fucking shoes and it brought back all the memories I never thought about until now. So what, when she turns to lead us to the back, all I can do is watch her ass move from side to side. Her hair also swishes, and I remember how she knew I like her with her hair loose, so she wore it like that all the time.

She stops walking, and if it wasn't for Helena pulling my hand in hers, I would have walked right into her. Which probably would have been a bad thing since she'd probably feel my dick and then think I'm some weird pervert. *You are a pervert*, my head is quick to call me out.

Sofia holds out her hand. "Please, have a seat." She waits for us to walk into her office before she follows us in. I wait for Helena to take a seat before sinking in one of the pink chairs. My eyes roam the room, as she walks around the L-shaped desk going to sit in her chair.

My eyes go to the shelves behind her as I see some of the pictures of her with her family. My eyes find a photo of her with a child in her arm. She holds the child on her hip as she smiles at the camera, her cheek on the child's head, and my heart sinks to my feet at the same time it lurches up to my throat. She's probably with someone. My eyes fly straight to her hands to look if there is a ring on her finger, seeing that there is no ring there.

I shake my head, asking myself: How fucking dumb am I? Here I am, sitting next to a woman who I asked to spend the rest of my life with, and here I am worrying about Sofia. I look over at Helena as she looks over at me, and I smile at her.

"Okay," Sofia says, looking at us and opening the folder on her desk as she grabs a pen. "I'm excited to start." She looks up at Helena. "Why don't we start with some questions so I can get a better idea of what I'm working with?"

"I'm so excited," Helena says as she looks at me.

"I know the first question that people usually ask is what the budget is, but before that, I would like to ask some questions to see if your budget is feasible." She looks down. "How large is the bridal party?"

Helena speaks up before I even have a chance to think about it. "I did a quick tally last night; I will have at least ten bridesmaids, so a good count is twenty." My head whips to the side to look at her, seeing if I heard her right. "We both have lots of friends." Um, no, we don't. I have lots of family members who I found out she doesn't even like. I look back at Sofia, who looks as if she's also surprised at that number, but all she does is make a note of it.

"What number are you thinking about for the guest list?" She looks back up and every single time she never looks at me. It's as if I'm not even here.

"Three to five hundred," Helena states.

"People?" I say out loud instead of in my head, and she chuckles at me.

"It's a big deal," Helena says. "You have to invite all your teammates, plus your family has lots of contacts that they will most likely invite." Oh, now she is okay with my family, I want to say but instead I look up at the ceiling. "I would hate to offend anyone by not inviting them," she tells Sofia, who just nods her head at her as she writes something else down. I wonder if she's making notes about how much this isn't at all like

I thought my wedding would be. I'd be lying if I said we hadn't discussed it while we were together. Both of us wanted an intimate wedding with just our family. Yes, that would probably be over two hundred people, but it wasn't anyone who we didn't know.

"I know you mentioned you wanted a black-and-white wedding," Sofia says to Helena. "Is it safe to say it's elegant?"

Helena pffts. "It's definitely going to be elegant."

"What is considered an elegant wedding?" I ask Sofia, and she has no choice but to look over at me. Our eyes meet as she starts talking all business. I've never met this Sofia. I'm used to the playful Sofia, who is always smiling, always snarky with me, but then always loving.

"An elegant wedding focuses on the luxurious elements that bring it all together." She folds her hands on top of the papers she's taking notes on. "It's like a five-star event. It's all about extravagance and beauty." She looks back to Helena. "Of course, it all depends on budget, but when it's as big as you want, little consideration is given to the cost."

"I love it already," Helena says to her.

"What month were we thinking?" Sofia now looks back at her notes.

"It has to be summer since he plays hockey," Helena reminds Sofia, and I want to groan that *everyone gets it*. Helena puts her hand on mine, and I just nod. "July would be the best to make sure everyone is out of playoffs."

"Are we thinking outside or inside?" Sofia doesn't even look up until Helena speaks.

"I would love both," Helena says, and in my head, I yell, *Of course you would.* "I would love to get married inside and have the party outside."

"We can do that," Sofia tells her. "Usually, the ceremony is inside unless it's a nice cool day and the bride wants a rustic feel. But then we can set up a tent that leads out from the ceremony space." Sofia avoids looking at me. "Will it be a one-day event?" My eyebrows pinch together at this question.

"We definitely need to have a rehearsal dinner." I look over at Helena and silently I have to admit I would hate to attend this wedding. "I'm thinking maybe two days before the wedding and then maybe a brunch the day after."

"I'm assuming with the guests coming in that you would need to provide accommodations?" Sofia asks, and all Helena does is nod. "So, we need to provide transportation from the hotel to the venue.

"The wedding will be an all-day event?" At this point, I don't even know if she is asking the question or telling us.

"It has to be," Helena says. "His family loves to have parties."

"Invitations." Sofia plods on. "I'm assuming that there was an engagement photo shoot?" She smiles, and for the first time, I see something flicker in her eyes, and I look down. What the fuck am I even doing here? This can't actually happen; she can't plan my wedding.

"We have not… yet," Helena says. "I would love to set it up."

"I can do that for you," Sofia assures her.

"We can ask my cousin Gabriella." I look over at Helena, who rolls her eyes.

"We can use the engagement photos for a *save the date* invitation," Sofia suggests. "I recommend this since this will be a big wedding."

"Wedding of the year," Helena sings and smiles.

"Sounds like it." Sofia smiles back at her. "Since it's so big, I suggest the *save the date* just so they know."

"When should we do this?" Helena asks.

"The sooner, the better," Sofia states. "Usually, people send out the wedding invitation four to five months before, so *save the dates* should be done seven to nine months out."

"Well, if Gabriella can't do it," Helena says hopefully, "we'll have to look elsewhere."

"We have a couple that we work closely with." Sofia tries to soften the tension. "We can look at that.

"Okay, the next questions are for the bridal party," Sofia says, and I want to get up and walk around, but instead my feet stay put.

"We have a bridal suite on-site," Sofia informs Helena. "I'm guessing that you would need makeup and a hairstylist, or will you be bringing your own?"

"Oh, I haven't thought about it," Helena says, and I want to laugh. Something she hasn't thought of, shocking.

"We have a list of people we work with. I'm thinking you would need three of each to help do the whole bridal party, plus the moms."

"And my aunts," I pipe up. "My cousins will most

likely also need that."

"We can't do everyone, Matty," Helena says, and I look at her, then back at Sofia.

"You must have more than three people on the list?" I ask, and she leans back in her chair. "Do you think we can set up the extra people at the hotel?"

"We can do whatever you want," Sofia confirms. "It's your wedding."

"Then I want to do that," I say, my leg now moving up and down with nerves. There is no fucking way that I'm going to have my family feel like they aren't included or that they don't matter. I don't even care anymore; I stand and stretch my legs.

"Would you like some water?" Sofia looks at me.

"If it's not too much trouble," I answer her and she pushes away from her desk, getting up.

"I'll be right back," she says, then looks at Helena. "Would you like some as well?"

"I'm fine." Helena smiles tightly at her. I wait for her to walk out of the room before I look over at Helena.

I don't even wait for her to say anything before I talk. "This is our wedding." She looks at me. "But my family is part of that wedding, whether you like it or not. I would do the same for your family."

"It's our wedding, not theirs," she declares, rolling her eyes. "We aren't paying for them to do their makeup."

"We aren't," I say, "but I am." I can't even imagine going to talk to my aunts and asking them to pay for their makeup. My father would kick my ass so fast, scratch that, my mother would kick my ass so fast.

"We aren't using Gabriella," she states as if she is going to win this.

"Then we aren't doing a *save the date*," I counter.

"Can we not discuss this here?" Helena says between clenched teeth when she looks over her shoulder as she hears the clicking of heels coming closer to us. "It's so embarrassing, and you're making this experience not fun."

I close my eyes, shaking my head before I walk back over and sit back down in the chair. Sofia walks back in with the water bottles on a silver tray. Helena grabs both bottles, handing me one. "Sorry about that," I say, not sure what I'm apologizing for.

Sofia sits back down. "Nothing to apologize for. Planning a wedding is a big deal." She smiles and looks over at Helena. "What about a dress?"

"I would love to have an original and I'm working on getting a designer." She smiles so big. "But I'm open to anyone you can suggest."

"I have a couple of names for you." Sofia smiles at her and my chest contracts as I think of her helping Helena with a wedding dress. I open the bottle of water, drinking it. The cold water hits me right away, and then she says, "We can do that without the groom."

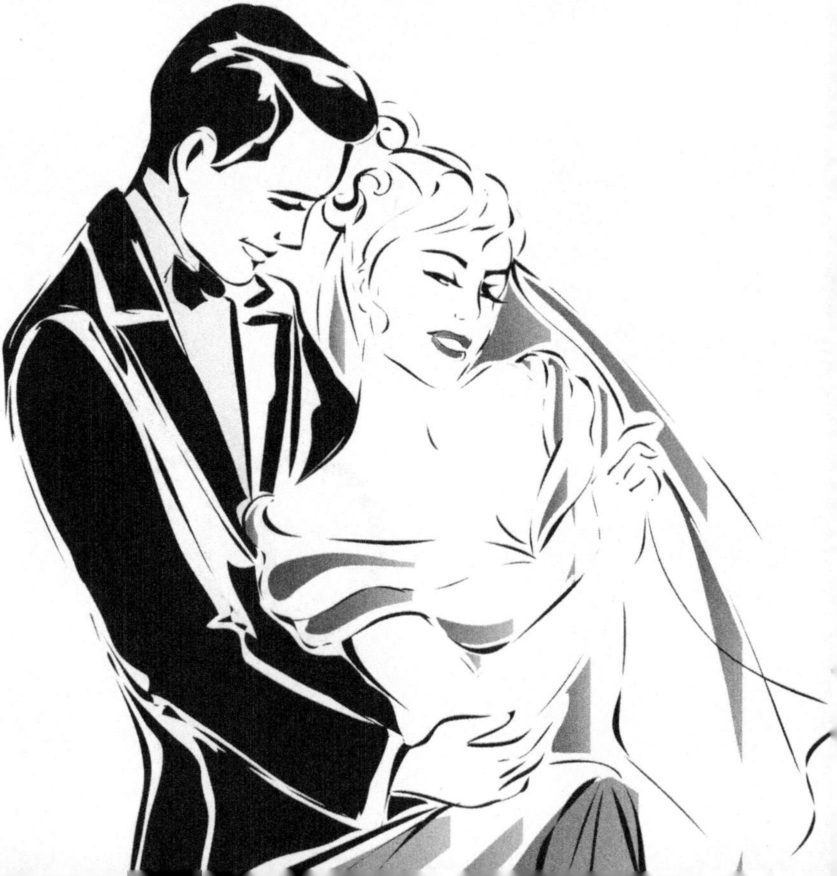

Nine

Sofia

I look down at the paper in front of me, not sure I can mask the fact that I'm going to help this woman pick out her wedding dress. I look at the paper with the rest of the questions empty, but I think I've done my part for the day. The rest of the questions aren't that important, and I can always reach out to her. "I think I have everything I need." I avoid looking back up, but I can't just look down at my papers until they walk out.

"What is the next step?" Helena asks excitedly, clapping her hands. If this were any other couple, I would probably be clapping my hands as well. This wedding is really going to be the wedding of the year and the commission will be amazing. Not only that but having this on my portfolio will be even more amazing.

"The next step is I take everything you told me and make a wedding plan," I tell her. "You can go over it and see if there is anything you think we should change or maybe there are things you see out there that you want to change things to." I go over the script I say all the time, ignoring the burning in the pit of my stomach. "After everything is said and done, we will have different days where we do different things."

"What does that mean?" Matthew asks.

"Well." I look over at him and fold my hands into each other and lean forward just a touch, knowing my tits will be pushed up. "One day, we will look at flower arrangements. Then the service setting, of course. We make a mock-up of everything that you chose so you can see exactly what it will look like on the day of your wedding."

"I love that," Helena says, her eyes have been lit up this whole time. She was the one doing all the talking all the time. The only time Matthew spoke up was about the makeup. This whole wedding is nothing like I thought his day would be. It's nothing like he said his day would be. When we were together, we would always talk about when we got married, but we were always on the same page. The only thing we wanted was our family and closest friends. Definitely not five hundred people.

"Wait until it's time to test the food." I smile at them both, this whole time avoiding looking at him.

"I'll work on this tomorrow," I state, instead of saying tonight, because how would that look, that I'm home alone at night? It screams I'm single. "Then send it over to you. If you have any questions, you can call me at any time. If you get home and discuss some of the answers you gave and would like to change something, it's not too late to change anything."

"This is going to be amazing," Helena says, looking at Matthew, who nods at her. The smile he gives her is as fake as fake can be. I can see the tightness in his shoulders. "It's going to be the best day of our lives."

I'm waiting for Matthew to say something, but he doesn't say anything, instead he gets up out of his seat. Helena follows him as she gets up, the smile never leaving her face. She holds out her hand for Matthew and he obliges when he slides his hand in hers, and a lump forms in my throat. I know what it feels like to be held by those hands, something I wish I didn't remember.

I follow them out, my eyes going straight to Matthew's ass. I shake my head and look down before Helena sees me checking out her fiancé. Once we go around the corner and into the waiting area, Helena stops and looks over at me. "Thank you so much, Sofia," she says, holding out her hand to me. She holds my hand in both of hers. "I'm so happy we decided to go with you." I make the mistake of looking over to Matthew to see what his face says to this statement, but he avoids looking at me.

"Thank you for putting your trust in me," I tell her and then look over at Matthew. "I promise to make your wedding amazing," I assure him, looking into his eyes as I stick out my hand, secretly calling him an asshole and a dickhead. He squeezes my hand a little bit more than he did before. I do the same thing, and when he drops my hand, I can still feel the heat from his.

He turns to look at Helena and puts his hand on her lower back to usher her out of the room. When the door closes behind them, I do what any average, sane person planning the wedding of their first love does. I walk back to my office and open the closet door, grabbing the half-empty bottle of sweet tea.

Kicking off my shoes as I walk over to my desk, I hear footsteps coming closer to my office. I look over to see the three of them walk in, just looking at me. Only after I sit down and take a shot of the sweet tea does Shelby start, "How are you feeling?"

I wait for the burning to subside from the sweet tea, as it burns all the way down to my stomach, and I have to wonder if it's the tea or the nerves at this point. I exhale a deep breath. "Like a concrete truck just ran me over." It's the most accurate description of how I was feeling during the whole meeting. I avoided looking at him and my stubbornness just told me that it's just another client.

"But was the concrete truck full?" Clarabella asks, and Presley just shakes her head.

"What difference does that make?" Presley asks, trying not to laugh.

"It makes all the difference in the world. With the concrete it would be fifty times heavier, if not more," Clarabella explains, and I just laugh.

"I think she's in shock," Presley suggests, and I just shake my head.

"I don't know if I'm in shock per se," I admit to them,

putting the cap back on the sweet tea. "But I do know that this might have been one of the hardest days I've had in my life."

"It's only going to get worse," Clarabella advises.

"What the hell is wrong with you?" Shelby screeches, throwing her hands up in the air.

"I'm not going to lie to her," she says, rolling her eyes. "What good would that do?"

"I don't know about you," I say, getting up and walking back over to put the sweet tea back where I took it from, "but I'm going home for the day." I slip my shoes back on.

"You should go home and get drunk," Clarabella urges and both Presley and Shelby hit her arm. "What? It's what I would do."

"This from the woman who slept with not her husband on her wedding night," Shelby says, laughing.

"I wasn't the only one." She points at her and Shelby gasps.

"I slept with Ace two days later," she defends herself, "two days is huge."

"If you say so," Clarabella says as they turn to walk out of the room. "Let me know if you need me."

"I will," I assure her, as I pack up the file and my laptop before I walk out of my office. I'm in a daze as I make my way home. My head keeps spinning around and around as I shut the car door with my hip before walking up the stairs to the front door, opening it by pressing in the code. I kick off my shoes as soon as I step in, walking to the kitchen and putting down my bags on the island.

My whole body aches, and I have to wonder if maybe I'm coming down with something. Walking over to the freezer, I take out one of my great-grandmother's chicken potpies she made me the last time I was with her. I put it on a baking pan before turning on the oven and placing it inside. I set the timer for forty-five minutes before I make my way upstairs to my bedroom. The bed is made since the cleaning lady was here today. I don't stop until I'm standing in front of my shower, opening the glass door, and turning on the hot water.

Once I'm undressed and tie my hair on top of my head, I step into the hot water. My head is still going around and around as I see his face. Always his fucking beautiful face. "This would be a lot easier if there was closure when we broke up," I tell myself as I turn off the water and step out, grabbing the plush white towel, wrapping it around myself. "No, it wouldn't," I answer myself as I put on a pair of cream, cashmere loose pants with a matching oversized, long-sleeved, V-neck sweater before making my way back downstairs. The smell of the potpie is filling the house. I walk over and grab the bottle of white wine from the fridge before opening the cupboard and taking down a crystal wineglass. Pouring wine to fill the glass halfway, I take a sip as I walk over to my bag, grabbing my laptop and notes from today.

Sitting on the stool, I open the folder and look down, seeing his name and then Helena's. I never thought this would be my reality. I mean, after we broke up, I had no idea what he was up to. He literally vanished from my life after a fight. My head wanders back to that fateful night.

The phone rang and I knew he just got off the ice. They were at an away game. "Hello," I answered him.

"Hey, baby," he said softly, and I couldn't help but smile when his voice would go soft like that. "Whatcha doing?"

"I was waiting for you to call," I told him. "That was a good win."

"It was the last minute of the game," he said, and I could have seen the smirk on his face.

"Are you still okay to go out?" I asked him of the plans we made when I got a call from the top event agency in Chicago, asking me to come in and meet them.

"You bet your ass," he said, and I got up. "Meet me at my place in about two hours. Gotta go, love you, baby."

"Love you, too," I said and hung up the phone. I spent an hour getting ready and headed over to his place. I sat on his stoop and waited for him. When he was ten minutes late, I texted him to see if he was okay, but got nothing. All it said was delivered. An hour later, I started to panic and called him, only for it to go straight to voice mail. I was pacing his porch back and forth, my phone in my hand as I watched the minutes tick by. I waited to see if the gray bubble would pop up, but nothing. I feared the worst when headlights pulled into his driveway. Not his truck but his friend Jake's. I walked down the steps, my heart beating in my chest, the fear had taken over my body. The car door opened, and he took one step out and then fell. I rushed to him but stopped when I heard him laughing. Jake rushed around the truck to pick him up.

"Is he?"

The fear left my body now that I knew he was okay and in its place was anger. "Wow."

"Hey there, baby," he slurred his words, and I just shook my head. "What is your problem?" He put his hands on his hips and, at that moment, it was the wrong thing to say.

"What's my problem?" I hissed out. "I just spent the last two hours wondering if you were hurt. I called you."

"Phone died," Jake said, but I took one look at him, and he shut up.

"It's not a big deal," Matthew huffed.

"I'm leaving," I said, and I walked past him, but he followed me.

"You're such a buzzkill," he said. His words hit me right in the heart. "I had a couple of drinks with the boys." He stopped when I turned around. "It's not that big of a deal."

"We had plans, Matthew," I reminded him, trying to get him to see my side.

"Plans change." He threw his hands up. "Whatever."

"Call me tomorrow," I said to him.

"Or how about I don't?" he said, and I turned around so slowly it was as if it was in slow motion. "If you leave, it's over." He's drunk *my head screamed at me. It was no use talking to him, so instead I just shook my head and walked to my car, leaving.*

I expected him to call me the next day, but instead I opened my door and there were my things in a box on my doorstep. That was the last time I spoke to Matthew.

The buzz for the oven makes me snap out of it. The feelings just as if it was back then, like a fresh wound being cut open again. I shake my head. "Fuck you, Matthew, and good riddance."

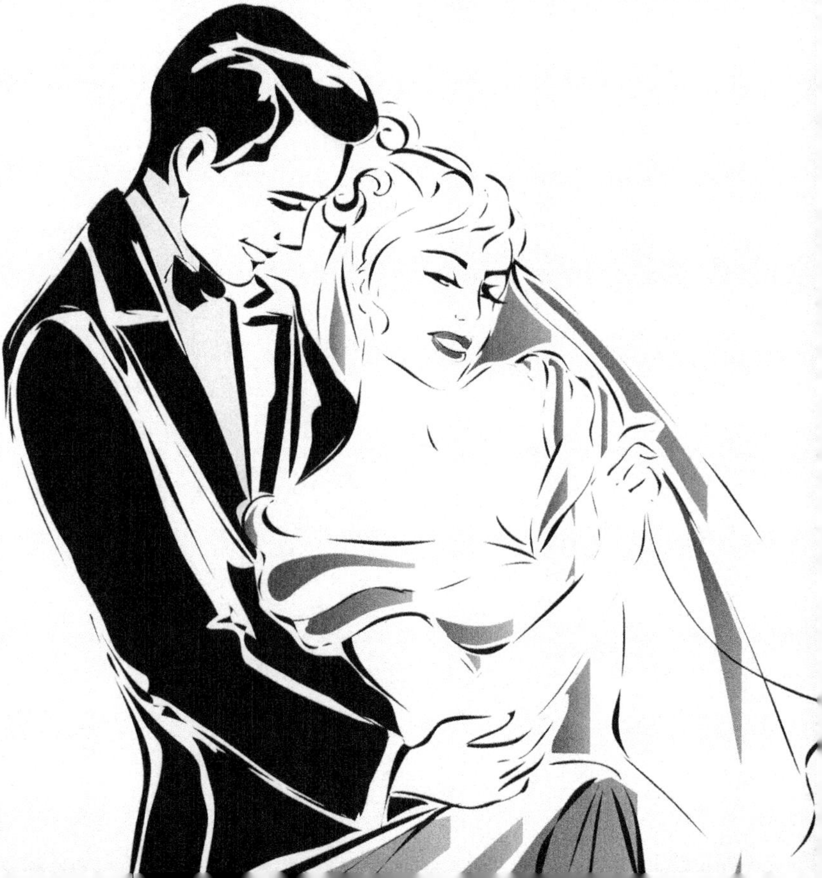

Ten

Matthew

"Push, push, push!" the coach yells as I'm skating down the ice with someone on my back. We've been on the ice for the last three hours. My legs burn from how much I've pushed them today. I hear the whistle blow and stop pushing my speed, skating the rest of the way down the ice.

My chest is heaving as I make my way slowly to move off the ice. I skate around a bit, getting my heartbeat back to normal. Getting off the ice, I walk down the corridor hearing the guys hooting and hollering. I don't talk to anyone as I make my way to my spot on the bench. I put my gloves up on the shelf, grabbing my phone and see I have a text from Helena.

Helena: Don't forget we are meeting at three.

I groan and put the phone down harder than I should and a couple of the guys glance over at me. Looking over at them as they question me with their look, I just shake my head as I undress and head to the shower. It's been ten days since the email from Sofia came through with the plan for this wedding.

To be honest, I didn't even pay attention to the plan. Never clicked the attachment, the only thing I focused on was her name and her phone number at the end of the email. A phone number I wasn't privy to. A phone number that was put in place after that fateful night. The night I fucked up so bad I've never talked about it.

I put my head under the hot showerhead and close my eyes. It's been ten days since the official wedding details came in. For the past ten days, I've been burying my head in the gym, in the game. Anywhere but what I am supposed to be focusing on and that is my wedding. Isn't it supposed to be a happy time? I thought it was, but it is turning out to be the worst time of my life.

Well, not the worst time of my life, that was two years ago when I was a fucking idiot. I turn off the water, grabbing my towel, and walk back into the locker room. It's pretty much cleared out, lots of the guys head over to the weight room after the ice training or to go eat.

I slip on my boxers and then my jeans when my phone rings. I pick it up and see it's Helena. "Hello," I answer as I put on my T-shirt.

"Hey, darling," she says, and I close my eyes. Since when did her voice make the sound of nails on a chalkboard? "I'm just reminding you about the appointment."

"Yup," I say to her. "I know, am I picking you up?"

"No," she huffs. "Do you not remember that I told you I had an appointment with the dressmaker?" Her voice is filled with annoyance.

"Must have slipped my mind," I tell her. "So I'll meet you there?"

"Yes," she hisses, "now I have to go." She disconnects the phone as I grab the baseball hat and put it on my head before slipping on my jacket.

Grabbing my keys, wallet, and phone, I head out. Unlocking my door and getting in my car, the phone rings again and I put my head back when I see it's my father. Usually, I'm more than happy to speak to him, but I know he's going to learn something is up. It's like he has Spidey senses.

"Hello," I greet, trying to sound as chipper as I can.

"Hey," he replies. "What are you up to?"

"Not much," I say, pulling out of the parking garage. "On my way to the wedding planner." I don't mention Sofia's name.

"Is that so?" I can tell his tone has changed. "What's going on?"

"Nothing." I try to fake it. I'm waiting for him to say something, but he doesn't, so I know he's waiting for me to say something.

"Cut the shit," he finally snaps, "you've been not yourself for the past, I don't know, two weeks—maybe even three."

I stop at a red light and close my eyes, even though he hasn't seen me in person, he has noticed the change in me. Now I question why hasn't Helena? "It's just." I inhale deeply before letting it out. "I don't know—all this wedding stuff."

"It can be overwhelming, for sure." He tries to calm me down.

"It's just." I look out the window and then hear someone honking at me. "It's just…"

"It's just what?" my father asks softly.

"I don't know, Dad," I tell him honestly. "I swear I feel like my life is spinning out of control and I can't get a handle on it."

"There are lots of changes coming your way." He talks me down off the ledge like he has so many times before. "You are going from single to married. You will be moving in with each other and starting your life together, it's a huge step."

"But that is the thing," I tell him. "Shouldn't it be easy?"

He just laughs. "Nothing in life is easy."

"I know, but knowing that you are going to start sharing a life with someone, shouldn't that be easy? It shouldn't be draining."

"You are right about that," he says, and I have to wonder if he isn't telling me this just to make me not feel like an idiot right now.

"The biggest thing you did in your life was propose to a woman and ask her to spend the rest of her life with you." I close my eyes, not ready to tell him I never really proposed. We were at dinner and discussing our future. The next thing I know, she's telling me she wants to get married next summer. I just went along with it because I thought that this was the next step.

"Maybe it's cold feet?" I ask and he just laughs.

"It could be." His voice gets low. "Have you talked to Helena about it?"

"No," I say right away, "I haven't spoken to anyone but you."

"Why don't you tell her how you feel?" he suggests. I want to tell him that if I told her how I felt, she would probably tell me it's stupid and it's all in my head.

I pull up to the office and see one car in the parking lot and park beside it. "I just got to the wedding planner. I'll call you later."

"Okay," he says, "don't be afraid to talk about how you're feeling."

Yeah, right, my head screams. If only I would have listened to that advice two years ago and not let my dumbass pride get in the way, maybe things would be different. Maybe, just maybe.

I walk up the steps and open the door to Sofia's office when I see a text from Helena.

Helena: *Running late at the dressmaker, be there soon.*

I panic when I see the text, getting ready to turn back around and go wait in the car, but the sound of clicking makes me look up and I see Sofia walking into the room. Her head is down, so it gives me a chance to study her without feeling like I shouldn't be looking at her. She's wearing another fucking skirt that hugs her hips and falls right at the knee. A tight black top shows off her perfect fucking tits. She always looks so elegant and put together. I mean she always did, even when we went riding horses, she looked like she just walked off the runway. Her hair is tucked behind her ear.

She must feel eyes on her because she looks up and sees me. Our eyes lock on each other as she comes farther into the room. My heart speeds up in my chest, which is now filled with nerves.

She looks around, not sure herself what to do. "Hello," she greets me, putting the file in front of her and I wonder if she's as nervous as I am. I wonder what she's been up to for the last two years. But more importantly, I wonder if she can ever forgive me.

"Hey," is the only thing I can say because my mouth suddenly runs dry.

She takes a look around, again not sure anymore. "Is Helena here?" she asks.

"She's at the dressmaker and she's running late," I reply, holding up the phone and she nods at me. "Um," I stutter, thinking about what to say next, "maybe we should—" I don't even have a chance to finish asking the question because she shakes her head.

"We should do nothing but wait for Helena," she states, and my stomach literally aches, and I hate it. I hate that this woman, who was once upon a time my best friend, the one I told my deepest secrets to, is now standing in front of me and she won't talk to me. *What the fuck did you expect?* my head yells at me. *You ended it with her in a drunken stupor and never went after her.* "How is your family?" I ask, knowing how much they mean to her. It was one of the things we had in common. My family is huge, and before her, I had never met anyone who could go toe-to-toe with my family.

"Fine," she answers curtly, and again, I fucking hate it.

"Sofia, I think we should." I take a step forward but stop when I hear the door open behind me. Looking over my shoulder, I see Helena. She is wearing tight jeans and a thick sweater.

"Sorry, darling," she says, walking to me and smiling up at me, getting on her tippy-toes and kissing my lips. "Have you started without me?" She looks over at Sofia, who just smiles at us.

"No," Sofia says softly. "We were just waiting for you. If you will follow me this way. I have three tables that I've set up as samples."

I follow her away from her office and down a corridor into a big room. "This room is nice," I note, looking around at the rustic area.

"It's not our style," Helena says, looking at me and then at Sofia.

"This is a setting area," Sofia informs her. "If you wanted to do it outside, a tent will have to be installed. This area is for smaller weddings and more for an intimate feel." I glare at Helena, who doesn't even feel fazed by my look, nor does she care. "Now this is the first table I have set up for you." She stops at a round table. "Obviously this is a smaller version of the table. I went with a white tablecloth, as you can see. You will see the large black plate on the bottom that never leaves the table until after the service." She points at the last plate with two white plates stacked on top of it. "I put together a sample menu that will go on each plate."

"I like it," Helena says. "I like the tall black vase." She points at the tall vase in the middle of the table filled with white flowers.

"I like the little ones." I point at the little square black vases that are smaller and filled with tulips and daisies. "It's easier to talk to the person across from you."

"Then I did this one a little bit more." She walks over to the table, and I hate everything about it. "Blingy," she says and Helena gasps.

It's a table with a black tablecloth and all the vases are clear with bling on them. The black-and-white plates in the middle have a black napkin inside of those rings that holds them together, again full of diamonds. "Now this," Helena declares, "is what we were looking for."

Sofia makes the mistake of looking up at me, waiting for me to say something, but instead I just look down at the table. There is chattering going on around me, but I just stare at the table setting. "I don't even think we need to see number three," I hear Helena say from beside me. Even though she walks over to the third table, but I don't, I just look from the first table to the second. Knowing I would never choose any of this.

"Okay, so I'll work on that," I hear Sofia say. "And I'll send you a couple of decorations that would add more bling," she says, and I can't even begin to think about more bling.

"Also, I would love the dance floor to be in white and our initials in black," Helena adds and Sofia nods at her as she makes a note.

"Sounds good," Sofia assures her as we walk back to the waiting area. "I'll work on that and send you guys the prices for each of those so you can look at them. Again, everything can be modified."

"Thank you so much!" Helena shrieks and claps her hands together all happy. "We will wait for your email." She turns to me. "Do you want to add anything?"

"No, I think I'm good," I reply, looking back at Sofia who is just standing there. "See you soon." I nod at her and walk out into the hot breeze.

"What is your problem?" Helena hisses out once we get to her car.

"I don't have a problem," I tell her, annoyed. "It's just too much," I finally say, and she rolls her eyes at me and folds her arms over her chest.

"Happy wife, happy life," she states. "Now, where are we going to eat?"

"I'm going home," I tell her. "I have an early morning." For the first time in our relationship, I lie to her.

"Ugh, fine," she pouts, "I'll go home and do more wedding planning."

"Okay," I say, leaning and kissing her lips before walking to my car.

"You've become so quiet lately," Helena says, right before I get in my car.

"Have I?" I ask, waiting for her to ask me why.

Waiting for her to ask me if I'm okay, but she doesn't, instead she just nods her head.

"Yes, and I don't like it." She turns and walks over to her car. "Don't ruin this experience for me." She gets into her car and takes off, leaving me staring at her taillights. I look toward the office, seeing a light on and wondering if I should go and talk to her. But just like two years ago, I turn around and walk away.

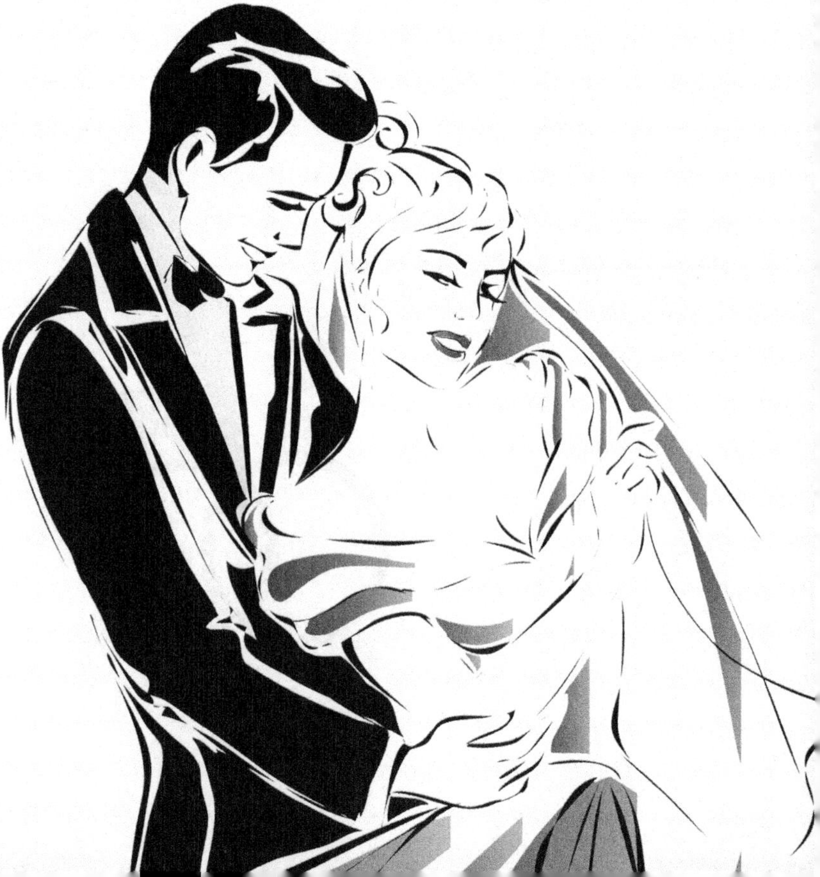

Eleven

Sofia

I'm standing in the conference room, going over different flower pictures in front of me. "Knock, knock, knock." I hear the voice coming from the hallway right before I hear the sound of the pitter-patter of feet running. "Charlotte, be careful." The minute I hear her name, a smile just fills my face.

"Sofia," Charlotte, my baby cousin, says running into the room, her voice bright and clear, matching the massive smile on her face. "Sofia, Sofia." I see her brown pigtails moving side to side as she makes her way over to me.

"Charlie, Charlie," I call her by her nickname, squatting down and opening my arms for her and she lunges herself into them.

"Sofia." She giggles my name as I bury my face in her neck blowing kisses. "That tickles." She squirms in my arms.

"Wow," my aunt Harlow says from the doorway, "you are wearing a white shirt and literally just took a toddler into your arms." She shakes her head. "Courageous." I look down at my white sleeveless shirt that I paired with my black-and-white checkered pants.

I smile at her and then look back at Charlie, who is playing with my hair as she looks at me. "She could be covered in red paint, and I would still want all the cuddles."

"I don't have red paint," Charlie says, looking down at herself.

"You don't," I tell her, and I bring her back to me to kiss her again. Ever since I was a young kid, my aunt Harlow was always by my side. We did everything together until she moved here about ten years ago. She came to attend the wedding of her ex-boyfriend, not knowing the wedding was going to be called off the same day. I heard from a couple of people that they started back again that very same night. Either way, she moved here, and Travis is Shelby, Clarabella, and Presley's older brother.

"Do I hear my little girl?" Clarabella says, sticking her head out of her office. "I have presents for you."

Charlie squirms out of my arms and runs out. "Traitor," I mumble, making Harlow laugh as she comes over to me and gives me a hug. "Where is Theo?"

"He's having a father/son day," she says with a

massive smile on her face. "Besides, I don't think Clarabella would be happy if he comes back here. Last time it was like the Roadrunner all over the place, and then he threw up in her office and didn't tell her." She tries not to laugh but fails. "Anyway, how is my favorite niece?" she asks and I give her the biggest hug.

"Amazing," I spout sarcastically.

"What is that tone?" she says, letting go of me.

I walk back to the table, and she follows me and looks down at the pictures of the flowers. "I'm in the middle of planning my first wedding." I look over at her as she moves the images around. "Matthew's wedding," I state, and her head whips to look over at me.

"Matthew who?" she asks, but I have a feeling she already knows what I'm about to tell her.

"No, you are not!" she shrieks out and throws her hands in the air. "You are fucking not."

"That's a bad word, Mommy," Charlotte says from the hallway.

"Sorry." She puts her hands on her cheeks. "Please explain to me what is happening right now?"

I laugh at her reaction, which I think is why I haven't told her. "Well, his fiancée, Helena, reached out to me." I start telling her the story as she pulls out a chair. I sit down next to her as I recap everything that has been going on. "The last time he came in, he was alone," I tell her, the pit of my stomach burning when I think back to the day last week. "He said we should talk, but I cut him off."

"Don't you think you two should have a conversation?"

she asks and I glare at her. She holds her hands up to me in a motion not to go after her. "I'm just saying, you guys didn't exactly have closure."

"I mean, it's pretty much self-explanatory that he breaks up with me and then dumps my shit at my door," I point out.

"But didn't you send his shit back with a guy?" she reminds me, and I roll my eyes. Did I get pissed off when he sent my things back? Yes. Did I do the most petty thing of all time and ask a hot guy to do me a favor? Yes.

"What choice did I have?" I ask.

"I don't know, maybe calling him and asking him if you could talk?" The glare I had on my face before is nothing like it is now. "I'm just saying that you two never got closure."

"Oh, nothing says closure like a box of your shit that he had at his house on your doorstep after standing me up for a date and arriving back home drunk." I shake my head.

"This explains why Grandpa needed me to bring you some extra sweet tea," Harlow voices, and I shake my head laughing.

"I might have called in a small favor." I hold up my hands and press them together. "Anyway, it'll be fine. Today we pick the flowers, and I think I'll be clear of him until it's closer to the wedding." She looks at me, not sure about what I'm saying. "In other news, guess who has a date tonight?" She opens her eyes even bigger now.

"Not from that dating app?" she huffs.

"Is nothing a secret?" I throw up my hands.

Harlow tosses her head back and laughs. "If you wanted to keep things a secret, why the hell would you let my sisters-in-law help you?"

"Good point," I concede, laughing. "Well, by tonight we are going to know if it's a good plan or a bad plan. But before then, I have a flower appointment in thirty minutes."

"Oh, this should be good," Harlow says, getting up.

"So good." I put my hands up in fists and shake them side to side sarcastically. Harlow bends to kiss my shoulder as she walks out of the conference room. I get up and take the pictures with me to the space we were in before.

The three tables are set up with the same plates as Helena chose at the last meeting and asked that I add more bling. I grab the flowers as I arrange them on the table the way I have them in the pictures.

I hear the bell ring, letting me know they are here. I look down at my watch and see they are five minutes early. I walk over to the door, opening it to the waiting room, and again he's alone. He's standing there in track pants and a matching track jacket. His baseball hat is backward, and I have this sudden vision in my head of him walking in and kissing me. It's so vivid that I'm stuck in mid step, making him look up at me.

"Hey," he says softly, his eyes look like he hasn't slept in a while and his face looks troubled. "Sorry, I came right after practice." He looks down at his outfit.

"No worries," I say to him, walking into the room, wringing my hands in front of me nervously.

"Would you like something to drink?" I ask at the same time I turn to walk to the kitchen.

"Water would be good," he replies to me as I walk over to the fridge behind the counter.

"Is it okay that it's in the fridge?" I ask and he nods his head at me.

I grab a bottle of water and bring it over to him. "Here you are," I offer, holding the bottle out to him. His fingers graze mine, and my body tingles. My eyes fly up to his to see if he felt the same thing I felt and, sure enough, he's looking at me.

"Thank you," he says softly as I let the bottle go. All I can do is nod at him because my heart has moved from the middle of my chest to my throat. I shake my hand, trying to erase the heat of his hand when the door opens.

Helena comes in, and I have to say that we could not be more different. It's a night and day sort of thing. She has light hair, whereas I have dark hair. Her eyes are also light, whereas mine are darker. Her skin is like a porcelain doll where I have a golden sun-kissed look.

"Sorry I'm late again," she mentions as she goes to Matthew, who smiles at her. "Hi," she greets him, tilting her head back and he bends to kiss her lips, but I turn away before I see it. I'm a glutton for punishment but I'm not a psychopath.

"Shall we?" I look over at them as I walk back to the room where the flowers are. I hold the door open for them. "To give a better picture of the flowers," I explain when they step in, "I had it set up with the place setting you chose." We walk over to the table.

"Oh, look at how pretty these are," Helena says of the chandelier candle vases she said she wanted. "This is exactly like I thought it would look."

"As you can see from this flower arrangement, I went with mostly all white flowers," I tell her of the bouquet of white roses that is tied together with a couple of black roses intertwined in them. The black roses have a diamond in the middle. I look over at Matthew to see what he thinks, but I don't even think he's listening. I mean, let's be honest, the bride usually has all the ideas and vision. The groom is just around for the ride. I would say one out of five grooms actually has an opinion. "The next one," I continue, "I added green in there to give it a more earthy feeling."

Helena hems and haws through the flower centerpieces. I'm very hands-on, so I'm right there creating the perfect piece for her. "That's it," she finally declares after what seems like twenty-five different changes she had me make.

"It's going to look stunning." I smile at her and take out my phone to take a picture of it, and it beeps in my hand.

Charles: Can't wait to see you.

Charles and I have exchanged a couple of messages over the last three or four days. I finally caved and agreed to go out for dinner tonight. I don't know what I was thinking.

"So what's next?" Helena asks as we turn to walk back to the front door.

"I will send you over some sample menus, and we can

set up some taste testing for next week."

The phone buzzes in my hand, but I ignore it. "If there is anything that you want to try that is not on the menu, all you have to do is tell me. Our in-house chef is very good at finding what we need." I'm about to say something else when the front door opens, and Charles comes in with a bouquet in his hand. "Oh, I'm so sorry, I'm early," Charles apologizes and all I can do is smile at him, while I secretly scream internally. *This is not happening,* I tell myself, *this can't be happening. Not here, not now, and of all people not with Matthew here.* My heart speeds up as I take a step to him. I can see Matthew look at him and then back at me.

"It's fine," I say, walking to him. "We were just finishing up." I stand in front of him and look into his brown eyes. "Do you want to wait in my office?" Please, God, don't make him say he doesn't know which one it is. I ask the universe to be kind to me.

"Oh, don't even worry about it," Helena says. "We took up too much of your time." She smiles at me and then looks at Matthew, who just sizes him up. "Have a great night."

"Thank you," I say to them as they walk out, and I swear I feel like I let out the biggest sigh of relief.

"I'm really sorry. I thought you said you were done," Charles says.

"No, no, it's fine." I try to play it off, laughing nervously. "It went longer than I thought it would be."

"These are for you," he announces, handing me the bouquet of carnations. *Don't judge him,* the left side of my brain says, while the right side says, *that flower is for funerals.*

"Thank you, I'm going to put these in water and then we can get going," I tell him, and he just nods at me. I walk over to the kitchen, taking a couple of glances at him while he takes a look at the pictures on the wall. He stands there in chinos and a sweater. He's about six foot three, and his black hair is curly. He pushes his glasses up from the middle of his nose.

Why are you doing this? I ask myself right before the other side of my head says, *she's trying not to think about the guy who just left.*

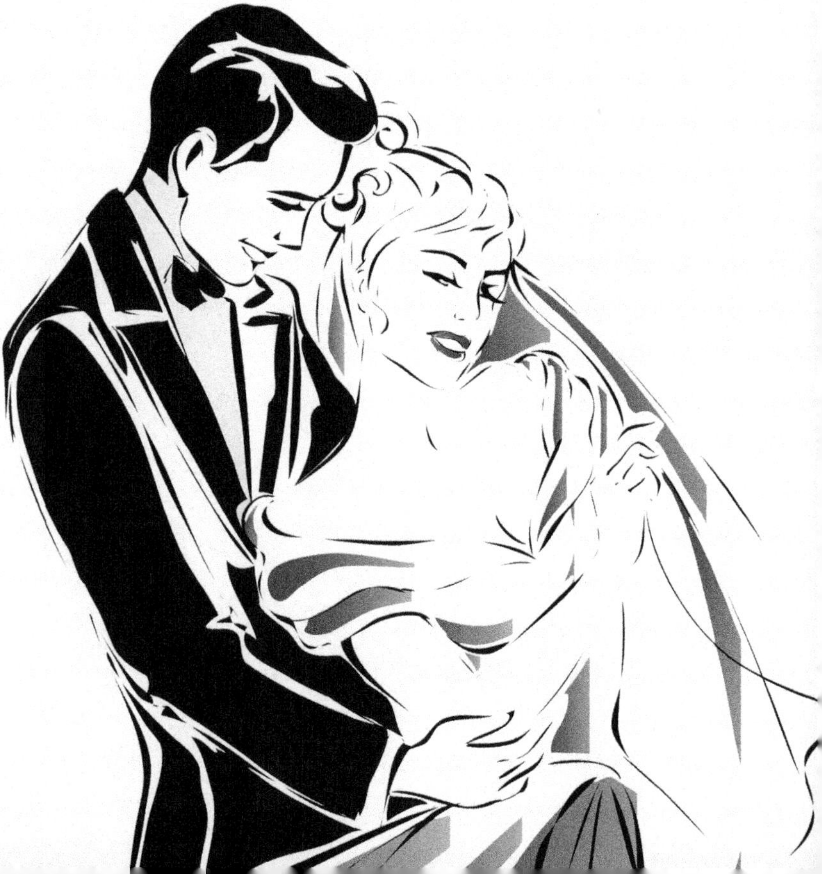

Twelve

Matthew

I walk into the house and toss my keys on the island in the kitchen. My head feels like it's going to explode. Sliding my jacket off and putting it on the stool, I walk over to the bathroom on the main floor and open the first drawer, grabbing the bottle of ibuprofen. I open the top and shake two out in my hand before popping them in my mouth. I turn the water on, bending to take some in my mouth to swallow the pills. I put the bottle back in the drawer, slamming it shut at the same time I hear the door close. What a fucking day this has been.

Getting to the venue ahead of Helena wasn't something I planned, but I also wasn't mad about it. The last time we were together, I tried to get her to talk to me about things, but she ignored me at every single turn. How the hell am I supposed to apologize to her if she won't give me the time of day? I just wanted to tell her I was sorry. To explain what happened was me being young and dumb, but she wouldn't hear me out. I mean, it could have been worse, she could have told me to go and fuck myself, which is something I think I would have done to myself. Or she could have easily kicked me in the balls, which is also what I deserved. But instead, we pretended we didn't love each other for two years. We pretended we barely knew each other when, in fact, I knew every single fucking inch of her with my eyes closed. She was my first love and I know they say you never forget your first love. I was just hoping I would be able to survive my first love.

"I'm here," Helena announces from the door, "and I got food." I close my eyes as my head falls forward. I put my hands on the white marble counter as I take a deep inhale and then exhale. The headache is now pounding even more. "Matty," she calls for me.

"In the bathroom," I say over my shoulder, and I hear her making her way toward the kitchen. I take a couple of minutes to myself before pushing off the counter and walking out.

The lights are all on in the kitchen as she moves around to grab plates. "Do you want anything to drink?" she asks over her shoulder.

"Just water," I tell her as I walk over to the fridge, grabbing a bottle of water. She leans over me, grasping the bottle of white wine she opened last weekend when she came for dinner. She walks over to the side, grabbing a crystal glass as she pops the cork out and pours herself a small glass.

I walk over to the bags on the island, reaching in and grabbing one of the takeout containers. "I got you chicken," she informs me as I pick up the second one and see it's chicken. I grab both containers and take them over to the stools. Placing one in front of her place, I sit down on my own stool and open the container. "Are you not going to use a plate?" she asks, coming over with two plates in her hand.

"No," I say, grabbing a fork and knife from her as she sits down on the stool beside me.

She sits down and plates her food before starting to eat. "So which flowers did you like the most?" she asks, and I shrug my shoulders.

"They all looked the same to me," I answer her honestly, without telling her my head was trying to focus on the flowers but instead I was trying not to run out of there.

"Did you like the new touches I added?" she quizzes me, grabbing her glass of wine and taking a sip. "I think more bling makes it more elegant."

"We can agree to disagree on that," I say, trying to just finish my chicken.

I know she wants to say something but instead she says nothing. She cuts a piece of her salmon before she turns back to me. "You're quiet." I don't know if she is asking me or telling me.

I look over at her and see her looking at me, her fork

down on the plate in front of her. "No, I'm not." I shake my head and avoid making eye contact with her. *I just need to shake this off,* I think to myself.

"Yes, you are," she retorts, her voice going higher at the end. "You don't call me anymore. It's always me who calls you." I try to find a comeback to say something to her, but for the life of me I don't remember when the last time I called her was. I mean, we talk mostly every day; I've been on the road quite a bit. Sometimes the time difference was an issue. I close my eyes, thinking that all I'm doing is making excuses for being an asshole.

"It's been a busy month," I say, avoiding looking at her.

"We haven't had sex in over six weeks." I look over at her, pretty sure that is wrong. "Don't even try," she warns me, her tone sounding more and more annoyed. "You've been out of it since we started planning the wedding." *No shit,* my head screams at her. I put my own fork down, knowing she isn't going to just let this slide. I also know, perhaps we should have this conversation. I know deep down inside this conversation is a month too late. This conversation should have happened the minute she told me Sofia was our wedding planner. I should have put my foot down and told her no. "Do you not want to do this?" she asks.

"What do you mean?" I look down at my hand on the island. My finger taps nervously as my heart speeds up now.

"Do you not want to get married?" The minute she says those words, it's as if my head just screams. I close my eyes for a second before I look over at her. I don't have to say a word to her. I don't say anything because all of the words feel like they are spinning around and around in my head as I try to find the right ones. But she doesn't give me that minute to compose them, and to be honest, isn't a minute too long? It should be a quick answer. "Oh my God, you don't!" she shrieks and pushes away from the island.

I watch her walk to the other side of the island as she stares at me. "I don't know." The words come out in a whisper as I admit it finally to her. I thought saying it out loud would be like a weight being lifted off my shoulders, but it's not like that at all.

"What the fuck, Matty?" she yells, her hands going up in the air. *Yes, what the fuck indeed*, my head doesn't help this situation at all.

I take a deep inhale as the pit of my stomach burns and the heat starts to rise to my neck.

"I don't think we should get married." The words that have been on the tip of my tongue for the last month finally come out. Shocking even myself.

I look at her, waiting for her to say something. Waiting for a sign that maybe we should get married. Perhaps we just need to talk this out. But when she says the next words, I know it would not have worked in the end. "Are you fucking kidding me? I just put in my order for my wedding dress." I close my eyes. Instead of telling me that we love each other and can work through whatever is going on, she's more worried about her wedding dress and the money she put down.

I take a second to look at her, seeing her eyes looking at me like she could kill me. There are no tears there because our relationship is ending. "I'll reimburse you," is the only thing I say to her, and if I thought her look could kill me before, I was wrong. This look would have me ten feet in the grave. "Fuck you, Matty," she hisses, "do you know how embarrassing this is going to be for me?"

I close my eyes as she huffs and rub my hands over my face. "You think this is easy for me?"

"I don't give a fuck about if it's easy for you or not. What the hell am I supposed to tell my family?"

I shake my head. "I have no idea. We could maybe just say that we are putting it on the back burner." I try to think of something to tell her.

"Back burner," she repeats what I said and even I want to shake my head at how dumb it sounded. "Fuck you, Matty." She turns and grabs her stuff. "Fuck you all the way to hell, where you are going to rot for doing this to me."

"Helena," I call her name before she walks out of the room. "I'm really sorry."

"I can't believe I was going to settle by marrying you," she says. "My mother said you were beneath me," she pffts, and I about laugh at how childish she sounds. "I mean, look at your family."

I stare at her for a good five seconds, giving her a chance not to say the next words about to come out of her mouth. She wants to shit on me, fine, I deserve it, but my family. "Watch it," is all I say.

"Or what?" She cocks her hip to the side. "You're a sad excuse for a man."

"Actually." I hold my hand up. "A sad excuse of a man would have gone through with the wedding and then divorced you." She takes one more look at me before shaking her head and walking out the door, slamming it as hard as she can behind her.

My head falls forward, and I don't know if I do a sigh of relief or if it's an *I fucked up* sigh. Either way, I push away from the island and walk over to the living room. I sit down on the couch and rest my head back. Looking up at the ceiling, I run the past hour through my head.

I try to piece the puzzle that is going on in my head as to when it all went to shit. When did it change? Was it always this way and I was just blind to it?

Getting up, I walk over and grab my jacket and walk back over to the couch. Looking at it, I know there is only one person who I can possibly call. There is only one person who I want to call right now. I dial the number, putting it on speaker. One ring leads to two and I know there is never three rings. "Hello," he answers before the second ring even finishes.

"Dad," I say, my voice monotone, "the wedding is off." I close my eyes as the words come out.

"I'm on my way," he says. "I'll be there tomorrow." I look down at the phone. "Are you okay?"

"I have no idea," is the only answer I can say. "I'm kind of numb, to be honest."

"It'll be okay," he assures me softly. "I promise you it'll be okay. I'm going to get things organized here and

I'll send you the details."

"Okay," I say. Even though I know I should tell him that it's fine, something about him coming to me makes it feel like everything is going to be okay.

I hang up the phone but never move from the couch. My phone rings five minutes later. When I look down, thinking it's my father, instead I see it's Christopher. "Hello."

"What the fuck happened?" he asks as soon as I answer the phone.

"Who told you?" I ask, closing my eyes.

He chuckles on his side of the phone. "They sent out the Bat-Signal."

For the first time since Helena and I broke up, I laugh, and it just feels lighter in my chest. I don't know why I'm surprised that it already made it to him. Actually, I'm surprised it took him five minutes. "It was all wrong, man," I finally admit it out loud. "All fucking wrong."

"Does this have to do with Sofia?" He was the only one I told that I saw her again.

"No," I answer without thinking twice. "This had everything to do with Helena and me."

"Well, I wish I could be there for you tomorrow." He laughs. "I'll FaceTime sometime soon, for sure."

"Thanks," I tell him. "I'll call you tomorrow. I'm going to go and—"

"Definitely not drown your sorrows," he jokes with me.

"Nah," I say, after the night that I fucked up everything, I never took another drink again. I was never not going to have a clear head. Actually, scratch that, the only time I would make an exception was if I won the Stanley Cup, otherwise it was always a no. "Thanks for checking on me."

"Always," he states before he disconnects. I put my phone down beside me, taking in the quiet of the house when the phone beeps beside me.

Looking over, I see that Helena texted me. I don't know what I'm expecting but it gives me a light of who she is.

Helena: I'm not paying the wedding planner.

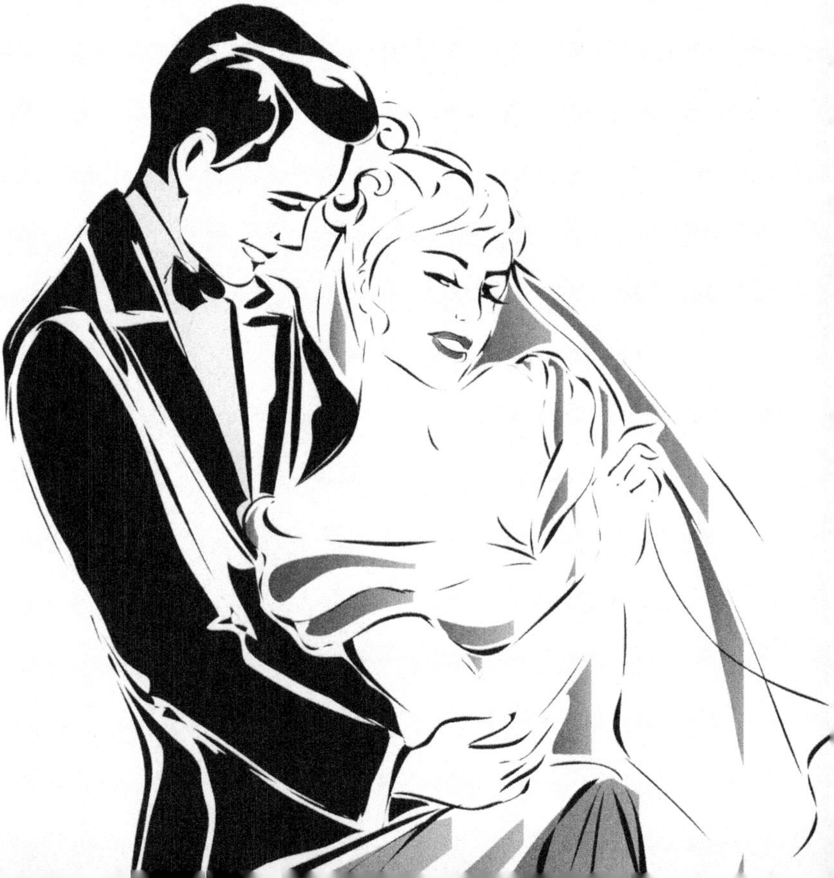

Thirteen

Sofia

I jog up the steps to the office, pulling open the door. Taking a look around, I see no one there waiting for me, which is weird since I had my date last night. "Good morning," I say loudly while I turn to walk down the hallway to my office.

"We are already in the conference room, waiting to be briefed!" Clarabella yells out.

"We have coffee and mimosas," Presley says, "without champagne because Shelby is a stick in the mud." I roll my lips. "And we have to work," she mimics Shelby.

"It's freshly squeezed," Shelby gasps.

I laugh as I pass by my office and walk right into the conference room. "So coffee and orange juice?" I say, looking at the tray that is in the middle of the desk, which holds a pot of coffee and a pitcher of orange juice with four glasses beside it. There is also a tray of croissants next to it with fresh fruit. "Oh, look at this continental breakfast." I pull out a chair and sit down, placing my purse to the side.

I grab a mug for the coffee and pour it, adding a splash of milk. "So?" Shelby looks over at me.

"So," I say, "it was nice." I try to sound optimistic.

"It was nice," Presley repeats and then looks over at Clarabella, who just shrugs before talking.

"I'm just going to say I was right." She looks at her sisters and back at me.

"Right about?" I ask, taking a sip of my coffee.

"I said that you didn't sleep with him last night," she finally says, and I gasp. "They said you would."

"It was a first date!" I look at both Shelby and Presley who glare at Clarabella.

"That is not even how it went," Presley corrects. "You said she wouldn't be doing the walk of shame."

"And I was right." She points at me. "She didn't even walk in here with a pep in her step. It was monotone, like her vagina."

"Ummm." I don't know what to say. "One, I wasn't going to sleep with him on the first date," I declare and then they all look at me. "And two, do you think I would come to work wearing the same thing as the night before?" I roll my eyes, looking down at my black jeans I slid on this morning with a white turtleneck and a plaid jacket. "I would at least go home and change."

"So did you have sex with him?" Shelby leans into the table, waiting for me to answer.

"No!" I shriek as they all look at me. "Okay, fine, it was a nice time. But…"

"Nothing good comes from a but," Presley says, leaning back in her chair, "not one thing. I love you but you're using your teeth too much."

"I love you but," Clarabella adds, "we can't have sex all day, we have a baby now."

I roll my lips trying not to laugh at them, but I can't help it. I throw my head back and laugh while Shelby just shakes her head. "I can top that; I love you, but your mother is in the kitchen."

"Ewwww." Clarabella winces. "You were going to have sex with Mom in the kitchen of your house?"

"No." Shelby shakes her head. "We were at Mom's house."

"Oh, for the love of God," Clarabella says, "it better have been in your room."

Shelby looks around the room. "You did not put your skanky ass on a communal area," Presley throws out between clenched teeth.

Shelby gasps out loud. "One, I don't have a skanky ass. He's my husband." She holds up her hand with her rings on it. "And two, what communal area? It's Mom's house."

"The bathroom," Clarabella says with a smirk. "Don't feel bad, we did it there also."

"I'm never using that bathroom again," Presley vows, looking like she is going to throw up.

"We put a towel down," Shelby says, looking over at Clarabella.

"We did not," she informs us, and now Presley pretends to vomit.

"Can you guys not wait to get home?" Presley asks them. "Like, it's Mom's house, what the hell were you guys doing that got you all hot and bothered that you needed to jump his boner?"

"Luke came in and brought me my favorite food," Clarabella clarifies.

"Ace was gone for two days, and when he came in, he gave me a look," Shelby explains, and I have to say I don't think I have ever lost my head about someone that just one look did it. *Liar*, my head yells. With Matthew, one look was all it took, and you were either down on your knees or pushed up to a hard surface, fuck, any surface. We did it in the closet of a restaurant once because he kissed my neck and told me I was fucking beautiful in my ear. "Anyway," Shelby says, "how was he?"

"It was fine," I repeat. "He was fine. It was just we didn't really have much in common."

"You don't have to have anything in common to get the D," Clarabella says and the other two agree with her.

"Ugh, fine," I concede, throwing my hands up like waving the white flag. "It was dull. He was nice, but I swear to God, I think I would have had a better time watching paint dry."

"What did you tell him?" Shelby asks and I literally bang my head on the table.

"Oh, you didn't tell him," Presley says softly, and I

just shake my head.

"What was I supposed to say?" I ask them when I finally put my head up. "It's not you, you are really a nice guy." I look at them and they must know I'm not finished. "That's the shittiest thing to say."

"Not if it's the truth," Clarabella states and now we all glare at her. "Hey, I'm a fucking unicorn, so it's never me, it's them."

"I don't think you should give up that easily," Shelby says, "maybe he was nervous."

"Yes, maybe he's dull outside and a freak in the bed," Clarabella adds, and I just look at her, my eyebrows going up and down. "What? It sounded like a good thing to say, but he probably just does it missionary."

I close my eyes. "I don't even want to know." I get up. "I'm going to call him later."

"Or ignore him," Presley urges.

"That worked great for you." Shelby gets up laughing. "Didn't you just have his second child?"

"I didn't ignore him," she says, avoiding looking at anyone. "I was busy."

I can't help but laugh before I walk out of the room and go to my office. The vase of carnations is on the side of my desk. I pick it up and walk out toward the kitchen with it. "Who died?" Presley asks when I walk by her office.

"He brought me these before the date," I throw over my shoulder, and she gasps out loud.

"You should have led with that before," she says, laughing. "I would have pretended I was vomiting in the bathroom before we even left."

I put the flowers on the counter in the kitchen before going back to my office and starting my computer. I scan my emails, surprised I don't have any from Helena with her questions on the flowers. Every single time we've had a meeting, she emails me at least five times with different questions.

I answer a couple of emails from new clients and set up five meetings for the following week. The girls head out to have lunch and I opt to just work, hoping I can get things done so I can go visit the family for the weekend.

The bells ring, alerting me that someone just walked into the office. I get up and walk out with a smile on my face that quickly fades when I see who is standing there. "Hi," I say to Matthew, folding my arms over my chest. A chill runs through me. "Is everything okay?"

He is in his track suit again with that stupid baseball hat backward. Why is that so hot, like why? Oh, I know why, because he used to wear it like that all the time so he could kiss you without it banging your forehead, that's why. "Yeah," he huffs, and I don't know why something seems off. "I came to give you this."

He holds a white envelope in his hand and for the life of me my hands stay stuck to me. "You can take it," he urges me.

My hand slowly reaches up to grab the envelope, my stomach burning when I think it might be a letter he's written to me since I won't give him the time of day. My name is written in the middle of it with a line under it. I turn it over in my hand, trying not to make him see that my hand is shaking. I see the top of a check when I open it and I don't know if I'm disappointed that it's not a letter or happy. "That is a check," he says when I pull it out and see that it's a check for the whole invoice of services, "for your services."

"Umm," I say, looking down at it. "You don't have to pay for the whole thing now," I tell him. "I know you are good for it." I look up, trying to make a joke, but everything about this feels off. Every time I'm alone with him it feels off. Like there is this huge-ass elephant sitting in the room and we aren't talking about it. But said elephant feels like it's crushing my chest.

"Actually," he says, and I finally look into his eyes, "I'm also here to tell you that the wedding is off."

The minute he says the words, my ears start to buzz. "Excuse me?" I say shocked, thinking maybe I heard wrong.

"I don't know if there were deposits made on any other things," he continues, ignoring my question. "If there is anything, I will cover that also."

I am at a loss for words, and I have no idea what to say. I keep looking at him, then down at the check and back up at him again. My mouth is going so dry I don't even think I would be able to swallow cold water. "Sofia," he says in almost a whisper.

I blink away the tears stinging my nose and my eyes as I look up at him, his eyes so dark blue it looks like the deep end of the ocean. You know when you go far out to sea and the water gets darker and darker, that is exactly what it looks like. I'm about to say his name when the door opens. Both of us look over to see Charles walking in with two coffees in his hands. He looks at me and smiles. "I'll go," I hear Matthew say, my eyes go back to look at him as he nods at me. He turns to walk out the door, nodding at Charles at the same time.

"I'm sorry," Charles says, laughing nervously, "it seems I really don't have good timing." I try not to let what just happened get to me, but I can't help it. All I can hear is *the wedding is off.* "I was in the neighborhood," he explains, coming to stand in front of me, "and I thought I would drop off some coffee."

I force a smile on my face because if not, I know my parents would kick my ass if I was rude. "Thank you," I say, reaching out and grabbing a cup from him.

"I got this one for you also, not knowing if you wanted regular milk or oat milk," he says of the other cup of coffee in his hand.

"That is very kind of you," I tell him, grabbing the other one.

"I was also wondering if you were free tonight?" he asks, putting his hands in his pockets, and I can't help comparing how different he is from Matthew.

"I'm sorry, I'm swamped all week," I tell him. "And then I'm going home to see the family this weekend." He looks at me awkwardly. "But how about I touch base with you next week?"

"That sounds perfect," he replies, his face filling with a smile. "I'll let you go." He leans in to kiss my cheek. "Have a great time with your family," he says, turning and walking to the door.

"Thank you," I tell him, "and for bringing me coffee." He leaves, and I let out a huge sigh, walking back to my office. Sitting down, I put the coffee to the side before looking back at the check, my name written in the comments section. I hear the girls walk back into the office and get up going to Shelby's.

She is sitting down reading something on her computer when she looks up. I put the check down in front of her, not saying anything to her. She looks down at it, then picks it up and looks at me. "What is this?" she asks.

"That is the check from Matthew and Helena's wedding," I say, trying not to freak out, "that has just been cancelled."

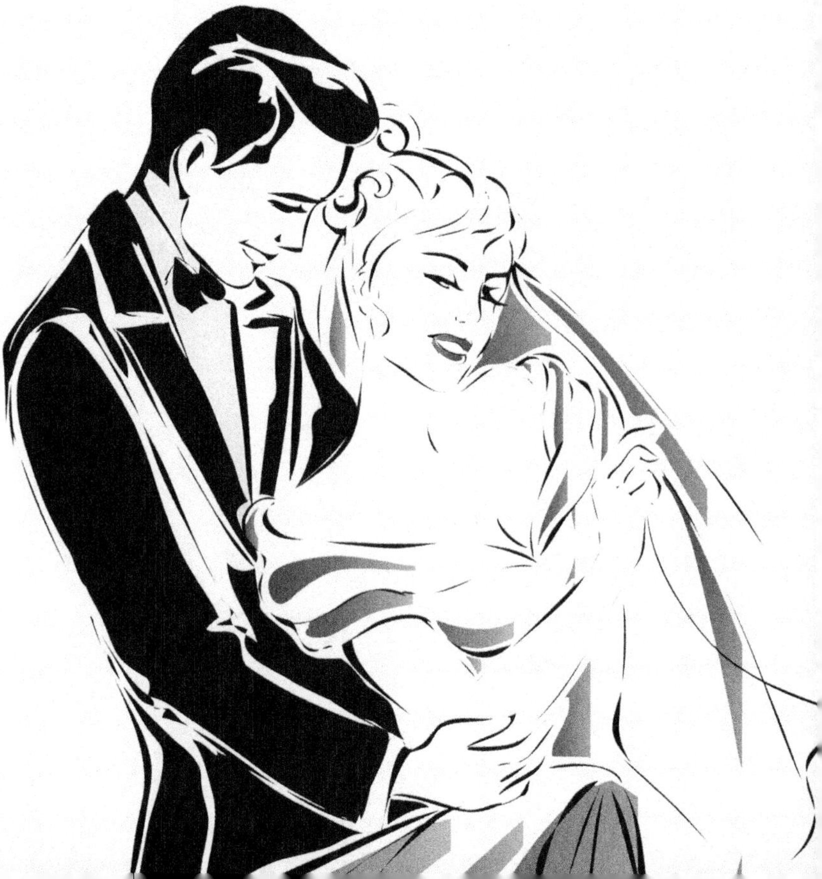

Fourteen

Matthew

I walk into my house, tossing my keys on the table by the door before making my way to the couch. Throwing myself onto the couch, I put my head back and close my eyes, letting out the biggest sigh of relief.

Fuck, today has been brutal. I walked into practice not knowing if anyone would ask me, but why would they? I went on the ice, did what I had to do, and then got my ass out of there, knowing I had to go to Sofia. I don't know what Helena was going to do or if she was going to call her, but I wanted her to hear it from me at least. How fucking dumb did that even sound? I wanted my ex to find out from me that the wedding she was planning was now cancelled. I practiced what I was going to say the whole ride there. How I was going to tell her that it was cancelled and ask her to sit down with me for a minute. I was almost there until her boyfriend walked in the room. I rub my hands over my face as I laugh, thinking how this is like a soap opera.

I'm about to lie down when the front door swings open. "Honey, I'm home."

"Matthew." I hear my father hiss at my uncle. "Too soon."

"You can take the stupid out of the guy, but you can't keep the guy from being stupid," my uncle Max says, and I can't help but silently laugh. For the first time in a while, I feel okay, or at least that things are going to be okay. I mean, I don't think anything is going to be okay until Sofia and I sit down and finally fucking talk. She can keep evading me for as long as she wants, but sooner or later, we are going to have a discussion. A discussion we should have had two years ago.

"That makes absolutely no sense," my uncle Evan says, and I get up, walking over to the entrance.

Looking down, I see the four of them are walking down the hallway like a boy band. "What is going on?" I ask them and look over to make sure no one else is walking in the door.

"You called," my father reminds me, when he's close enough, he grabs me by my neck and pulls me to him. "I called Evan."

"Who called me," my uncle Matthew says, hugging me once my father lets me go, after the hug he slaps my arm.

"And we all know that he doesn't go anywhere without this one," my uncle Evan says. "M&M for life."

Matthew and Max both moan. "That fucking nickname will probably be on my tombstone."

"Oh, it will," Evan assures him, slapping my arm, "even if I have to spray-paint it."

My father heads to the living room while my uncle Evan heads to the fridge, as Max and Matthew walk over to look out at the yard. "What's going on?" I look at all of them. "It looks like an intervention."

"Bite your tongue," my father scolds. "Come and sit down."

"Yes, come and sit down so we can hear all about it," Evan says, walking over to the couch, sitting on the other side. "We should order pizza or something."

"This isn't a slumber party," Max says, sitting down next to him laughing.

"I was also going to add in beer," Evan says to him.

"Come over here." My father motions for me with his head.

I groan, throwing my head back, knowing I'm going to actually have to tell him the whole story. I walk over and sit next to my father. "Should we, I don't know, get something to drink?" Evan says to us.

My father and I both yell, "No!"

"Jesus," Matthew says, holding up his hands, coming over and sitting next to Max. "Okay, so what's going on?"

I put my elbows on my knees and take a deep inhale, my head hanging forward. "I don't know how to put this," I start, "it's just, we decided."

"We?" Matthew asks and I close my eyes, knowing that with the four of them, there is no way I can get away with anything. If one lets me off the hook, it's just because the other one knows he's going to get me. It was always like that growing up. We would get away with it with one of them, and as soon as we would celebrate our victory, the other one of them would sweep in and crush our souls.

"We started the wedding planning." I look up at the guys as they just stare at me, waiting for more. "And, I don't know, it's just like everything she picked would be the opposite of what I would have wanted."

"You called off your wedding because you didn't have the same decoration taste?" Evan asks, almost laughing.

"It was more than that," I say. "It just…" I shake my head and look down at my hands that are gripped together. "It felt wrong."

"It's better that you did it now," Matthew says, "than get divorced later."

"That's what I told her, but she didn't take it as well," I tell the guys and then take a deep breath. "There might be more."

"There might be or there is?" Max asks as he puts his elbow on the arm of the couch.

"Well, I didn't know she was looking for wedding planners." I look at them and then to my father, who hasn't really said much. "We went for our consultation and—"

"Did you fuck your wedding planner?" my father

says between clenched teeth, and I just stare at him and shake my head. I mean, I did screw her, but not recently. He lets out a huge sigh of relief. "I would hate to have to kick your ass."

"I would do it for you," Evan says, glaring at me, and I just shake my head, not sure that by the end of this, he won't kick my ass.

"I walked in, and Sofia was there." I say her name out loud and my uncle Matthew is the first one to hold up his hand.

"Sofia?" He repeats the name, making sure he heard right. "The Sofia?"

"The Sofia." I say her name in a whisper.

"The woman you were in love with?" Max asks and my chest gets tight and all I can do is nod at him.

"But you guys broke up?" my father asks and I take a deep inhale.

"We did," I admit, "sort of."

"Sort of?" Evan says and I just stare at him. "Oh, there is so much more." He points at me. "And I have a feeling I'm going to have to kick your ass."

"I have the same feeling," Matthew agrees, glaring at me, and when I look at Max, he just shrugs.

"No one is kicking anyone's ass," my father declares. "You never told us."

"I guess there is no time like the present." I rub my face and get up, the nerves getting the best of me. "We were at an away game," I start, thinking back to the fucking day I wish never fucking happened. "We won by the skin of our teeth and the guys wanted to go and celebrate." I can hear their voices clear as day in my head. "Let's just go and have one drink, they said, and I knew I should have just said no and gone home. But I didn't, of course, I was like, one drink and then I'll leave." I start walking the room, pacing. "Especially since I knew Sofia was waiting for me to take her out." I close my eyes. "We were going to go celebrate her getting into Chicago events." I look at the guys, who still don't say anything to me. "I kept checking my phone and then the guys there were relentless, 'Stay, have one more.'" My hands go into fists. "'Stop looking at your phone, Petrov.'" The burning starts in my stomach. "'You're so pussy-whipped.'" I look up and close my eyes, pinching the bridge of my nose. "So I kept drinking with them to show them I wasn't pussy-whipped." The minute I say the words, all four of them groan. "Needless to say, I was shit-faced, and when I got home, she was there waiting for me all dressed up. Her face was filled with worry because she couldn't get a hold of me." I swear I have to rub my chest as I see her face again, like it was just yesterday and not two years ago. "She was frantic with worry since I never answered her calls or texts because my phone had died somewhere along the way. She tried to walk away from me and I—"

Max gets up. "Did you touch her?" He asks the question, and if I didn't know better, I think he would have hit me first and asked the question after if I wasn't related to him.

"Of course not," I reply, and he sits back down. "But I wasn't kind to her either. I told her to stop complaining and then I broke up with her."

"While you were drunk?" Evan asks. I refuse to look over at my father for fear I will see how disgusted he is with me.

"Yes." The word comes out in almost a whisper, but loud enough that I know they all hear me.

"Oh, for fuck's sake," Matthew curses. "But you went to see her the next day, right?"

"No, there is more," I admit, and his head goes back, and he lets out a hiss. "My friends were there telling me I didn't need her. She was holding me back. She had no right to be pissed at me, it was my night." I wish I would never have listened to them. "So after she stormed away from me, I went into my room and packed up all her shit." I swallow the lump in my throat. "And dumped it at her door that night."

"You fucking idiot," Matthew says, "you fucking, fucking idiot."

"I know!" I shout "You don't think I fucking know this? I got up the next day and it was all a blur. Like, I remember bits and pieces, but when I sat up in bed, I saw all of our pictures gone. I saw my bedside table where she kept all her stuff on it empty." I want to vomit, just like I did that day two years ago. I got up out of bed and I was going to go over to her when the doorbell rang. I ran, thinking it was her, but instead it was one of her guy friends and he had a box in his hand. The box I left at her house. I thought for sure it was her stuff back, but he shoved it in my hands, and when I looked in, it was all of my stuff. I was destroyed, but when I turned around, all the guys were there." I shake my head. "I let my pride win."

"Oh, Matty," my father says softly, and I look over at him and he has his own tears in his eyes.

"Your pride?" Matthew says, his voice going higher. "Have you met her family?"

"Yes," I admit to him.

"You did her dirty like that?" he hisses, shaking his head.

"I didn't do her dirty like that," I finally say, and even I know I did her dirty like that.

"You threw away two years because you had shitty-ass friends, and you caved under peer pressure," Evan states calmly. "Did you even love her?"

"More than anything," I admit for the first time ever, my voice breaking. "I called her a couple of times, but her number was changed," I also admit for the first time. "I tried to go see her, but she was gone by then."

"Helena," my father says, "did she know?" I just shake my head.

"No, when we walked into the room, she pretended she'd never met me, and I did the same." I sit down, thinking about how fucking nuts this is. "She acted like I was a stranger."

"You love her." My father doesn't even skip a beat. "You can say what you want about Helena and whatever bullshit excuses you want to tell yourself to make you feel better." He doesn't mince words. "You were dumb and stupid." He looks down. "Trust me, if anyone knows anything about caving to peer pressure, it has to be me."

My father has been clean and sober since before me and he never, ever hid it from me or shoved it under a rug. "But, son, think about it. You are living your life, and the minute you see her again—your whole life is shaken."

I want to tell him he's wrong, but I can't. I let his words sink in. "You have to admit your faults, and from the story you told me, you better fucking be ready to fucking beg her to talk to you again."

"Dad, I tried," I explain to him. "I was early one day, and I tried."

"After what you did to her, you're lucky she didn't cut off your testicles and make potpourri out of them," Evan says, and my father laughs.

"You have to stop listening to Zara," my father urges. "You tried, and she didn't listen. That doesn't mean you are off the hook. Then you have to prove to her that you aren't the asshole who broke her heart because you wanted to be manly." I'm about to tell him I know, but he holds up his hand. "Whatever the outcome is, you have to close the book, the story is still waiting for an ending." His words make more sense than I could have.

"You met her father?" Max asks, and I nod my head. "You're lucky he didn't come after you."

"What's her family name?" Matthew asks.

"Barnes," I say, "Sofia Barnes."

"Why does that name sound familiar?" Matthew says, earning a moan from Max, who rolls his eyes.

"You don't know everyone on the planet," Max declares.

"Casey Barnes," Matthew says, and I look over at

him.

"That's her grandfather," I say, shocked that he actually knows him.

"You fucking dumbass." Matthew jumps up, then looks at my dad, who just stares at him. "CBS Corporation."

"The security firm?" I ask, and he puts his hands on his hips. His jaw tightens, and I swear I see a tic in the vein on his forehead. "That's her grandfather?" I ask.

"Holy shit," Evan blurts from beside Matthew, his phone in his hand. "This guy is—" He looks up at Matthew.

"He could make you disappear, and not even I would be able to find you," Matthew states, and I swallow down. "Everyone, calm down." We all look at him, then look at Max, because he's the only one who can reel him in. "You think I'm powerful?"

"One," Max says, getting up, "no one thinks you're powerful except for Karrie." He holds up a finger. "And two, if she told him, he would have already been paid a visit."

"Is he in the mob?" I ask, my hands going into my hair.

"You wish," Evan says. "This guy trained with the Navy SEALs for fun." He laughs and I look over at my father, I'm sure the blood has now drained from my face.

"Everyone needs to just relax," my father says, getting up. "Max, please take him out of here before his head explodes." He points at Matthew, who just shakes his head.

"I'm going to ask around," Matthew comments, "put

out some feelers." He looks at us, and Evan just laughs at him getting up.

"Oh, Tony Soprano, time to get you home and in a robe." Evan slaps him on the back before looking at me. "You better make this right." All I can do is nod at them because I know if I don't, I'm going to have these four kick my ass along with her family.

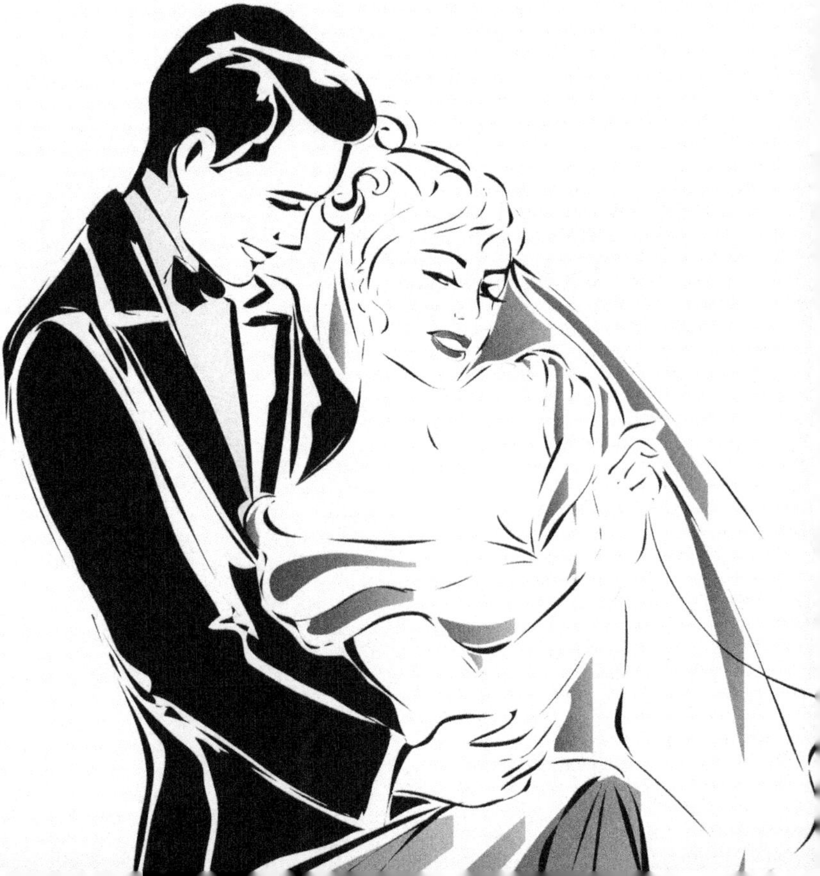

Fifteen

Sofia

The wind blows my hair as I make my way down the single road that leads to my parents' house. The sun is shining so bright in the sky that it's like a *welcome home* hug. I put my hand out the window, moving it through the wind, just like I used to do when I was a teenager. The crunching of rocks under my wheels fills the silent car.

I don't even have it in park before my father comes out of the house. I can't help but smile as he stands there in jeans and a flannel button-down shirt, and his dirty-ass cowboy boots that I think he's had since I was five on his feet. Our eyes meet, and he smiles so big his eyes light up. "My baby girl is home!" he shouts, coming down the five steps toward me. I have enough time to turn off the car before he opens the driver's door.

"Hi, Dad." I smile at him as I unbuckle my seat belt. He doesn't even give me a chance to get my bearings before he literally pulls me out of the car and gives me the biggest hug I've gotten. Well, since the last time, when he said he hadn't seen me in a year but was actually only a month.

"She's home." He lifts me off my feet, his arms still wrapped around my waist. "Hazel," he yells for my mother, "she's home!"

"Dad, you are acting like I'm returning from war," I tell him as he puts me down and holds my face in his hands.

"You look tired," he says, and I sigh at the same time that my mother opens the door and slams it shut.

"You did not just tell her that," my mother scolds, putting her hands on her hips. She's wearing jeans and a T-shirt. Her T-shirt looks like she has jam on it, and I can only imagine that she's been baking since this morning when I called and let them know I was on my way. I knew two days ago I was coming, but I didn't want to let them know because I knew they would make a big deal out of it. Hence, my mother baking. When we moved back to town when I was five, my aunt Savannah offered my mother half of her coffee shop if she would do the baking. Needless to say, it worked out so well that my mother now has an industrial kitchen and has all her baked goodies shipped out around the United States, Hazel's Sweets.

"What? She looks tired," my father states again, dropping my face. "They are working her too hard."

"Oh, would you hush?" my mother says, pushing him aside. "No one likes to be told they look tired. Why don't you just tell her she looks like shit."

My father gasps. "How can she ever look like shit? She looks exactly like you." He smiles at her, thinking he's complimenting her but missing the mark.

"Reed," my mother warns, "I would stop talking if I were you." She takes me in her arms and kisses my cheek. "You feel skinny," my mother says, and I close my eyes.

"That's what I thought also. I'm going to call Grandma Charlotte and tell her." He takes his phone out of his pocket and walks away from us.

"See, now he forgot about how tired you are," my mother says, and I laugh at her. "This is a nice surprise," she says. I just smile because I'm afraid if I say something, anything, I'll burst out in tears.

She looks into my eyes, and I know she can tell I'm not okay. But the sound of a truck approaching makes me look down and get myself under control. I blink away the tears that have threatened to come out being in my mother's arms. "Well, well, well," I hear my grandfather Casey say as he steps out of his truck. "My first grandchild has returned."

"I've got to say." I put my hands on my hips as I watch him walk over to us. He is wearing blue jeans that look like he rolled around in the dirt with and an even dirtier shirt. His boots look like the soles are falling off them. "I'm surprised I didn't get stopped at the city limits." I shake my head. "You must be slipping in your old age."

He claps his hands together and howls out laughing. "I got you pegged as soon as you rode into town. I just thought I would give your dad a couple of minutes with you before I whisk you away," he says, wrapping me in his arms. I smell him, and he smells like home. The smell of when I was five and he found out I was his granddaughter, he would hug me tight and pretend he wasn't crying, but I would feel wetness on my shirt.

"Are you crying?" I would ask.

"Nah, it's the sky sprinkling you with happiness," he would say, and I believed every single word he said.

"Are you ready?" he asks, and my father gasps.

"She literally just got home," he hisses at his father, "it's been five minutes."

"Four minutes and some change," my grandfather says, "but Grandpa Billy is saddling up her horse as we speak."

My father throws his head back. "You can't entice her away with her horse," he says, and he knows that he totally can.

"Remember when he bought her a pink tractor because she asked him to and then her lower lip quivered when she said it's okay that he has no money," my mother says to my father as I laugh.

"That tractor is still in the barn, by the way," my grandfather tells her. "It was an investment."

"She rode it five times." My father laughs. "Okay,

let's go riding," he says, clapping his hands.

"No way." My grandfather holds up his hand to stop him. "This is our thing."

"How is it your thing?" my father asks him. "I was the one who taught her how to ride."

"Not well," my grandfather retorts before looking at me. "You even came dressed to ride." I look down at my white riding pants I put on this morning, knowing that I would be riding, and a button-down, long-sleeve jean shirt that is tucked in the front. The shirt rolled up to the elbows shows off the watch he bought me for graduation and the love bracelet my parents bought me when I turned eighteen. "You have your boots at the barn."

"I'll be back." I walk over and kiss my mother and then my father. "And you get me the whole weekend." His eyes light up.

"Until Sunday night?" he asks.

"No." I shake my head. "Until Monday morning."

I get into the truck with my grandfather, and I'm pulling up to my great-grandparents' place in a matter of minutes. The whole family lives about five minutes from each other in every single direction. My grandfather owns most, if not all, of the land in town. He may be the biggest tech guy out there, but his heart is at the farm.

I get out of the truck and practically run toward my horse. My great-grandfather is standing there holding her reins. "Sunshine," he calls me, and all I can do is smile at him. He wears the same thing as my grandfather but with his cowboy hat on his head. The only time he takes that thing off his head is to go to sleep.

"Grandpa Billy," I say his name as I run to him, just like I did when I was a little girl. He gives me a hug with only one hand. He kisses my cheek. The horse sniffs me as I get closer to her and rub her neck. "Hi, Peaches," I coo softly, "I missed you. I'm going to go change into my boots and come back." I rush over to the area where everyone has a locker with their name on it. We are so many that we had to have three rooms. I open my locker, kicking off my sneakers and putting on my riding boots. Before walking out, I see the barn is empty, the horse is now outside. I make my way to my horse, which is right next to my grandfather Casey. He is on his black stallion as he holds the reins for my horse. I put my foot in the stirrup and swing my leg over. "Just like riding a bike." I wink at him as he laughs.

We take off side by side slowly, and then when we are in the clear, we both push our horses. I put myself lower to pick up more speed. I don't know how long we ride, but when he stops ahead of me, I slow my horse down as we make our way over to the creek for the horses to get some water.

"That felt good," I say, getting off my horse and leading her to the water.

"What's got your bees in a bonnet?" he asks and I just look down, kicking myself for thinking that I was covering up my shit.

"Nothing," I say softly. The sound of birds chirping in the distance fills the quiet forest. "Just thinking of work," I lie to him. He looks at me and I know he knows I'm lying, but he just lets it be. "Just working through something."

He just nods at me. "You know I'm here, right?" he reminds me, and I can't help the tear that escapes as I wipe it away. "Whatever it is you need, we are here."

"I know," I reply softly, and he drops it. We ride back, and instead of going back to my grandfather Billy's barn, I ride over to my house.

My father is outside when I ride up. "I'll take her back," he offers when I hand him the reins. "Mom's inside." I walk up the back porch steps, taking off my boots before walking in. The smell of strawberry and lemon fills the house.

"Something smells amazing," I say, walking into the massive kitchen my father has built for her, the basket of muffins on the counter.

"Don't you touch that unless you wash your hands," she scolds with her back to me, and I roll my eyes. "Then get your skinny ass on that stool so we can talk."

I groan as I walk to the big stainless-steel sink, turning the water on, and washing my hands. I grab a strawberry muffin as soon as my hands are clean, sitting on the stool while my mother drizzles icing on her lemon cakes. "So talk," she says, and I just look at her.

"I don't know what to say," I answer her honestly as my heart speeds up in my chest, and instead of enjoying the muffin, suddenly my stomach rises to my throat. I've been a fucking mess since he came into the office and told me the wedding was cancelled.

"How about you start with why you look like someone told you Santa wasn't real?" she asks as she side-eyes me.

I look down, wondering how to say the next words but all words escape me. "I got my first client," I say, and she looks over, smiling.

"Knew you would," she states.

"It's Matthew." I say his name and her hand stops mid drizzle. "Yeah, that."

"He's getting married?" she asks in a whisper.

"No," I reply. "Well, he was but the wedding is now cancelled."

She puts the fork down. "What?"

"I don't know, Mom," I say, frustrated. "I don't know anything. All I know is that I was fine. I was over him."

She looks at me with her eyebrows going higher. "You were over him." She picks up the way I phrased it past tense.

"I am over him," I cover quickly, but then I put my hand on top of my head. "I thought I was.

"He's been out of my life for the last two years." I slap the island. "I didn't even think about him except when it was the day of his birthday and our anniversary," I admit for the first time ever. "But why, in just a couple of weeks, is he now consuming my thoughts all the time?" My voice goes louder and louder as I get more and more frustrated. "This whole thing is pissing me off because I'm not supposed to give a shit."

"Maybe it's because you didn't get closure," my mother suggests softly, and I tilt my head to the side. "Sending his stuff back to him with a guy who he always thought was into you isn't closure."

"He could have called me." I glare at her now.

"Didn't you change your number?" She folds her arms over her chest, mimicking me. "Bottom line, Sofia, you need to sit down and talk to him."

"About what?" I throw up my hands. "About him being an asshole and breaking my heart? About how I waited to see if he would chase me but was let down because he was never coming after me? About how I loved him so much that every person I've dated since him I compare to him?" The tears escape and run down my cheeks. "I don't want to talk to him. I don't want to discuss it. He had his time to discuss things with me and what did he do? He sent me back my stuff."

"Sofia, a lot has changed in two years. You are both different people." She tries to be the voice of reason. "You owe it to yourself to talk to him. If not, you'll be forever comparing everyone to him." She picks the fork back up and continues to ice the cake.

My phone pings from the couch and I get up, walking over to it, not sure what to say to my mother. Taking it out of my purse, I look down seeing the text from the man who I just can't escape all of a sudden.

Matthew: Can we talk?

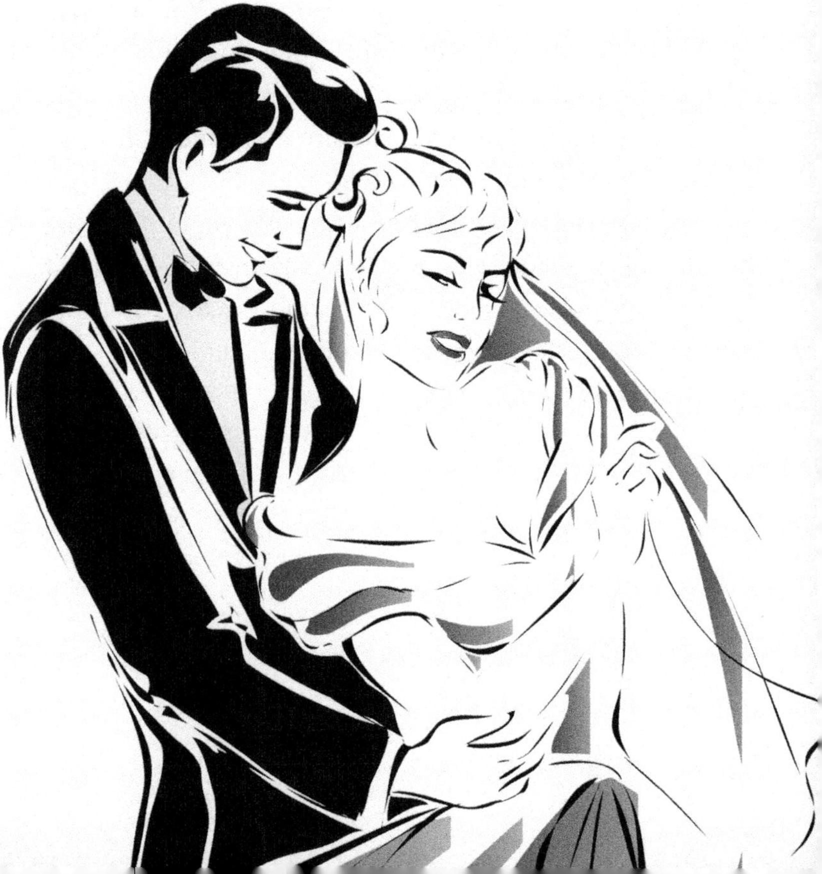

Sixteen

Matthew

I walk out of the plane, ducking my head, holding on to the side rail as I take the steps down to the tarmac. The breeze runs through me as I make my way to my car, the sun in the sky slowly going down. I open the door to the back seat, throwing in my carry-on bag before I sit down in the driver's seat. We were gone for one game on the road, so I don't have that much I took with me. I take my phone out and power it back on, looking down to see if I got a text. The circle keeps going around and around as it finally loads up. The pings coming one after another showing me I missed four texts.

Opening up the text app, I see I have one from my mother.

Mom: Just thinking about you.

I want to laugh because I know she wants to say a lot more. I know she has a lot more questions for me, but I also know my father is holding her at bay. The second one is from my sister, Zara.

Zara: I heard the news that you escaped the ball and chain. You must feel one hundred and four point three pounds lighter. Let me know if you need to talk.

I skip the one from Christopher and go to the last text I sent her, two days ago.

It's been two days since I sent her the text asking her to talk, and it's been crickets. All it says is delivered. I was lying down in my hotel bed, watching I don't even know what, when all I wanted to do was talk to her. All I wanted to do was hear her voice. I couldn't explain it, so I pulled up the email I had saved from her in my inbox. Instead of calling her like I wanted to, I sent her the text. I placed the phone on my stomach, thinking that she would get back to me but nothing. Nothing for the last two days. I start the car and begin driving, but instead of going to my house, I drive straight to her office. I spot one car in the parking lot and park next to it.

Getting out, I see that the sun is almost gone now. I jog up the steps to the office, pulling open the door. Taking a step in, I see there is no one there. I walk into the middle of the room and look around. The same room where, two months ago, my life changed yet again. I look over at the pictures on the walls, trying to calm down the erratic beating of my heart.

What the fuck are you doing here? my head asks, and

I don't even know if I can answer. Is she even here? I have no idea. The only thing I know is this is where she goes, so I had to show up.

I hear the sound of shoes coming closer and closer when she steps out of the hallway. She looks at me, shocked. "Matthew," she says my name in a whisper. "Are you okay?" she asks, stepping closer to me, which gives me a chance to take her in.

She's wearing white jeans this time, and I think it's the first time I've seen her here in jeans. She has a brown belt on, and a light beige, long-sleeved sweater with cuffs rolled at her wrists. Her hair is back and in a ponytail.

"I texted you." That is the only thing that comes out of my mouth, and I have to be thankful it isn't a declaration of love because, at this point, I don't know what is going on with me. I've been trying so hard to do the right thing this whole time that I haven't been my true self. I've been biting my tongue and suppressing everything so now I feel like I'm a ticking time bomb, and with just one push, everything is going to pour out of me.

"Oh, yeah, sorry," she says, avoiding my eyes. "I was…" She stops talking and finally looks up at me. It happens in slow motion really, or maybe it hits me like a freight train that I didn't know was coming. It was in this room that my world got rocked not long ago, and I finally realized she was the one. That it's always been her and I'm pretty fucking sure and I can bet my life it will always be her. "What is going on?" She puts her hands in front of herself as she wrings them together, and I know she is just as nervous as I am.

"We need to talk." I can hear my father's voice in my head. *You have to go lightly. It's been two years. You are both different.* It's only because of that I'm not pulling her to me and kissing the shit out of her. Just the thought has me rock hard. Looking down, I make sure my shirt is covering how I feel.

"We don't, though." Her tone is filled with sass. A vision of me pushing her against the wall, with my hands outstretched beside her head, while I devour her mouth, showing her how much we have to talk about fills my mind. I can literally taste the kiss on my lips.

"I owe you a dinner." The minute the words are out of my mouth, I know I should have chosen other words. I know this because all she does is glare at me, which makes me want her even more. "Can I take you out to dinner?" I ask, knowing she is going to say no. Also knowing that this time it's different, she isn't getting rid of me so easily. I'm not the stupid kid I was before.

"No," she replies without even thinking twice or pretending to think about it and then letting me down.

"Please," I say softly.

She just looks at me. "What do you want?" She asks the same question I've been asking myself since I let out what really happened between us. I know what the end goal is, I just don't know how to get there.

"Just to talk to you," I admit softly. "I just want to talk to you. I think we should talk." My heart flies from the pit of my stomach to my throat, and I'm thinking about getting on my knees and begging her if I have to.

"Fine," she huffs and then takes a deep inhale. "Why

don't I text you when I'm done and we can meet?"

I swear to everything, I want to jump up in the air and raise my hands over my head in victory while I celebrate. I can't help the smile that fills my face. "I'll take it." I nod. "I'll wait for your text."

I start to walk out of the room, ready to escape while I can, and then I stop suddenly. I turn to her. "This isn't like a trick, right?" I look at her, getting lost in her eyes, wondering what she's seen in the past two years that I haven't. Wanting to know all the memories she's made. Well, maybe not all the memories. I don't want to know shit about who she dated.

"What isn't a trick?" she asks.

"That you say what I want to hear and then never contact me." I put my hands on my hips.

She rolls her eyes at me. "You know where I work." She raises her hands toward the walls, and I can't help but throw my head back and laugh. Like real laughter that I haven't had in a while. "How far do you think I can get before you realize I'm not contacting you?"

"You got that right," I tell her in a way that she has to know she can run but she can't hide. "See you later."

I jog down the steps to her office, making my way to my car. Once I get in, I pull up her name, and instead of texting her, I call her. I'm more surprised than anything that she actually answers instead of sending me to voice mail. "You just left," she says instead of saying hello. "I literally still see you outside." She walks out of the door, standing at the top of the stairs. I just look up at her, wishing I could take the elastic out of her hair.

"I know." I laugh, my finger tapping the steering wheel. "I was just wondering how much longer you think you will be?"

"What?" she says into the phone while still looking at me.

"If you aren't going to be long, I can wait for you," I tell her, and she just shakes her head.

"I have an appointment in thirty minutes, it should last maybe an hour. I will text you when I'm done." All I can do is stare at her. "I promise I won't ghost you." I'm about to say something when she continues. "At least for today anyway."

"I'll wait for your text, then," I say into the phone, and she turns to walk back into the office. "You look beautiful, by the way." She stops mid step, never turning back around. I couldn't not say it. It's been at the tip of my tongue since I first saw her again, which makes me the biggest asshole ever.

"I'll talk to you later." That is all she says before the door closes and the line disconnects. I pull out of the parking lot and head toward my house. My body is filled with nerves and what feels like endless energy. Even though my body is exhausted from the game we played against LA, I feel like I could run a 5k.

Pulling up the phone feature on my screen, I call my father, who answers after one ring. "Hey," he says, "how're you doing?"

"Um," I say nervously. "Do you think you can come down this weekend?" I ask.

"Of course." He doesn't even wait a second before

answering me. "I will, however, have to bring your mother, or else I won't be able to return to this house," he says, laughing. "Apparently, according to her, I will lose some precious body parts that I would very much like to keep."

I laugh, knowing how hard this must be for her. "Yeah, bring the whole family," I tell him. "We can even do family lunch at my place on Sunday."

"Are you sick?" my father interrupts me. "Did you get hit in the head?"

I laugh again, twice in less than an hour, this must be a record. "Nah," I reply, leaving out that I'm hoping Sofia also joins us so they can meet her again. "Just miss you guys."

"Okay, I'll make a few calls," he says.

"Put out a few feelers," I mimic my uncle Matthew.

He laughs. "We'll catch up this weekend, yeah," he says. "Now I'm going to go and make your mother happy with the news."

"Thanks, Dad," I tell him as I park my car, "for everything." He says he loves me before he hangs up and I get out and walk into my house and wait for her to call me. I was kidding before, if she doesn't call me—I know exactly where I'm going tomorrow morning.

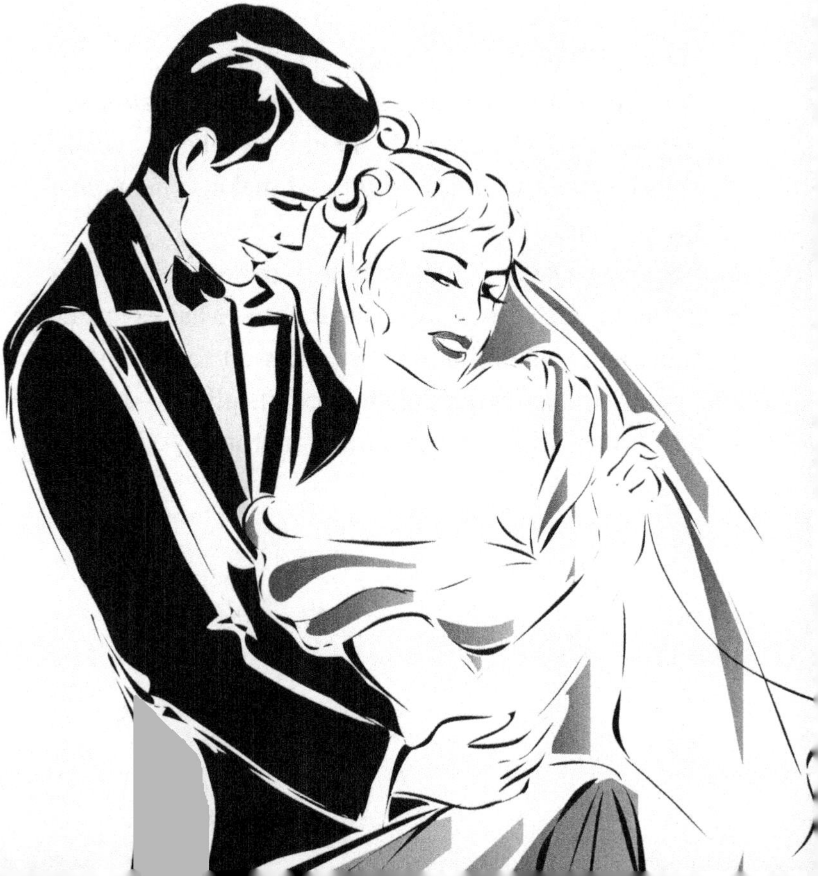

Seventeen

Sofia

"As you can see," I say as we walk into the big venue space, "we can accommodate up to a thousand people." The bride and groom look at me with big eyes. "There are walls that retract on both ends." I point at the walls of the slide, making the space bigger. "Or we can make it more intimate by closing two more retractable walls." I point over to the side where two more walls are now open but can be closed.

The bride walks around the space, taking it in as I stand to the side giving her time. My head has been in a spin since they walked in. I'm trying not to think about the reason it's in a spin, but that reason showed up ten minutes before the couple arrived. I had no time to compartmentalize it. I can still hear his voice. "You look beautiful." I wanted to turn around and throw my phone at his car, but I refrained and pretended it didn't get to me. What the hell was happening to me? I went two years perfectly okay without him, and now it's as if no time has been lost. "Would we be able to come back with our parents?" the bride asks excitedly.

"Of course," I answer her. "We can even do a setup with tables so they would get the look of it." She looks over at the groom, who stares at her with such love in his eyes. "What do you think?"

"I think that if this is what you want"—he smiles even bigger at her—"then this is it." He looks over at me. "What do we need to do next?"

I nod at them and proceed to tell them the next steps. They sit in my office as we go through a couple of things. It's after seven by the time they leave and I lock the door, walking back to my office to finish the paperwork. I sit down at my desk, looking down, knowing I can do this in the morning and I'm just stalling at this point.

When I got the text on Saturday, I ignored the pull to answer him right away. I put it down and walked away, spending the weekend with my family. Riding my horse, catching up with my cousins, going to the bar on Saturday night, and two-stepping until my feet hurt. I drank way too much, which ended up with the memories of him that I locked away coming out in full force. Sunday was spent at the family barbecue where I laughed more than I have in a long time. That night, I decided I was going to ignore the text and pretend that it didn't happen. I even deleted the thread so I wouldn't be tempted to answer him. In my head, there was nothing to talk about even though, according to my mother, I needed closure.

I stare at my phone for what seems like forever. "What if I don't text him?" I wonder. "What is the worst that can happen?" I lean back in my chair and look out the window at the darkness. "He shows up tomorrow and forces you to talk to him in front of the girls." I close my eyes and decide to bite the bullet. Might as well get this over with. I think of texting him, but then I would just be waiting on him to answer me.

I take the deepest breath I've ever taken before I press the button to call him. "Please don't answer," I beg the universe to help me out. One ring turns into two and my heart starts beating really fast. "I'm hanging up after three rings," I mumble to myself as the second ring stops, and as soon as the third one starts, he picks up.

"Hey," he says, his voice groggy, and it sounds like he was sleeping.

"You're sleeping?" I say softly, my neck feeling warm as the nerves float through me. "I should have texted you instead." The words come out of my mouth instead of staying in my head.

He laughs and something else goes on inside me, but I'm not going to pay any attention to it. "Were you hoping I wouldn't have answered you?"

"No," I say, laughing nervously. I know I'm lying and sadly I know that he also knows it was a lie. "Why don't we do this tomorrow?" I try to push it off.

"Can't," he says right away, and I hear rustling from

his side of the phone. "I have a game tomorrow." I close my eyes.

"We can do this next week." I am literally pulling at straws to cancel this thing all together. "Or how about the week after next?" I swing in my chair side to side, trying to come up with even more reasons.

"Are you done?" he asks and I stop mid swing.

"I am," I start but then quickly add in, "But you sound exhausted." My voice goes low.

"I'm fine. I can rest later." His voice sends shivers running through me and I feel bad for not answering him before. Maybe we could have had this conversation on the phone and not face-to-face.

"Matthew." His name rolls off my tongue so naturally. I think it's the first time I've called him that since he came into my life again. "We can honestly do it another time. I promise I won't blow you off or pretend I'm sick." I chuckle. "Or someone died."

"No, it's fine," he says adamantly. "Where do you want to meet?"

"I have no idea." I think of places that we can meet at. Maybe I could mention Luke's place, but then what if we run into people I know or who know Harlow or the girls, and then it's like front page news?

"Do you want to come here?" he asks. I am already shaking my head, but curiosity gets the best of me.

"Where is here?" I close my eyes once I say the words. It's none of my business where here is. Since the engagement was called off, is he living in a hotel? Did she move out of the house? Did he move out of the house? There are so many questions I want to ask, but I also know it's none of my business.

"I live in town," he replies, and I gasp.

"You live here?" The shock in my voice must be apparent because he laughs at me.

"Where did you think I lived?" he asks.

"I have no idea," I tell him the truth. "I hadn't really thought about it."

"We need to catch up." The minute I hear those words, my stomach gets tight.

"Why don't we do it at another time?" I again try to push it off because maybe I'm just not ready to catch up. Maybe we've caught up and we should just leave it at that.

"Sofia, you have three choices, you can come here." His voice is clear now. "I can come there or we can meet." I wait five seconds to see if he is going to give me a fourth option. "So you pick, what's it going to be?"

My leg starts to move up and down. "Why don't you come to my house?" If we are going to do this, I'm going to do it on my turf. Besides, do I want to go to his place where Helena's stuff is probably still lying around the house? Or is it?

"Are you sure?" he asks as I hear a door closing.

"No," I answer honestly, "but you won't let up, so this is where we're at."

He laughs. "Can you send me your address? I'll go and get food and then head to your place."

"Or we can just have coffee," I suggest, tapping my desk.

"Send me the address, Sofia. I'll send you an ETA once I get it."

"Okay," I say.

"I'll wait on the phone while you send it."

"What?" I ask, not sure I heard him right.

"Sofia, you are already a flight risk." I close my eyes, rolling my lips. "So I'm not going to let you go until I have your address. Or, option number four." I wait for it. "I pick you up at work and drive you home."

"Wow," I respond, shocked that he knows me a bit better than I thought. "As if I would not send you my address. I'm insulted."

"Nice cover-up, Sofia." He laughs. "I'm still waiting in my car."

"You're in your car?" I fly out of my chair. "How?" I look around for my purse and rush to get out of my office. "You were literally asleep five seconds ago."

"I fell asleep on the couch waiting for your call," he explains. "Then when you called, I got up and walked out the door. Now, do I come get you or do I meet you at your house?"

I open the text thread, typing in his name I stored before deleting the text.

Me: *3216 Elm Street*

"There," I tell him once I press send.

"Got it. I'll be there in about thirty-five minutes."

"See you then," I say, disconnecting before he keeps me on the phone longer. I rush around the office grabbing my jacket and bags before hightailing it out. I get in the car and make it home in twenty minutes. The whole time

I'm playing how the conversation is going to go in my head. Each time preparing what to say to him.

I park in the driveway and run up the stairs, punching in my code. I dump my bags at the door and kick off my shoes, turning on the lights in the hallway and then the kitchen once I make it there. I even turn on the lights in the adjacent room and to the fireplace also.

"Oh, come on," I scold myself, quickly turning it off. "Why don't you put on 'Let's Get It On'?"

I pace around the room, making sure that nothing screams romance, or I want to have sex with you. "Why would he think you want to have sex with him?" I am literally having a conversation with myself. "I don't want to have sex with him," I tell myself while I can hear my cousins laughing at me from Saturday when I said the same thing, and in the next sentence mentioned how good-looking his dick was. "Should I change?" I look down at the outfit I put on this morning, right before I left my parents' house and drove straight to work. "Yeah, why don't you slip into something a little more comfortable?" I mock myself. "Maybe some lace and your garter.

"You need to calm down and get a hold of yourself!" I shout at myself, walking into the kitchen and grabbing the bottle of sweet tea. "One shot and then you just need to chill out. This is going to be fine." I unscrew the top off the bottle and take a swig of the tea, and it burns all the way down for a second. "There, now, just relax and stay professional," I tell myself, feeling my cheeks starting to get hot. I put my palms on them and they feel like they are on fire. "What if he thinks you're getting all hot and bothered because he's coming here?!" I shriek, running over to the sink and turning on the cold water. Wetting my hands, I place them on my cheeks, I'm not even done with the first cheek when the doorbell rings. My head flies to the side as I think about not answering it for one second, and it is as if he can hear my thoughts.

"I'm already outside, so you can't pretend you aren't there," he says, and I glare, "and I'm blocking you in."

The only think I can think of is, "Asshole."

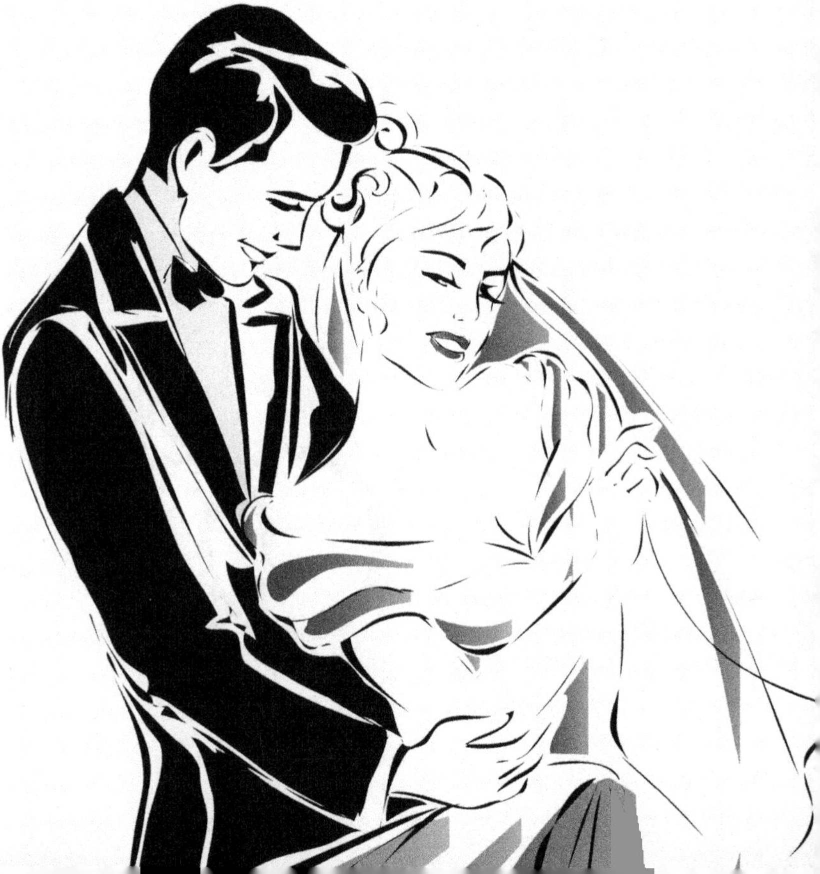

Eighteen

Matthew

I ring the doorbell, my hands shaking. I look down at my shoes and then look up again, not hearing anything from the other side of the door. I look back to the driveway where I parked my car right behind hers. "I'm already outside, so you can't pretend you aren't there," I say loudly to the door, knowing she is debating whether or not to answer it, "and I'm blocking you in." She tried to cancel this about fifteen times in the span of a ten-minute conversation. "I'll just sit out here on your stoop and eat," I announce to the door and then hear the lock turn. My heart is hammering so hard in my chest, the second I hear the noise I wonder if she will be able to hear it.

The door swings open and I see her and my heart slows down right away, knowing she's right here. "I was in the bathroom," she says. "Come in." She moves aside and I walk inside, going straight to the hallway.

"Figured I owed you dinner," I say to her as she closes the door and walks to stand in front of me. "And maybe an apology," I try to joke with her, but from the look she gives me, it falls flat.

"Maybe?" she huffs. "Maybe?" She walks over to the door and opens it up. "Get out." She points outside.

"Okay, fine," I cave. "I definitely owe you an apology," I say softly. "I owe you a lot more than that."

She closes the door and folds her arms over her chest. "Go on." She doesn't move from in front of the door.

I knew we would be doing this, but I thought for sure it would be while we were eating. I put the food down beside me, just in case she does kick me out of her house, at least she is going to eat. "Wow, so we are doing this right away," I start, looking at her. "I'm sorry."

"For what?" she asks, her eyes going into slits. I wish she would give me an option to talk, but I've riled her up and she's ready to go to war with me. I can see it in her eyes that are so dark now, and all I want to do is hold her face and kiss her until her eyes are light again. I also know from the look she is giving me, if I do that, she is going to shoot me in the ass and then the foot.

"For fucking everything," I finally admit.

"Oh, no." She shakes her head. "You wanted this little chat. You are going to get a little chat. Let's start with you not calling me to cancel the plans."

I close my eyes, not wanting to do this, but knowing I have no choice. I brought this on myself and it's time to face the music. "But instead of calling me and, you know, cancelling, you made me worry that you were hurt somewhere." I just watch her because she's right. I'm about to tell her this but she holds up her hand. "So what do you do? You come home and I'm annoyed because you aren't on the side of the road bleeding out?" I am about to laugh but I roll my lips. "Not only are you not bleeding out, you're drunk as a fucking skunk. And what do you do, Matty?" She cocks her head to the side and folds her arms over her chest. Her chest is rising and falling as if she ran a marathon.

I hold up my hand. "You want to do this; you call me by my name. To you I'm Matthew," I remind her, "and I know what I did. I fucked up in ways that I can't even explain." I finally start talking, the words coming out like word vomit. "I fucking fucked up so freaking hard that there are no words I can say that can make it forgivable. You have to know, Sofia, it was the booze talking."

"You broke up with me drunk, and then the next day sent me all my stuff!" she yells at me. "The next day!" She throws her hands in the air. "You can't blame the booze on that!"

"That is where you are wrong," I say gently. "I did it that night." The words come out soft. "I was so pissed that you just left, I stormed in the house and started packing up your stuff." Her arms fall to her sides. "So I'm even more of an idiot, I know. But when I woke up the next day, it was a blur. I swear to you, Sofia, I didn't even remember that I packed your stuff up. I woke up and saw all your things gone from the side table and then bits and pieces were coming back. But then I was coming to you when David," I say, his name raising my eyebrows, "knocked on my door and presented me with my own box." She rolls her eyes. "Yeah, David; the same David I told you had his dick wet for you. He was returning my stuff to me with all of our pictures cut in half."

"He did not!" she declares, not looking at me. "And you are missing the point." She looks at me. "You fucking broke my heart!" she yells at the top of her lungs, anger filling the room. "You fucking shattered me!"

"Do you not think I broke my own heart?" I ask, hating I hurt her so deeply. "You don't think that it killed me just as much as it killed you?"

"I have no idea," she says softly. "You know why, you didn't even bother to come and see me, to come and talk to me. To do anything."

"I tried to call you a week after," I tell her, "but your phone was already disconnected."

"Oh, it was fucking disconnected two days later. Two days I waited for you to come and see me. Two days, telling myself, you know that he's going to come, just you wait." She shakes her head. "I was wrong."

"There are a few things I've done in my life that I regret," I tell her, swallowing the lump in my throat. "That night is number one on that list. I lost the best thing that has ever happened to me. I lost the woman I loved more than life itself. I lost half of my soul that night."

"Well, you got it back." She laughs. "You were getting

married." She shakes her head. "I don't know what you wanted to do tonight. I don't know why it matters, to be honest, we have moved on."

"I'm so sorry," I apologize to her instead of telling her that I haven't moved on, I don't say the words. *Two years later, and one look at you and I'm right back in it.* "I'm sorry I hurt you. I'm sorry I broke us. I'm so fucking sorry," I say in a whisper.

"You are two years too late," she says and my heart shatters in my chest.

"Didn't you always say it's better late than never?" I point at her, hoping she throws me a rope because I'm in the water and it feels like I'm drowning.

"Okay, fine, I accept that you are a horse's ass." She looks at me. "What do you want?"

Everything! my head screams but my mouth is in control. "To be friends." Saying the words feels like acid in my mouth.

"I am not going to be friends with you." She shakes her head.

"Why not?" I ask, shocked. "I'm a good friend!" I shriek. "I'm a very good friend."

"I have enough good friends," she informs me.

"Everyone can use more friends." I put my hands in my pockets because my cock has decided that this is the part where I show her how much I want to be her friend.

"Not me, but thanks." She cocks her head to the side and with her hair up it gives me access to her neck.

"Okay," I concede, walking toward the door and her. I see her eyes turn a touch lighter, and I even see the disappointment on her face. "Thank you for taking the time to talk to me." I lean down, and our eyes lock right before I kiss her cheek. "See you soon, Sofia." I walk to the door and she hasn't moved from the spot she's in. "I got you a burger with cheese and bacon and fried pickles." I open the door, hoping she says not to go, but I know her. I know she's going to let me go. I deserve it. I know it. She knows it. But what she doesn't know is that I'm not going anywhere.

I'M WALKING OFF the ice, and for the first time in a long time, I slept like a champ. Of course I woke up with the biggest hard-on of my life, even after taking a shower and jerking off to her, twice.

As I walk into the room, sweat is pouring off my face. I put my stick against the wall and walk over to my spot on the bench. Grabbing my phone, I see that I have a message.

Rhonda: Package was delivered this morning and was accepted by Sofia Barnes.

I smile as I put my phone down and hurry up in the shower. I put on shorts and a T-shirt with a team sweater. I grab the baseball hat, putting it on backward, my wallet and phone. "See you tonight, boys," I say, rushing out of the room and to my car.

I arrive at her office twenty-five minutes later; the traffic was insane today. I go up the front stairs two at a time, pulling open the door and stepping in. A woman

mine to TAKE

is standing at the desk. "Hi, can I help you?" she asks, looking me up and down.

"I'm here to speak to Sofia Barnes," I reply, smiling at her. She picks up the phone and calls her. The woman turns around so I don't hear her talking.

She turns around and puts the phone down. "She'll be right out," she says before she walks out of the room and down to where I know Sofia's office is. I hear her heels before I see her.

She's wearing a white tight skirt that goes to the middle of her calves but has a slit in the front that goes to her knees, the black shirt she is wearing is cut too low in the front for my liking, "What are you doing here?" she asks, smiling, but I can see she's pissed. Her teeth are clenched together.

"I was making sure you got my gift," I tell her, smiling. This morning I rushed into the rink and got one of my jerseys, and then hit up Rhonda, the public relations girl, asking her for two tickets to the game tonight. Then I begged her to make sure Sofia got it. I made it on the ice with a minute to spare. I now owe her a signed jersey from my grandfather.

"I did." She nods her head at me.

"And?" I say, waiting.

"And nothing, I got it." She folds her arms over her chest, making her tits push up.

I take a step closer to her. "Are you going to come?"

"No." Fuck, she is so beautiful. "I don't like hockey. I'm more a football fan these days." Her eyes go a shade darker when she lies. And she moves her eyes from side to side.

"You are lying." I point at her.

"I'm not lying," she huffs.

I fold my own arms over my chest. "Then you definitely should come so you can see why you miss it." I step even closer to her.

"I don't miss it," she insists so fast that she doesn't have a chance to hide the lie.

"You know I can tell when you are lying." I laugh.

"You don't know me, Matthew," she declares and I close the distance between us, standing toe to toe with her.

"Oh, I know you, baby," I say softly, right before I step away from her. "See you tonight," I tell her once I get to the door, "and wear my shirt."

I open the door to step out. "When pigs fly," is the last thing I hear before the door closes behind me.

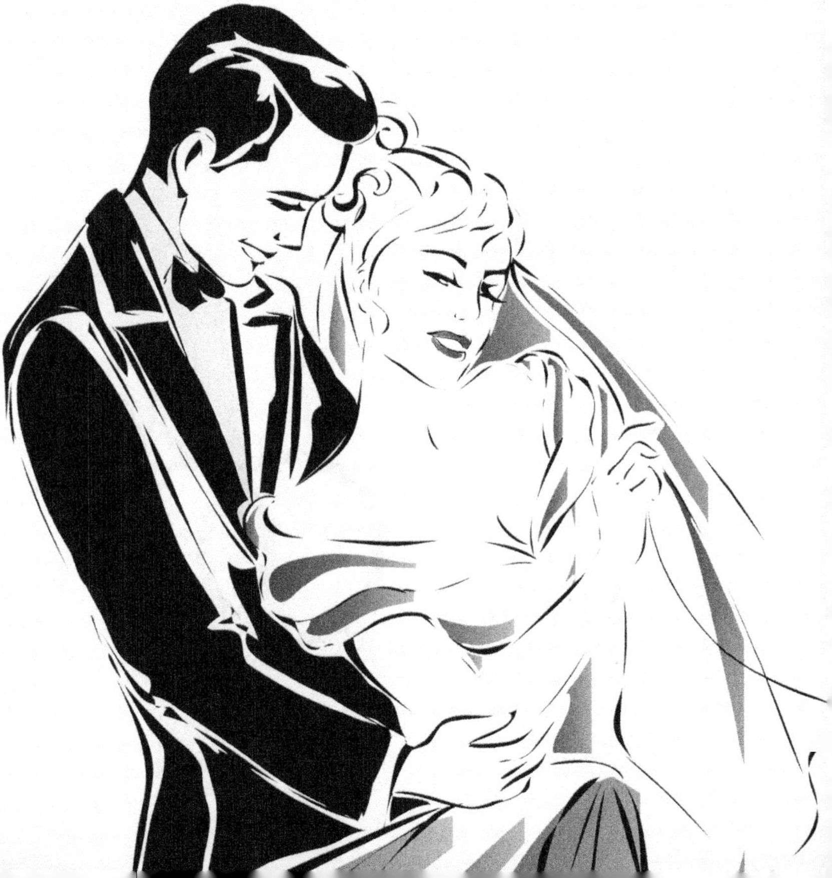

Nineteen

Sofia

He steps out, and the door shuts right when I say, "When pigs fly." I stare at the door for a couple of seconds before the anger surges through me. I walk over and open the door right as he opens his car door. "You can't just keep doing this, Matthew."

He looks up at me, the smirk on his face going straight to a smile, making me want to kick him right in the shins with pointy-ass shoes on. "What can't I be doing, Sofia?"

"Well, for one, you can't just keep showing up here where I work," I start there, "and two, you have to stop this whole thing."

"I'm just coming to visit a friend and see if she wants to come and watch a hockey game." He folds his arms over his chest and I wish he hadn't because his arms just seem bigger.

"I'm not your friend, Matthew," I inform him. "You asked me to talk and we did, but it's time for us to both move on." I stare at him, hoping to see something in his eyes to tell me he's heard what I've said, but his eyes just twinkle. "I'm not doing this with you. I'm not playing this game." Instead of giving him any chance to answer, I grab the door handle, stepping in.

"Nothing with us is a game," he calls out right before the door shuts, giving him the last word. I think about going back out there and telling him to fuck off.

"Motherfucker!" I shout, and now I hear the sound of heels clicking on their way to me. They come out of the hallway one at a time. All of them looking around.

"What's going on?" Shelby asks like she has no idea, when in reality she probably knows the whole story.

"Nothing." I shake my head and walk back into my office. I know I said nothing, but I also know they are not just going to let me go like that. I walk into my office, seeing the vase of tulips that was delivered along with the white box in the chair. I didn't even get a chance to open the box, all I did was open the card that was in the flowers. I honestly thought they were from my dad, so I opened the envelope all happy until I read the fucking note.

Sofia,
Hope you can make it.
Your friend,
Matthew

To say I was shocked was an understatement, when he left my house last night, I felt like we broke up yet again. I picked up the bag of food before I walked into the kitchen. I put it directly in the fridge before turning off all the lights and walking upstairs. I was numb, to say the very least, as the conversation we had played over and over in my head. It was a conversation that was two years in the making. It was a conversation I had played in my head over and over for two years. I told him how much of an asshole he was and how he broke my heart. What I wasn't ready for was his side of the story. For the past two years, I thought it didn't bother him. I thought he wasn't as affected as I was, but the way he said, *"There are a few things I've done in my life I regret, and that night is number one on that list. I lost the best thing that had ever happened to me. I lost the woman who I loved more than life itself. I lost half of my soul that night."* I thought my legs would have given out right then and there.

Everyone said there was no closure. Well, we have closure now. The door is slammed shut and locked. The book is now closed, and we can both move on. Except something says this is far from over.

"You got flowers?" Clarabella asks when she walks in and goes to sit down calmly.

"Yes," I say, pointing at them. "And something in there," I tell her as she picks up the white box and shakes it side to side.

"It could be a bomb," Presley teases, chuckling. "You know what it isn't?" She waits for us to say something.

"His dick."

"Definitely not his dick," Shelby declares and I just gawk at her. "I've seen him, he has to be packing to walk with all that swagger." I just roll my eyes because Matthew Petrov owns his swagger and he is, in fact, packing below the belt.

"Well, are we going to open it or are we going to play guessing games all day?" Clarabella asks as she hands me the box.

"It's probably something to irritate the fuck out of me." I grab the box and undo the satin bow on top before flipping the top of the box open and moving the white tissue paper to the side. "Oh my God," I say, looking down at the white shirt.

"Is that a hockey jersey?" Clarabella asks, trying to roll her lips so she doesn't burst out laughing.

"Unfortunately," I confirm, putting the box down and taking out the shirt. I don't have to turn it over to see that it has his name on the back.

"What is going on?" Presley looks at me, then back at the shirt and then to the flowers.

"Nothing," I deflect, shoving the jersey back into the box. "Less than nothing. He sent me flowers and tickets to the game, and apparently that."

"Code purple!" Shelby shouts.

"We are all here," Clarabella states, then turns to me. "Are you going to wear this?"

"Not a chance in fucking hell!" I shout. "I'm not even going to the game."

"Oh, here we go," Clarabella starts, "you are going to

go to the game tonight."

I stare at her, my eyebrows pinching together. "Oh, no, I'm not." I shake my head at the same time.

"Just don't drink any booze because you might end up having sex with him," Shelby advises. "I drank on my fake honeymoon, and well, we had sex. A lot."

"I drank when I ran away from my wedding," Clarabella adds. "Definitely had sex that night."

I look over at Presley, who just laughs. "I had sex all the time, there was no need to drink."

"You were drunk the first time you asked him to take your virginity," Clarabella reminds her.

"Oh, yeah," Presley remembers, "definitely don't drink."

"I am not going, so that is a nonissue," I tell all of them.

"If you don't go, he'll know he got to you," Shelby says, folding her arms over her chest.

"If I go, he wins," I counter.

"Unless you go and make him eat his heart out," Clarabella announces.

"I don't want to go." The words come out of my mouth before my head says, *I want to go.*

"We spoke last night." I fill them in on the small details I'm sure they are going to freak out about, and the minute I say the words, they all gasp. I hold my hand up to stop them from talking. "It's over. He said his piece. I said mine, and we are moving on." I look at the three of them and they all burst out laughing. "What?"

"He's been here four times since he broke up with his

girlfriend." Shelby tilts her head to the side.

"Actually, his fiancée." I point at her. "He was engaged less than a week ago, and now he wants to come up all in my space and uproot my life?" I shout, shaking my head. "No fucking way. Fuck that."

"You're going," Clarabella states, "if only to tell him you don't need him."

"I just told him I don't need him." I point behind me to the window. "So I don't have to go."

"That was a mating dance if I ever saw one," Clarabella declares. "He looked like he was going to fuck you against the door, with or without us looking out the window."

"Mating dance?" I say, not sure I heard her right. "I was literally telling him how much I hated him."

"That just gets it going even more." Presley laughs. "I used to tell Bennett at least once a day how we weren't a couple."

"But everyone knew that you were," Shelby remarks. "The only one you were fooling was yourself."

"Ladies," I say softly, "I am not going."

"You have to," Shelby says, and she is usually the voice of reason between the three of them.

"I don't have anyone to go with," I finally say, "and I'm not going to a hockey game by myself."

Clarabella holds her finger in the air before walking over to the door. She sticks her head out of the door. "Addison," she calls the new receptionist who started working here this week. With the expanding business, we needed to hire someone to do most of the paperwork and return phone calls.

Addison comes into the room and looks at all of us, the smile on her face falling. "Am I in trouble?" she asks as she tucks her blond hair behind her ear.

"No!" we all shout at the same time, and the frown turns back into a smile.

"That guy who was just in here?" Clarabella asks her.

"The hot one?" she asks, and all I can do is roll my eyes. He's not that hot, and I don't know why I'm bothered she thinks that.

"Yes, him," Clarabella confirms, turning to me to smile as if she made her case.

"He's not that hot." I throw my hands up in the air.

"Now you're fucking lying." Shelby points at me. "Addison, what are you doing tonight?"

She looks at her and then me. "Probably some coloring and then maybe some Play-Doh, and if it's really a crazy night—painting." She smiles. Her daughter is four years old and she is a single mom, and from what she said, the father is not involved at all.

"Not tonight, you aren't. You're going to the hockey game," Shelby tells her, and her eyes go big.

"Um," she says, "thank you so much, but I don't have any babysitters." She twists her fingers in front of her. "And I don't have the extra cash to hire someone."

"I will take her," Shelby says with a smile. "The girls have a great time when they are together." Addison's eyes go even bigger.

"I haven't been out without her since she was born." I put my head back, feeling like an asshole if I'm the one who ruins her one night out.

"This is insane," I finally say out loud. "Are we just going to forget that he was engaged less than a week ago?"

"Let me ask you something," Shelby says, and from her tone, I have a feeling she's going to come at me with guns blazing.

"How was he during the wedding meetings?" She puts her hands on her hips.

"Oh, good one." Clarabella claps, pointing at Shelby.

"He was like every other groom," I lie through my teeth. Folding my arms over my chest, one look at them and they can see through me. "Okay, he was off a bit, but that is only because it was awkward that his ex was planning his wedding." I look at her. "How do you think Ace would feel if you were planning his wedding?"

Clarabella just laughs. "She'd be burning that fucking church down." She looks at Shelby. "Don't even try to lie."

"Not even going to try," Shelby says. "Have you discussed with him what happened with the fiancée?"

"No," I gasp. "Not one part of me wants to know about his relationship with his fiancée." I look at them.

"Well, another reason to talk to him again," Clarabella says.

"It's over," I tell them and I look at Presley, who is the most sensible at this moment, "with everything."

"So we aren't going to the game tonight?" Addison asks, and I just look over at her.

I take a deep breath, looking at the flowers and the

tickets. "Just for the game." I look over at everyone squealing, pointing over at the white box. "But I'm not wearing that fucking thing."

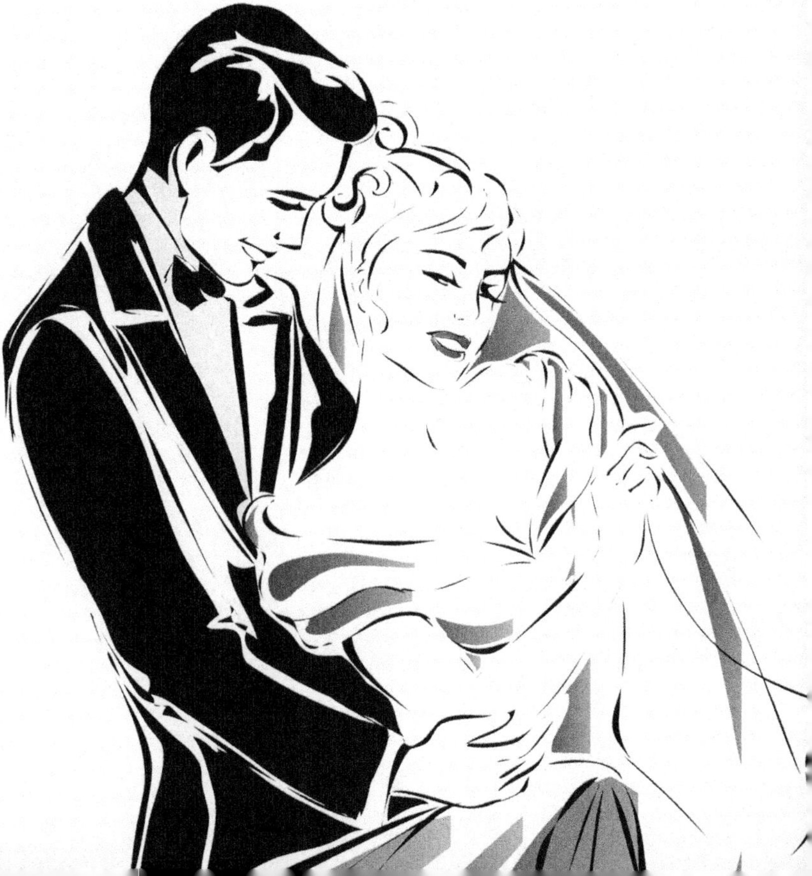

Twenty

Matthew

The soft alarm bells wake me from my dream, right before I take Sofia. My eyes flicker open in the darkened room. I look around for a second, making sure it was a dream and not reality.

I reach over, and the covers are cold. "Just a dream," I mumble, grabbing the phone from the bedside table and turning off the alarm before throwing the cover off myself and getting out of bed. When it's a game day, I always get a two-hour nap in during the day. Usually, I have trouble falling asleep, but because I didn't sleep well the night before, I crashed as soon as I put my head down. It could also be because I saw Sofia right before I went to bed, or it could be that I'm feeling in my skin for the first time in a long time. I can't explain it, but I'll be asking my father about it this weekend when he comes down.

Pressing the button to open the dark-out shades, I make my way to the walk-in closet. Half the closet is empty of course, since it's so big. I turn and go to my suit rack, grabbing a blue suit. Taking the hanger off the rack, I place it on the island in the middle of the room that has drawers. Sliding the pants off the hanger and slipping into them, I turn to grab a white button-down shirt. Tucking it in, I button it all the way to the top, then open the top drawer and grab a dark-blue tie. I finish getting dressed, then I run my hands through my hair before walking out of the house and into my car.

I get to the rink and see the camera crew set up there to take pictures and videos of the guys arriving. I grab my phone and walk in, nodding to the crew before texting Sofia.

Me: What time are you going to be here?

I don't know if she is going to answer me. Fuck, I don't even know if she is going to come. From the look on her face when she came out of her office before, I'm lucky I wasn't struck down by lightning. Right before I put the phone down, I send her a picture of a flying pig.

I undress five seconds after arriving, which defeats the purpose of arriving in a suit, but rules are rules. I make a pit stop in the team kitchen, preparing a protein shake before I go into the gym and get on the bike. I start to pedal slowly, warming up my legs, and decide that I'm going to scroll Instagram. My fingers are already typing in her name. I see that she is private, and the little circle picture is of her with three other people, but I can't see or zoom in. I press follow and send her a message.

Me: Hi, friend.

I laugh at my joke, also knowing how mad she is going to get. I put the phone down as I watch the huge television screen in the room. I speed up my pace, pushing myself but not that hard. I slow my pace before getting up and joining some of the guys to warm up. When it's time to go and suit up, I check Instagram to see if she accepted my follow, only to be shown that I have to request to follow her again. "Oh my God." I chuckle. "She denied me." I shake my head and go to the messages, seeing she saw the message and left me on unread.

My heart skips a beat because I know how good the chase is going to be, but better yet, I know how worth it it's going to be when I make her mine. I put my phone down before undressing and getting into my gear. The music in the room is blaring as I close off my head, it's time to work.

Grabbing my gloves and my stick, I skate out onto the ice. My skates glide over the shiny surface; there is nothing quite like skating on fresh ice—I mean, it comes after pond ice, which is the best thing I've ever skated on. During Christmas break we've started to rent houses up north where the family skates all day long. It's the best.

My eyes scan the people standing around by the boards, fans holding up signs and banging on the window. I don't see her. I stand on the side, waiting for someone to pass me the puck before I skate to the goalie and take a shot. I'm skating back to the side when I look up to the seats she has tickets for, and then I see her. Standing there wearing black pants and a black leather jacket with a scarf around her neck, she has her hair loose and looks ahead with a beer in her hand. The one thing she is missing is the jersey with my name on it. *All in due time,* I tell myself as I wait for her to find me on the ice. When she does, my face goes into the biggest smile I think I've ever had. So big my cheeks hurt. I give her a chin up and then smirk at her.

In true Sofia fashion, she holds one hand up and flips me the bird. I throw my head back and laugh at the top of my lungs before she turns to talk to the woman beside her. The same woman I saw this afternoon when I showed up. "Could be worse, she could have come with a guy," I tell myself as I skate off the ice for us to get it ready for the game.

I skate to the middle of the ice, the sounds of the crowd cheering for us. I hold my stick in both hands as I wait for the referee to come over with the puck. Cole, my center man, stands there ready to go. I am on his right and Nick is on his left. "Let's play a clean game," the referee says to both teams. I put my stick on the ice and wait for the puck to drop.

The second the puck touches the ice, the music shuts off. Cole loses the face-off, giving Toronto the puck. The defenseman skates the puck into the neutral zone and then passes it across the ice to the right side. My stick comes out, trying to block it, but it is too short. They bring the puck in the zone, setting up their play. The guy takes a shot on the net and it bounces off the goalie's pad and goes toward the right side. The defenseman coming into the zone grabs the puck, turns, and passes it to the middle of the ice, but Cole intercepts it. I'm already out of the zone with him as the defenseman follows us. He speeds up in the neutral zone as he passes me the puck. I take it over the blue line, passing it back over to Cole who is closer to the goalie. Instead of taking a shot on the goalie, he quickly passes it back to me and I put it in the back of the net. The red light in back goes on at the same time the fans jump to their feet. Those around the glass slap it to celebrate with us. I put my leg up before I skate over to Cole, jumping on him. The crowd goes wild as I look up at Sofia and give her another chin up. She just shakes her head and she claps her hands. *Football, my ass,* I think to myself as I head over to the bench and skate down the line, high-fiving everyone.

The three periods are over, and we end up winning four to two. It's always a good time after you win. I'm named first star, so I skate around the rink, tossing three pucks into the stands. Saving the last one for her section, I toss it over the glass toward her but it is snatched out of the air way before it even gets to her.

I rush to the locker room and take my phone, sending her a text before the media is let into the room.

Me: Meet me downstairs.

I press send, waiting for a second, and when I don't see the three dots pop up, I call her. Dialing her number, I put my finger to my other ear to block out the sound of the guys celebrating while I walk into the hallway, where it's a bit quieter. She answers after three rings. "Hello," she says and I can hear people around her.

"Where are you?" I ask.

"Trying to get out of here." She laughs. "Where are you?"

"I'm in the locker room," I tell her. "Come meet me."

"Don't push your luck," she says, chuckling.

"Come on, I need to thank you for showing up." I look around. "Plus, I have a puck here."

She laughs. "Go toward the escalator that leads to downstairs," I instruct her. "Once there, follow the signs that bring you to media."

"Ugh," she groans, and I hear rustling from her end. "Five minutes—I have to be somewhere," she says, and I squeeze my phone tighter.

"See you soon," I say and hang up before I piss her off by asking her a million questions about who she's meeting.

I stand here at the entrance of the media corridor, hearing some of the fans walk by, my back pressed against the wall. The drops of water from my hair fall onto my jersey. I peek my head out and then I see her walking around the corner with that girl, the two of them talking and laughing together. I get a chance to look at her without her knowing and it all makes sense to me now. Everything my father said to me when I asked him how he knew my mother was the one.

"You aren't supposed to think you found the one. You are supposed to know. If it's the one, there isn't that

question. There aren't any questions, it just is. There is no second-guessing when you know it's the one."

He's so fucking right. It's nothing that I can explain. It isn't like it's written in a book or flashing lights are pointing at it. You just know, and standing here watching her, my stomach gets tight, my chest contracts, and I feel like I can walk on water.

She must sense me looking at her because she turns her head toward me. She looks around and then holds up a finger to tell me to wait a minute, while she then points up toward the ladies' bathroom. I nod my head at her as she disappears from my sight.

"Damn," I hear from beside me, seeing Brady from Toronto standing there still in his gear. The only thing off is his skates. The opponent's locker room is right next to where I'm standing.

"Who's the chick?" He crosses his arms over his chest.

"Fuck off, Brady." I motion with my head toward his changing room. Brady all but laughs in my face and claps his hands.

"If she was yours, would you even have to tell me to fuck off?" He pokes the bear with a stick. I stand, going toe-to-toe with him, but because I still have my skates on, I'm taller than him.

"Let me put this in words that you are going to understand," I say between clenched teeth. A couple of people from Toronto have stuck their heads out of the room. "If you even go next to her, I'm going to make sure you are eating from a straw for the next four months."

He chuckles and is about to say something when the captain of the team comes out and grabs Brady by his shirt. "Go get changed," he tells Brady.

I stare into his eyes. "Is that clear enough for you?" Brady takes one more look at me before he turns and heads back to the room. The minute he walks away from me, another thing hits me, shocking me even more—my uncle Matthew has been right about everything.

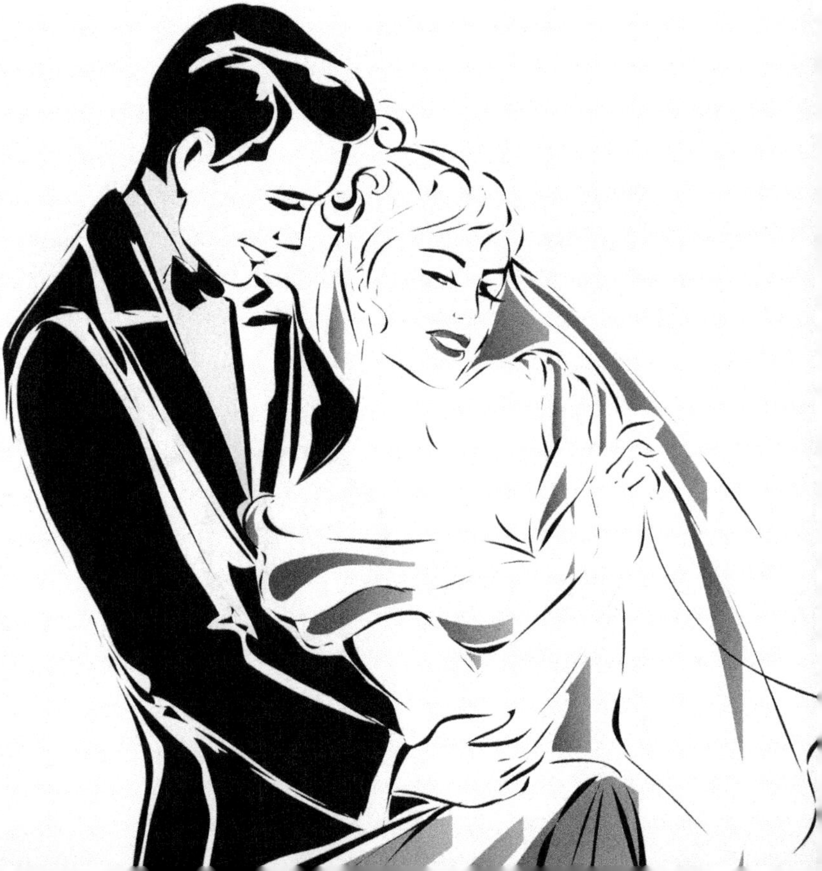

Twenty-One

Sofia

I flush the toilet and walk out to wash my hands at the same time Addison rushes back into the bathroom. I put my hand under the soap dispenser and I'm about to wash my hands when I see her face. "I think we should go," she urges, looking over her shoulder and I'm afraid something happened to her.

I put my hands under the stream of water to rinse off the soap. "Is everything okay?" I ask before walking over and snatching some brown paper from the dispenser and drying my hands.

"We shouldn't go out there," she says and looks over at the doorway.

"Why?" I ask.

"You know your guy?" she asks, her voice going low as she wrings her hands in front of her.

"He's not my guy," I correct her, and she just rolls her eyes at me.

"Okay, well, the guy who wants you and you want him," she states. "He literally threatened a guy who was asking about you."

"Why?" I gasp, shocked. "What?"

"He's going to be eating from a straw." My mouth opens to say something but nothing comes out. She fans herself now. "I haven't been with anyone since my daughter was conceived, but if you weren't interested in him…" She winks at me, making me glare.

"This is crazy," I huff before I kick her in the shin for even thinking about Matthew that way.

I walk out and see he's waiting with his hands on his hips. He looks up when he hears me coming. "Good, you're here," he says. "I have to go and talk to the press." He points with his thumb behind him. "But do you want to go and eat?"

Yes! my head shouts out, but my mouth says, "I have to work tomorrow." I turn to Addison. "And I have to get Addison home."

"Fine," he grumbles, looking around, "then give me ten minutes, and I'll walk you out." The look on his face is one I don't think I've seen before.

"I don't need you to walk me out," I assure him, and he just stares at me, his teeth grinding down.

"Fine, then I'll leave with you now." He bends to start untying his skates. "Then be fined for not talking to the press." He looks up once he's got one of his skates untied.

"Oh my God, you are such a dick," I say out loud.

"Is that a yes?" he asks, his mouth going from a side smirk to a smile. His hair is still dripping wet from the game.

"It's an *I have no choice.*" I throw my hands up and I see some of the players walk out of the room. One of them lingers looking at me, and Addison nudges me with her elbow.

"Good enough. I'm going to go change and meet the press."

"And shower," I stick in there, "you stink like molded cheese and feet." I fan my nose.

"Okay, how about you drop off Addison?" He motions to Addison. "Nice to meet you."

"Thank you," Addison says, "for the tickets to the game. I had so much fun."

"Anytime," he replies, "as long as you bring this one." He points at me.

"I'm standing right here," I tell him, waving my hand in front of his face, and he laughs. "I'm going to drive Addison home, and then I don't know, I guess you can text me."

He looks at me for what feels like forever, my feet want to step forward to him and kiss under his chin. I haven't seen him in action in a long time, and I swear to God, the minute I saw him skating, I gushed from my vagina. "Five-second look," he says, and I can't help but burst out laughing.

"Whatever, Matty." I say his nickname more to annoy him than anything else.

He glares at me. "The guys usually head over to Luke's Bistro," he says. "Do you know where that is?"

I laugh. "That's Clarabella's husband's place."

"Good, so people will know not to fuck with you," he states, looking over his shoulder. "Bernard," he calls to the guy who is standing inside the door wearing a blue suit. The guy walks over to us. "Bernard, this is Sofia, my"—he looks at me and my eyebrows go high—"friend, and Addison, my other friend."

"Nice to meet you," I say, nodding at him, wondering what is going on.

"Do you think you can escort them to their car and make sure that no one—" he says, and I turn away without saying a word to him. "Where are you going?"

"Away from you," I toss over my shoulder, Addison rushing to keep up with me. "Goodbye, Matty."

"Matthew!" he shouts his name. "Text me when you get in the car and you're on your way."

"Absolutely not," I retort, not bothering to look back at him as we make our way over to the escalator. "He's so infuriating," I say, looking over at Addison. "Are you okay?" I ask, and she shakes her head and laughs, looking down.

"Clarabella said something about a mating dance the other day," she says as we get to the top floor where we walked in from. I follow the signs to the parking garage, some of the fans still lingering along with the concession stand workers who are closing up. "I didn't quite understand it, but now, after watching that"—she looks over her shoulder—"I get it."

"Ugh," I groan as we walk toward the parking garage. "Matthew and I have a history."

"From the looks of it," she notes, "I don't think it's history."

"He broke up with me when he was drunk two years ago," I tell her, and she stops walking, "and then a couple of months ago hired me to plan his wedding with his fiancée."

"I had a one-night stand and ended up having a baby," she finally says, and my eyes almost pop out of their sockets. "Met this guy at a bar. He was so hot." She smiles. "Had the hottest sex of my life with him. Then woke up and cringed that I just had a one-night stand, and instead of staying and talking to him, I did the walk of shame at six in the morning. Six weeks later, I was pregnant, and when I went back to tell him, he was moved out and gone."

"Oh my God," I say, putting my hand to my mouth. "Fine, you win."

"I did win," she declares. "I have the best kid that you could ever have. Avery is all me just with her father's face," she says sadly, "and for the rest of my life I'm going to make sure she never feels like she missed out by not having a dad."

I walk over to her and give her a hug. "If it makes you feel better, I didn't meet my dad until I was five." She gasps. "He and my mother had a one-night stand before he left for the military, and then surprise, out came me.

Five years later, she went back to town because her grandfather died and my father was also back in town."

"Wow," Addison says.

"Yeah, plus I've met Avery and she is the coolest kid I've ever met. And I have a lot of practice with cousins," I assure her as I slip my arm in hers. "I want you to promise me something."

"Oh," Addison says, "I won't tell anyone about tonight."

"I don't give a shit about that. I want you to promise me that if you ever need help, you'll come to me."

She looks down. "Thank you," she says softly. "My parents disowned me when I had Avery." I put my hand to my chest. "They refused to have a daughter who had a child out of wedlock."

"Addison," I murmur softly, my heart literally breaking for her.

"My sister and brother." She wipes away a tear, and now I feel like an asshole for making her feel bad. "They didn't want to piss off Mom and Dad, nor did they want to get their trust fund taken away, so they just found it was easier to pretend I didn't exist. When I had Avery, I dressed her up in the cutest outfit I could find and went to see them. I thought for sure once they saw her, they would come to their senses." She smiles through the tears. "Needless to say, they slammed the door in my face and pretended I wasn't even there."

I cross my arms over my chest. "Excuse me, but they are assholes," I tell her, "and they don't deserve to have you or Avery in their lives."

"Thank you," she says. "Getting this job meant everything to me. Just being part of a team and not just a number."

"You aren't just a member of the team," I explain to her. "You're now family. I mean, dysfunctional, but still."

"I'll take it," she replies as we get into the car. I start the car, and she just looks at me.

"What?" I ask, and she tilts her head to the side.

"You have to text him that you got in the car," she reminds me, and I glare at her.

"If you think I'm going to do what he says to do, you have another think coming." I shake my head. "He's lucky I'm going to meet him, and the only reason I'm going to meet him is because he'll probably show up at my house or at work."

She snickers beside me. "This is going to be fun," she says, clapping her hands.

I shake my head, not bothering arguing with her. I drop her off at Shelby's house where she left her car and Avery. I pull out of the driveway and my phone rings. I look at the center console, seeing that Matthew is calling.

"Are you calling to cancel?" I say cheerfully, and he just laughs.

"I'm calling because you never texted me," he huffs. "Where are you?"

"Where are you?" I answer his question with a question as I make my way into town.

"I just got out of the shower," he actually answers. "Are you at the restaurant?"

"I am not," I say, and he doesn't even wait for me to answer him.

"Fine, I'll come to your house," he mutters and I laugh at him.

"I'm on my way to the restaurant, don't get your panties in a twist."

"Okay, I'm leaving in ten, so I'll meet you there."

"Yeah, yeah," I say and hang up on him. I pull into the parking lot at the same time as Luke is walking out.

"What the hell are you doing here?" he asks when I get out of my car, looking at his watch. "It's ten o'clock on a school night."

"I know," I huff. "I'm meeting a friend."

"The hockey player?" he asks, and I gawk.

"Is nothing sacred?" I cross my arms over my chest, and he laughs.

"The restaurant is closed for the team." He chuckles. "But Clarabella did say you went to the game tonight." He looks around. "She would be very interested to know that you came here." I start to talk, and he holds up his hand. "I'll save that for you to tell her." He comes over and kisses my cheek. "Go in the back so no one sees you walk in."

"Thank you," I say, walking over to the back door. I smile at the cooks as I make my way to the front, sliding onto a stool at the bar.

"If it isn't Sofia," Anthony, the bartender, says. "My night just went from sucky to amazing." He winks at me and I just laugh. Anthony and I have worked side by side behind the bar a couple of times when we were stuck at the venue and had to call in help. "What can I get you?"

"I'll have a white wine, please," I tell him and he nods and walks away. I'm about to take my phone out when I feel the stool next to me being pulled out.

I look over and see him, his hair still wet from the shower. The smell of his cologne hits me right away, and suddenly, I'm back in the whirlwind that is Matthew Petrov. I'm about to say something to him when he shocks me with his question. "Is that a friend of yours?"

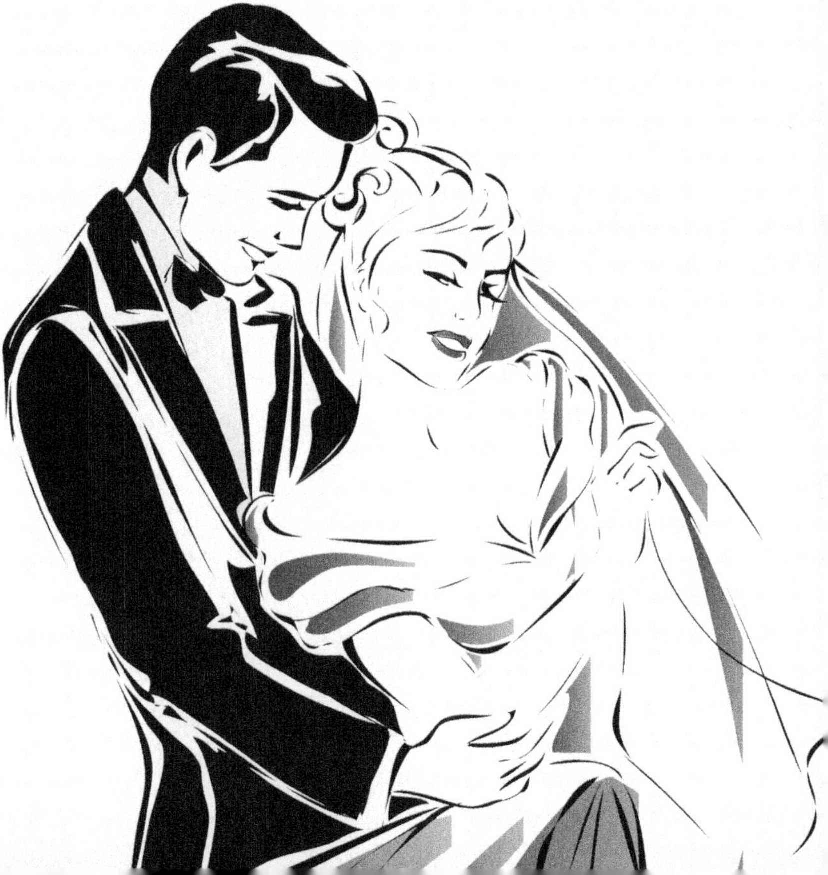

Twenty-Two

Matthew

I stand here for a couple of seconds waiting to see if she is going to answer me, putting my hands in my pants pockets before I do something stupid like drag her away from here and anyone else who wants to look at her. She looks over at me. "Anthony and I are friends actually." I smirk at her answer. The minute she agreed to meet me, I ran back in the room, gave two interviews that I rushed through, and ran out of the shower not even waiting to dry my hair. I tucked my tie in the jacket pocket and hightailed it to her. When I walked in, it took me two seconds to find her at the bar.

"Where is the girl?" I ask, looking around.

"She had to get home to her daughter," she replies,

and I'm even happier it's just the two of us. I mean, I would have taken her any way I could.

"Here you are," Anthony says, coming back over. He puts a white square napkin down on the bar before he places the glass of white wine in front of her. He smiles at her before he turns to look at me. "Can I get you anything to drink?" he asks.

"I'm good," I tell him, instead of doing what I want to do and that is throat punch him. He nods at me before walking down the bar. "Should we grab a table?" I ask, looking around to see that most of the guys came out tonight. There are definitely more people who come out after a win than when we lose. It's usually a hit or miss for me. If Sofia wasn't here, I would have gone home, but nothing could have stopped me from talking to her.

"Yes." She nods, grabbing her bag and holding her hand up for Anthony, who comes back over. He walks as if he's on a catwalk, and if I thought I hated him before, I was wrong. "Can I get the bill?"

"I've got it," I assure him. "We're going to go to the table. I'll settle up at the end."

"No problem," Anthony says. "Besides, that one was on me."

Do you know those cartoons where you see the guy getting hit on the head with a frying pan over and over again until he sees stars? That's what I think of when he says this.

"Aren't you the sweetest?" Sofia plays with him, and I have to bite down. "Next time, it's on me."

Never going to happen, I almost say out loud, but

instead I put my hand to her lower back, guiding her to a booth in the back of the restaurant. She slides into the booth, while I take off my suit jacket and toss it at the end of my side of the booth before sitting in front of her. I roll the sleeves of my shirt up to my elbows once I unbutton them.

"Have you eaten?" I ask while I look down at the menu that was placed on the table before we even sat down. We usually rent out the whole place so no one is coming up to us while we enjoy our meals.

"I ate a hot dog at the game," she says, grabbing her glass of wine, "and a pretzel." She takes a sip and looks around.

The server comes up to the table. "Hi, I'm Suzanna. Can I get you anything?"

"I'll have the grilled salmon with steamed veggies," I tell her, then glance at Sofia, who is now looking down at the menu.

"I'll take a small house salad and a plate of fries." She looks up, smiling at the server, who nods at her before turning back to me. "Can I get you anything to drink?"

"I'll have a water," I tell her, handing her my menu for her to take the hint and leave us alone. Ever since I walked in here and saw her, all I knew was I didn't want to share her.

"Coming right up," she chirps, walking away from us. I look back over at Sofia, who is still looking around.

"What are you doing?" I ask, turning my head and looking around, wondering if she saw someone she knew.

She finally looks back at me, tapping her finger on

the base of her wineglass. "Is this going to be something they talk about tomorrow?" she asks, and my eyebrows pinch together because I have no fucking clue what she is talking about.

"I have no idea what you mean by that," I say, leaning back on the booth and stretching my arms across the back.

"Well," she says, grabbing her glass again, "not too long ago, you were engaged." She brings the glass to her lips. "And I was your wedding planner," she adds, right before she takes a sip to stop herself from talking.

"Things change." That is the only thing I can say. I hadn't really announced that the engagement was on. And if it wasn't for Helena's post on social media with a picture of the ring, no one would have caught wind of it.

"But do they?" She puts her glass down, and Suzanna comes over with the glass of water for me.

"They do," I confirm, grabbing the glass and finishing half of it.

"Let me ask you something." She looks me dead in the eyes, and for the life of me, I can't remember a time I didn't love her. Which is the strangest thing because I haven't seen her in two years.

"You can ask me anything," I tell her. Now it's my turn to tap the table nervously.

"After we met the first time." I tilt my head to the side. "Why did you come back?"

The pit of my stomach burns with this question. "I didn't," I finally say, "I wasn't planning on it. Actually, the minute we walked out of the office, I turned and said we weren't using you." Her eyebrows go up at this declaration. "Helena told me at the last minute she booked you."

"You didn't try to convince her otherwise?" she asks the loaded question. It's the same question Christopher asked me when I told him we were using Sofia. It will probably be the first question my cousins will ask me once they find out.

"I figured if I did." I look around, not ready to admit the next part. "She would want to know why."

Sofia's eyes almost bulge out of their sockets. "So she didn't know about me?"

"No." I say the word and see the hurt in her eyes, right before she builds the wall back up, making my heart hurt. I want her to ask me why. I'm ready for her to ask me why. She might not be ready for it, but I am. Except she doesn't ask me another question. Instead, she picks up her glass of wine and looks away from me as she takes two gulps.

I'm about to tell her why I never told Helena about her when Suzanna comes over with three plates. She places my plate in front of me, then the plate in front of Sofia, placing the plate of fries in the middle of the table. "Enjoy," she says to us before walking away.

Sofia's eyes stay glued to her plate of salad, grabbing the fork next to her as she tosses it around on the plate. I grab my own fork, flaking a piece of salmon away. We eat in silence as I ponder the questions I want to ask. I look up at her a couple of times and notice she isn't even eating the salad. She's just playing with it on her plate.

"What's the matter?"

"Nothing." She doesn't look up at me, and although we haven't been together in two years, I know that tone doesn't mean nothing. It means she's pissed. I used to always love it when she gave me this tone. I knew the fight would be worth it, because when we made up, it was electric.

"You sure aren't acting like nothing is wrong," I say, not sure if I should.

"I'm just a little bit annoyed and confused is all," she finally declares. "You come to meet me, don't want to use me, use me anyway, and never even mention to your fiancée that we knew each other." She shakes her head. "Actually, forget it. I don't even care, to be honest. It's none of my business." She takes a bite of her salad.

"Is that you asking me why I didn't tell her about you?" I take a bite of my salmon, waiting for her to answer me.

"Not in the least. I don't really care." I know it's a lie. She knows it's a lie.

"Well, considering we didn't just know each other..." I make sure she knows I hate the way that came out of her mouth. Her eyes now fly up to me. "I didn't tell her about you because I wasn't sure what to say."

"I don't know how your relationship worked." She takes a sip of her wine. "Nor do I care, but you should always go with the truth."

"I would never lie," I tell her, grabbing a piece of carrot, "which is why I didn't tell her about you."

"That makes no sense." She puts her glass down.

"Doesn't it?" I take another bite of the salmon, just so my hands are busy doing something instead of being on the table tapping it. "If I told her about you, she would have had questions." I look at Sofia. "Questions I would have had to answer." I raise my eyebrows, wondering if she gets what I'm saying.

"How was I supposed to tell my fiancée that my wedding planner was the only woman I've ever loved?" She doesn't say anything. "How do you think that conversation would have gone? Because she would have asked me if I still had feelings for you and the answer would have been yes." She opens her mouth and closes it again, no words coming out. "How do you think that would have gone? 'Helena, I think we should not go with white-and-black flowers because they look horrible.'" I grab another piece of salmon. "'Oh, and by the way, did you know Sofia and I dated and lived together for two years?'" I shake my head, angry because maybe I should have said those words. "Are you dating anyone?" I say right before I pop the piece of salmon in my mouth, wanting to kick myself. Did I actually say those words out loud? Do I want to know the answer to this? One thousand percent. Am I ready for the answer? Absolutely not.

I avoid looking up at her, not sure I can handle it. "Yes," she replies, her voice high and tight. I close my eyes as the answer sinks into my brain. The minute it does, a rage washes over me.

Suzanna comes over. "Are you finished?" she asks of my almost empty plate, and I nod my head.

"I'm done also," Sofia says, pushing her plate to her, "and can we have the bill, please?"

"It's all taken care of," Suzanna relays. "Have a great night."

Sofia grabs her purse from the seat and slides out of the bench. I guess this means we're done.

"I'm done," she announces as I grab my jacket in my hand and slide out to stand in front of her. "You don't have to leave. I can see myself out."

I don't bother saying anything to her, instead I hold out my hand for her to walk ahead of me. I hold up my hand to a couple of the guys as I walk out. My hand itches to slip it into hers as we walk around the building and toward the back, where I see her car parked, but she's one step ahead of me.

The sound of her shoes clicking is the only thing that makes noise. There isn't even another car on the street. "This is me," she says from the back of her car.

I stand in front of her. "How serious is it?" I tilt my head to the side, waiting for her to answer, hoping like everything that it isn't.

"None of your business," she retorts, her eyes staring straight into mine. I nod my head at her. "We are two friends having a conversation." She throws my words back in my face. I smirk at her, always knowing those words would come back to bite me in the ass.

My whole body fills with nerves. I make sure my eyes never leave hers when I say the words, "The last thing I want is to be your friend and we both know it."

She lowers her eyes just a second before looking back

at me. "I know a couple of things." She crosses her arms in front of her. "One, I didn't want to be here but you didn't give me a choice." The lie comes out of her mouth so smoothly. We both know she didn't have to come here tonight, but she did, and I don't know who I'm going to owe that she is here, but I will pay them double. "Two, what I also know is that we shared something"—she takes a deep breath in—"a while ago, but now it's gone."

"What if I want it back?" I ask the loaded question.

She pffts out, cocking her hip to the side. "You think I'm going to be your rebound?" She points at herself.

I can't help but chuckle, my whole body on alert. My hand clenches my jacket so tight I think my fingers are turning white. "You aren't anyone's rebound or second choice." I take a step toward her, my feet not even caring what my head is saying. At this point, I'm not thinking about anything but her. I stand so close to her I can feel her breath on me. "You're the fucking first choice every single time." The words come out in almost a whisper. My hand drops my jacket to the ground and flies to hold her face. She gasps just as my lips touch hers and I feel like I just walked into heaven.

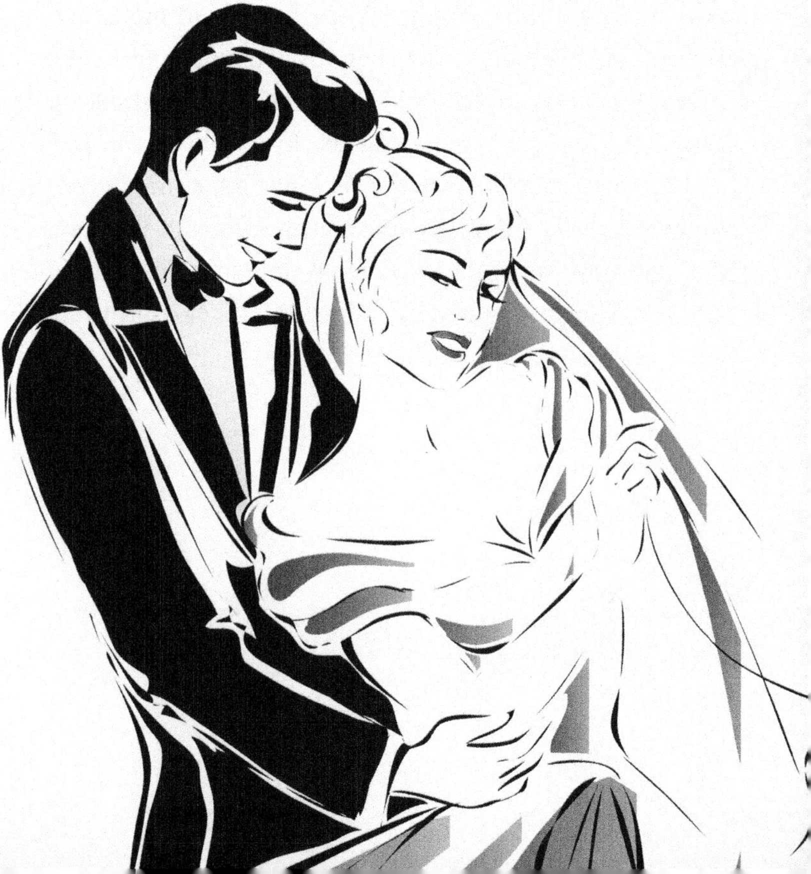

Twenty-Three

Sofia

Everything happens in slow motion, or at least it feels like that. One minute I'm sitting down in the booth and he's saying things I need to compartmentalize, and the next, he's asking me if I'm dating someone. The fucking balls on this guy, he literally asked someone to marry him. Now he's asking me if I'm dating someone and if it's serious. I wanted to stab my fork in his eyeball. The audacity of him, and now his lips are on mine and I want to hate it and tell myself to push him away. But the minute his tongue slides into my mouth, it's like the first time all over again, except now it's going to be worse because I remember what it's like to be kissed by Matthew.

His hands move from my face and are buried in my

hair as he pulls me even closer to him. His head moves to the side to deepen the kiss, and I forget it all. I forget that I'm pissed at him. I forget I wanted to slap him across the face. My hands move on their own as they go to his hips and then up his sides, slowly moving to his chest where his heart beats under my palms. Our hearts beat almost at the same rhythm. I want to push him away from me but I get lost in the kiss. I get lost into everything that Matthew Petrov is. He's charming, he's beautiful, he's funny, he's the love of my life, yet he's also the one who broke my heart.

He moves his nose against mine. "Matthew." His name comes out in a whisper or a plea, I don't really know nor do I trust myself if he's touching me.

"I love when you say my name." His voice is a whisper also, right before he comes back to kiss me. I close my eyes for a second and tell myself I never had a last kiss with him, so this is going to be the last one, but even my head laughs at me. My tongue fights with his as they go around and around and around.

My hands fall from his chest and I take a step back from him. His hands fall from inside my hair as my head tingles from his touch. My lips are still wet from his kiss as both of us just stare at each other. My eyes move over his and then down to his chest to where my hands just were. "You kissed me."

"You kissed me back," he counters, not even caring that he kissed me outside in the middle of a parking lot where anyone could have seen us.

"You kissed me," I repeat as my lips tingle from the

kiss and I want to wipe his taste off my lips, but my hands stay glued to my side, "in the middle of a parking lot."

He looks around. "I guess this is where it happened." He bends to pick up the jacket he tossed on the ground.

"I told you I was dating someone." I put my hands on my hips. "And you didn't even care."

He holds up his hands to make me stop talking. "You were lying." I glare at him. "Every single time you lie, you blink faster than you normally do." He points out something that I was working on not doing.

"I'm not dating anyone in particular," I say a half truth, and he just looks at me with that dumb smirk I hate.

"Yes, you are," he declares. "I'll see you tomorrow, Princess Sofia." He stuns me by turning around and walking over to his car, getting in, and driving away.

"Motherfucker!" I shout to the back of his car as I get into my own car and drive away. I get home and storm into the house, slamming the door behind me. "That fucking jackass." I toss my purse on the table before walking upstairs and getting undressed. "I would have had to tell her I still had feelings for you," I mock his words, putting on a pair of shorts and a tank top. Pinning the hair on top of my head, I walk into the bathroom to take off my makeup. "I should have not gone to the game." *I am going insane,* I think to myself. I'm having a full-blown conversation with myself. "I should have gone with my gut and ignored it." I brush my teeth after tossing the wet cloth in the wash pile. "Go and show him you aren't affected by him." I shake my head at the words. "Yeah, that worked out great for me." I walk out and turn off all the lights before sliding into bed. "He kissed me without a second thought." I sink into the pillow. "Was it good?" I say to absolutely no one. "Yes, it was, but it's probably because I haven't kissed anyone in a long time." I laugh at myself. "Yeah, let's go with that. I was desperate for someone to kiss me."

I toss and turn most of the night, only falling asleep for a couple of hours. Finally, I give up at six in the morning and grab my phone. Opening Instagram, I see that Matthew Petrov has requested to follow me. Again, I do what I did the day before, I press the delete button. As soon as I press the delete button, I go onto his Instagram. Because he plays hockey, he's not on private, so I can lurk on his page and no one knows but me. I scroll down to the six pictures he has, seeing the last picture he posted was this summer. It's him with his cousin, Christopher, and I zoom the picture a bit more to see that he's with the actor Romeo Beckett. All three in a tux with the caption: *He won the trophy and took home the girl. Congrats on the wedding, Gabriella and Romeo.* I slide right and see a picture of Gabriella and Romeo at the altar, their hands holding each other's, her hand in the air with her bouquet, his hand in the air with the Oscar. I scroll down to see that not one post has Helena in it. Not one post about them getting married. Not one post about anything to even say he had a girlfriend.

I'm about to go down the rabbit hole and type in Helena's name when I hear a soft knock. I stop mid type to make sure I didn't just hear it in my head. The sound comes again except just a touch louder. I sit up in my bed, tossing the covers off me before walking to the door and sticking my head out to make sure I heard it from downstairs. The knock comes again. "What in the hell?" I mutter, walking down the steps and looking out the peephole. "Oh my God," I mumble as he looks straight into the peephole.

I don't even know how he knows I'm here, but he says, "I brought you coffee." He's holding up the tray of coffee in one hand. "And breakfast."

I unlock the door and open it just a bit, my eyes meeting his. His face goes into a big smile as I take him in. He's wearing shorts and a blue T-shirt with his baseball hat on his head backward. "What are you doing here?"

"I wanted to have breakfast with you," he says, my feet moving backward to open the door for him. He takes a step in and stares at my outfit. My nipples are hard and poking through the tank top I'm wearing. "Good morning," he greets me before bending his head and pecking my lips. He walks into the house as I close the door softly.

Looking down at my tingly nipples, I scold them softly, "Traitors," before following him down the hallway.

"Seriously," I say to his back, "you can't just show up here."

He grabs one of the white cups of coffee, turning and handing it to me. "If I would have called you and asked you to have breakfast, would you have said yes?"

"No," I reply, crossing my arms over my chest in protest.

"Exactly, so I improvised." He holds the cup up even higher so I can take it from him.

"Perhaps you shouldn't," I retort between clenched teeth as I grab the white cup from him.

"I got an everything bagel with egg and sausage or sesame seed with egg and bacon," he states, opening the bag.

"You can take both those and eat them in your car." I point over at the door, but he just laughs as he takes both sandwiches out of the bag and opens them on the counter.

"We can each have both."

"I don't want to have breakfast with you, Matthew," I tell him point-blank. *Yeah, she doesn't want to have breakfast with you because she wants you to eat her vagina for breakfast*, my head screams. I'm so afraid I've said those words out loud, I hold my lips together tightly.

"It's just breakfast." Matthew pulls out a stool for me and then another one for himself as he sits on it.

"You aren't going to leave, are you?" I ask the question as my feet move toward the stool, and I get on it.

"Not until you eat, and we have a talk," he says, pushing the food toward me.

"I don't think there is anything left to talk about," I say, picking up one half of a bagel and taking a bite.

"We need to talk about last night," he counters, taking a bite of his own sandwich.

"Which part should we discuss?" I ask. "Should we discuss that you never told your fiancée about me, or maybe we should discuss the fact you kissed me without even thinking twice."

"If you want me to tell Helena about you, I will, and that kiss was good." He takes a bite. "Great even." He chews. "It's the best kiss we've ever had."

I shake my head. "Unbelievable," I mumble before my mouth agrees that the kiss was the best we've ever had.

"When I saw you for the first time again," he starts, "it felt like a box I locked two years ago was suddenly opened, and I saw the light again."

"Hold on while I go get the violin and you sing me a sad song," I mock him. "You were fucking engaged to another woman." My anger now comes out. "You literally asked another woman to spend the rest of her life with you."

"No, I didn't." He shakes his head and all I can do is gasp at him.

"I met your fiancée!" I shout, pushing away from the island. "Literally, I was planning your wedding."

"But I never asked her to marry me." I stare at him, not sure what the hell he is saying to me. "It was just like she said we should get married, and I was like, yeah okay. Then we were engaged." My mouth hangs open. "It was just sort of the next step." He shrugs his shoulders. "Truth be told, we should have moved in with each other first."

"You weren't living with her?" I ask, my head spinning with this information.

"Nope. She sometimes stayed over, but not really," he

explains and I don't know what to say. The minute we became a couple, we spent almost every night together, if I didn't go to him, he would come to me. I can count on one hand the nights we didn't spend together. "I thought it was the logical next step, but I quickly saw that it was a mistake. I'm sorry I hurt her." He looks up at me now. "I'll be forever sorry for that, but I can't hate it too much because it brought you back into my life." He taps his fingers on the counter nervously. "The minute I saw you, I knew it was wrong."

"What if you hadn't seen me?" I ask, my voice no more than a whisper. "If you never saw me again, you would have married her."

"I don't think so," he says as if nothing happened. "Something felt off from the beginning, but it really came to light when I saw you."

"This is not happening right now." I put my hand on my forehead, trying to see if I have a fever and am delirious.

"My family is coming down this weekend to attend the game, and I'd like you to come also," he informs me as if he didn't just drop a bomb in my lap.

"Absolutely not. Are you out of your mind?" I don't know if I'm asking him or telling him.

"Could be," he concedes, smiling at me as he gets up. "Either way, I want you to come this weekend."

"I have to get ready for work," I tell him because I can't think of anything else to say. My heart is speeding so fast in my chest that it's all I hear in my ears.

He comes over to me and looks in my eyes while he

pushes away the hair from my face. "You are beautiful," he says softly before he bends his head and kisses me until I have trouble remembering what we were just talking about. "I'll call you later." He rubs his nose with mine before walking out and closing the door behind him.

Just like that, he's gone as if I dreamed the whole thing. I blink my eyes a couple of times, and I'm about to pinch myself. "Did this just happen?"

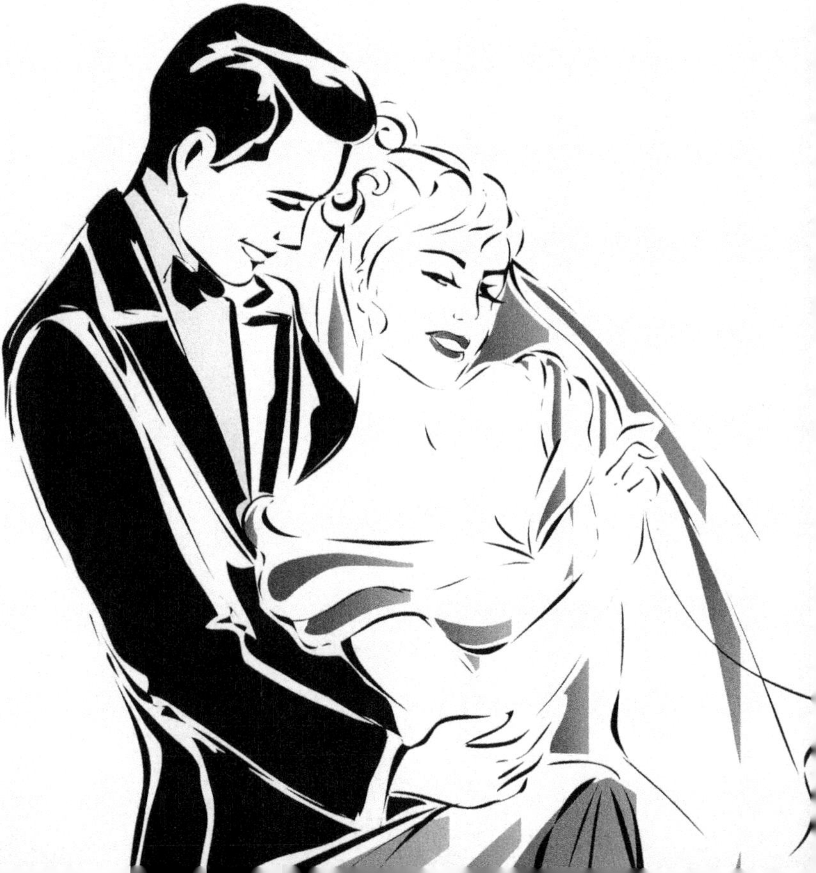

Twenty-Four

Matthew

"We leave Sunday morning until Wednesday," I hear someone say from the other side of the room.

Everyone groans, including me. "Back-to-back games in Philadelphia and then Pittsburgh."

"Pack your hats and coats, people." I turn to see the public relations guy say, "They got snow two days ago."

"Snow isn't that bad," I state, getting up and slipping on my sweater with the team logo in the middle and my number forty-five on the corner of it in small numbers. "If it's snowing, it means it's not below zero outside."

"Good point," Brock says from his side of the bench. "Remember last year when we went to Winnipeg, my nostrils froze walking off the plane."

I laugh at the guys telling stories of when it was the coldest, grabbing my phone and keys. "See you tomorrow, boys," I say, walking out toward my car. Pushing the steel door open, I step into the underground parking lot.

Looking down at my phone, I pull up her name and smile when I press the call button. I unlock my car door as it starts the second ring. "Ugh, hello," she says, huffing.

"Good afternoon," I greet, my voice chipper.

"What do you want, Matthew?" she returns, and I can just imagine the scowl on her face.

"Do you want to have dinner with me?" I ask, knowing full well what her answer is going to be.

"No," she declares, not surprising me.

I roll my lips to stop myself from bursting out laughing. "Okay."

"Goodbye." She disconnects and my chest fills with this feeling of fullness.

I pull out of the parking garage and the next person I call is my father, who answers after the first ring. "Hey," he greets.

"Hey," I reply, pulling out and going toward my house. "What's up?"

"Not much, just going to go and ask your mother what she wants to eat for dinner," he says. "What about you? What are you up to?"

"Not much. Going to go home, grab dinner, and head to see Sofia," I share, waiting for him to say something.

"So you spoke with her?" he asks softly.

"I did," I confirm, taking a deep inhale and then letting

it out. "I think it was the hardest conversation I've ever had."

"Did you two clear the air?" I think about how to answer this question because it's not so cut and dry.

"When she told me I broke her fucking heart." I can hear her voice in my head. "I hated myself." I swallow the lump. "I was the one who was supposed to protect her and I am the one who caused her pain."

"Have you said that to her?" My father is never going to judge you. Not once. He's going to sit down and talk things out. I don't answer him before he says, "Communication is key, Matthew." I pull into the driveway of my house, leaning my head back against the headrest. "If you don't tell her how you feel, she'll never know."

"You're right," I tell him, rubbing my hands over my face. "I have to tell her everything and not hold back."

"You also have to prepare yourself for the fact that she may have moved on," he warns me, and just the thought shatters me. At just that thought, my heart which felt so full before now feels like someone has reached into my chest and ripped it out. "It's not an easy thing to do, trust me, I know." He breathes out heavily. "When I couldn't go to your mom and I had to wait out the year, it was the longest time of my life. Knowing she could move on at any second motivates me to be the man she deserves. And now look at us," he says, and I can picture the smile forming on his face.

"Didn't she threaten to cut off your junk last week?" I chuckle.

"Which means she loves me something fierce." He laughs also. "Don't waste any more time, Matthew."

"I won't," I assure him. "Can't wait to see you this weekend."

"Same," he says, "now I'm going to go and wine and dine my woman."

"Never say that to me again." I close my eyes. "Now I'm going to imagine you two having sex in the kitchen."

He laughs. "Wouldn't be the first time."

"Too much, Dad," I tell him. "I love you, goodbye." I hang up to the sound of him laughing his head off.

Getting out of my car, I jog up the steps to my house, opening the door and kicking off my shoes before walking straight to the stairs. I take off the sweater and pants right beside the unmade bed and slip into it. I press the button to close the blackout curtains at the same time I put a one-hour timer on my phone. I put my head down on the pillow, closing my eyes, and the only thing I can think of is Sofia.

I don't even know if I nap during the hour, all I know is the alarm rings and I reach over and grab it, turning it off. I turn on my back and open my Instagram, where I pull up Sofia's name. It says this account is private and it's giving me the blue button option to follow her, again. I press follow, and it lets me know that it's been requested.

I shake my head, bringing up my call log again and pressing the phone logo right next to her name. It rings three times before she finally answers it, and truth be told, I thought she wouldn't. "Hello," she answers.

"Where are you?" I ask as I throw the covers off me, pressing the button for the shades so some light comes in.

"On my spaceship headed to the moon." She shocks the fuck out of me, and all I can do is throw my head back and laugh.

"Fuck, you're funny." I get up, holding the phone to my ear with my shoulder as I get dressed.

"Do you want to come to my house for dinner?" I ask, even though it's a wasted question.

"No." She doesn't even skip a beat with that answer.

"Shocker." I laugh. "Okay, I'll come to you."

"Ugh, why?" she questions. "There is no reason for us to have another meal together."

"We need to talk," I tell her, thinking about what my father said.

"We already did," she says, her voice going soft. "We spoke twice or was it three times? Either way, we said what we had to say."

"I thought of other things to say," I inform her. "Are you at work? Do you want me to swing by there and pick you up?"

"If I was at work," she starts, and I put the sweater over my head, "how would I get to work tomorrow if you picked me up?"

I walk down the stairs and chuckle. "I'd drive you to work," I state as she groans. "Either way, I get to see you again."

"Matthew," she grumbles in frustration.

"Sofia," I counter, my voice going soft, "one more

dinner."

"Why don't I believe you?" she huffs.

"Why do you keep denying my follow request on Instagram?" I ask as I grab my keys and head out the door.

"Because there isn't a reason to accept it. It's for my really, really close friends."

"How close do we have to be?" I ask, getting in my car.

"You have to know certain things about me," she challenges.

"Go," I tell her.

"Favorite color."

"Blue, but not a light blue like the sky, a darker blue like navy but not so dark that it looks like black." I smile when she doesn't tell me I'm wrong. "Next?"

"Favorite food?" she asks, not telling me my answer was wrong.

"Depends," I tell her. "On a lazy day you like pretty much anything your grandmother cooks. On a quiet date night, you like either steak or salmon, you can do either, sometimes both. When you are out drinking, definitely a cheeseburger with bacon, loaded. The greasier the better. You like fries, your favorite kind are crinkle cut, with ketchup."

"You're annoying," she says, and I can't help but laugh.

"Favorite person in the whole world?" she says, thinking she can trick me.

"If it isn't your horse," I start, "it has to be either

Grandpa Billy or Grandma Charlotte."

"Goodbye," she says and hangs up as soon as I pull up to her house and see her car is there.

I jog up the steps and ring the bell, hearing her walking toward the door. "The person you are trying to reach is not at home," she announces behind the closed door. "Please go away."

I knock on the door. "I have to answer more questions to make sure you accept my follow request on Instagram."

"If I accept you, will you leave?" she asks, and I put my hands on the doorframe leaning in.

"What fun would that be?" I prod when I hear the lock turn and the door opens. She stands in loose-fitting pants with a matching long-sleeved sweater that falls off her shoulder, which is bare and begs to be kissed. "Hi," I greet, moving in before she slams the door in my face.

She closes the door behind me, and I turn to face her. Her back is to the door, her hair loose like I love it. "Fuck, you're beautiful," I state right before I take her face in my hands and then run my hands into her hair. My lips lower onto hers, my cock getting hard the second her tongue touches mine. I'm lying. My cock was hard the minute she opened the door.

"You can't do that," she says when I let her lips go, her voice in a whisper as she slowly opens her lips.

"Do what?" I ask as I push myself even more into her. I rub my nose with hers and bend to kiss her again.

"Say things like that," she explains. "Tell me I'm beautiful. Kiss me when you want. Friends don't talk and do things like that."

"I'm not your friend," I assure her right before my lips claim hers again. This time she arches her back into me as her hands go around my neck and into my hair. My hands slide out of her hair, and one wraps around her waist as I push her into the door. We both groan when she must feel my cock. I lift her by the waist and she wraps her legs around my hips.

"Sofia," I whisper her name, "I didn't come here for this." I bite her lower lip.

"Then what did you come here for?" she asks, and I see her eyes have gotten a touch darker.

"I came just to be with you," I tell her the truth. "I came because I can't stay away from you." I attack her neck, sucking in. "I came because all I want to do is be with you. I'll take anything you have to throw at me, just so you know. I'm not going anywhere, Sofia."

My lips crash to hers as I turn and walk up the stairs. I don't know what is going to happen, but whatever it is, I want her lying down, and I want to be able to see everything. I make my way down the hall to the only open door, stepping in and seeing it's definitely her bedroom. Her bed is made, of course, her throw pillows at the top of the bed. The little love seat sits in front of the bed.

"Bed or couch?" I ask, taking my lips away from hers as she slides off me and stands in front of me.

"I don't care," she says, putting her hands on her hips and getting up on her tippy-toes to kiss under my chin before she slides her hands under my shirt. My body shivers under her touch at the same time my body becomes more alive than it has in years. It's as if my body was asleep and one touch from her and it was on again.

"Kiss me," she whispers, and I do exactly that. My lips meet hers, my tongue slides with hers at the same time she is fisting my shirt, moving the material up my chest. The kiss starts off slow, but it ends with us fighting each other to get the kiss deeper. She lets go of my lips to pull the shirt over my head. "One for one," she hisses as my hand flies to the hem of her shirt, ripping it over her head and seeing her standing there with nothing fucking on. Her perfect tits just open to me, her nipples perky and begging to be sucked, bitten, and pulled.

"Fuck," is the only thing I can say as my hands come up on their own and palm one in each hand. My head goes down as I take one in my mouth, biting down right before I suck it between my lips. Sofia hisses, and when I look up, her eyes are closed. I move from one nipple to the next doing the same thing.

Her hand comes up to my head, her finger pushing the cap to the floor where my shirt is and so is hers. I trail my tongue from her nipple to the middle of her chest and down her stomach, bending onto my knees in front of her. Kissing her stomach, my hands are on her hips, and in one fluid motion, her pants are around her ankles.

She stands there in the tiniest pair of panties I've ever seen in my life. The white lace shows everything to me, including the little landing strip she always has. My hands squeeze her hips tight, making sure she doesn't go anywhere. "Are you wet for me?" I ask, my eyes on her landing strip. My hands pull her to me as my nose rubs against her clit. "I want to savor this." My voice is clear and tight, my cock straining to get out and in her. "But, fuck." My tongue comes out to lick her through her panties, the sound of us both moaning fills the room.

"More," she pleads, her head falling down as she watches me move my hand from her hip to the side of her panties, pushing them aside. Her breath hitches right before my tongue licks between her folds. "Yes," she hisses, right after my tongue turns around her clit in circles, round and round, right before sucking it in. Her legs open just a touch more, giving me more access. "More," she begs and the hand holding her panty to the side is now opening her folds up so I can slide two fingers into her.

"Yes," she hisses again as my fingers move in and out of her, her hips meeting me halfway. Her pussy squeezes my fingers, and fuck if it isn't heaven. "I need more," she says and I know what she needs. Sofia and I did a lot of things really, really well, but what we did exceptionally well was not be shy when it came to the bedroom.

If I wanted her to suck my cock, all I had to do was ask. If she wanted it hard and fast, all she had to do was ask. We dated for two years, and after one week, I slid into her; from that day we used to have sex twice a day, sometimes more. I knew every single inch of her body. I knew every single freckle she had. I knew what every single touch meant and now was no different. She wanted it hard and she wanted it fast, and I was going to give her what she wanted.

I get up off my knees and wrap my arm around her waist, picking her up.

"How do you want it?" I ask, looking down at her as she smiles at me.

"Hard and fast," she says, and I laugh.

"You were getting it hard and fast to begin with," I tell her, my mouth devouring hers as she wraps her legs around me, trying to get even closer to me. Our mouths are in a frenzy to get deeper into the kiss. I put my knee on the bed and set her down, falling on top of her, my hands by her head holding me up by my elbows. Her legs are still wrapped around my hips, but her hands are now going to my pants. She pushes them over my hips, my cock springing free. Her hands grip the base of my cock and I moan but her mouth swallows the sound. She moves her hand up and down my shaft before I break the kiss. "At this point, it's going to be really fast," I warn her, but instead of listening to me, she just attacks my mouth.

"Less talking." She moves away from my mouth, nipping at my jaw. "More." She moves her panties to the side, rubbing my cock up and down her slit. "After you fuck me, I'm going to clean you up." She places my cock at her entrance. "But only if you fuck me like you mean it."

"Challenge accepted," I tell her, slamming into her in one fucking move, my balls slapping against her ass. My pants are in the middle of my thighs, but I don't give a shit. I have one goal and one goal only, to fuck my girl hard and fast. I pull out until the tip and then slam back into her. Her back arches off the bed as she slides her hand between us. "Legs," I demand of her and she lifts her legs to drape over my shoulders. I press into her harder than before, the sound of skin slapping fills the room, along with her moan every single time my balls slap against her ass.

"Right there," she moans.

"Eyes," I tell her, and she opens her eyes to look at me, "watch me fuck you." She looks down between us, my cock hammering into her while her finger strums her clit faster and faster. I can feel that she's almost there. I bite back my own orgasm as her pussy grips me so tight I don't think I will be able to pull out, but I do. She is fucking soaking my cock, dripping down my balls. Her eyes close as I pound into her faster and faster. My thrusts become shorter and shorter until I pull out and plant my cock all the way in her.

"I'm close," I declare, pulling out this time slowly as she comes down from her orgasm. "Where do you want it?"

"Where do you want to put it?" she asks, her hips lifting to match my thrusts. "My mouth?" she asks. "My tits?" She rolls her nipples for me. "Or inside me?"

Fuck, all three end with me winning. "My mouth," she finally decides, "to clean you up." I slam into her one more time, then pull out. She sits on her ass, her mouth swallowing my cock. Her legs spread to the side of me, leaving her open.

Her hand grips my cock, moving up and down. My arm leans down and slides two fingers into her. "Gonna fuck you with my fingers," I tell her as she cleans herself off me, "the same time you suck my cock and we both come." Her eyes look at me while she jerks me off faster and faster. My fingers are fucking her just as fast. "Take it," I tell her as she swallows me to the back of her throat. "I'm there." I know she's going to swallow whatever I give her but giving her the choice. "Come on my fingers," I instruct her and she moves her hips up to meet my fingers, her moan vibrating on my cock as I come down her throat. I come like I've never come before in my life. She fucking swallows every single last drop and groans when I slide my fingers out of her.

"Now that," I observe as I hold her face in my hands, "was hard and fast." I kiss her lips and she smirks at me.

"I don't know about you." She licks my lower lip back and forth. "But I think we can do it harder." Her hand works my softening cock. "I want you naked." She licks the tip of my cock, while one hand tries to push the pants lower on my legs.

"I'll take off my pants when you let my cock go," I tell her, and she looks up at me and pouts. "After that, I'm going to lie down in the middle of your bed. You're going to work my cock," I inform her, getting off the bed and kicking my pants away from me. "And while you do that, you are going to slide that sweet-ass pussy on my face." She closes her legs at her knees. "Panties off," I order her, lying down on the bed, "and get up here and sit on my face."

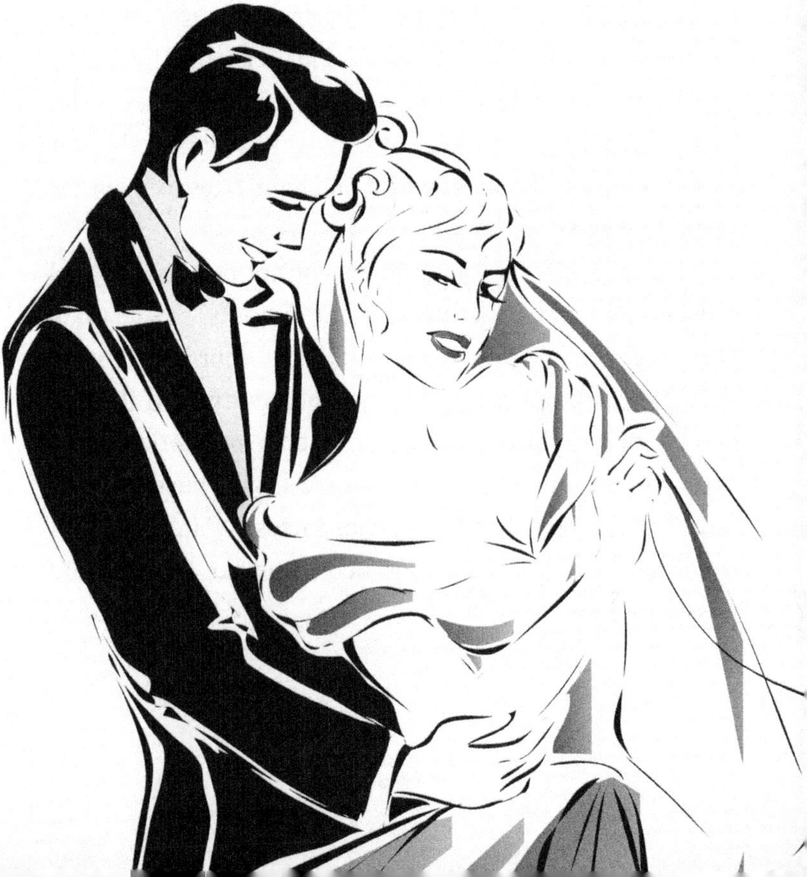

Twenty-Five

Sofia

The alarm bells start to ring softly at first. I try to open my eyes but they feel so heavy. I'm about to reach out to shut it off when I feel this added warmth on me. Or maybe it was there all along but I'm just feeling it now. My breast is held in a hand while his front is pressed to me. "If you keep wiggling that ass," he mumbles from behind me, "we are going to get started on round five." My eyes fly open and it all comes back to me. Matthew showing up, me attacking him. Having sex in my bed. Having sex in the shower. Having sex on my kitchen counter. Then again having sex right before we finally fell asleep. Having what I thought was the best sex of my life and then having it again only to think that was better. "Sofia," he says my name, his face buried in my neck as he starts giving me soft kisses, "you need to turn off the alarm."

"I can't move," I tell him as his hold on me gets tighter.

"I got it," he says, not releasing his hand on my breast but instead reaching over me with his whole body, turning it off.

"It's not even six o'clock," he says, lying back down behind me.

"Um," I start to say as the reality of everything that happened sinks in. "Matthew." I close my eyes, taking in the heat that is seeping into me from him.

"No," he scolds softly, his face buried back in my neck, "don't you even think about it."

"Think about what?" I ask.

"Whatever it is you are going to say," he says, his breath tickling my neck. "Don't think about it."

This pisses me off, so I turn in his arms, shocking him enough that he lets go of my breast. "Oh, face-to-face." He smiles at me, pulling me into him. His arms wrap around me but then he slides one hand to my ass where he squeezes before hitching my leg around his hip. "That's better," he states, his cock at my entrance. "Hmm," he hums, right before he slides into me. My pussy is still a bit sore from last night, but I can't help but moan. "Made for me," he voices as he slowly fucks me, "you can't deny it." My head doesn't listen to anything that I'm screaming out, because my back arches to get even closer to him. "That's it, baby." His thrusts go faster. "Say it."

He flips me to my back and my legs open even wider for him. He puts his hands to the sides of me, getting up and thrusting into me harder than before. "Say it."

I can't even control myself, my body wanting all of him. "Shut up and just make me come."

He chuckles and gets to doing just that. "Where do you want it?" he asks, and I think about it for a second.

"I don't care," I tell him and he groans, thrusting one more time before sliding out of me. Now, I'm the one who groans, and he just slams into me one more time before I come again and so does he.

He rolls to the side, taking me with him. "Morning."

"I have to get up," I inform him, not trusting myself not to say something stupid. Like do you want to stay home all day and have more sex? Or better yet, do you want to do this again tonight?

I turn away from him, sliding out of bed. "I'll go make you coffee." He gets out of bed and my mouth waters. Matthew two years ago was in top shape and perfect. He had the perfect abs, the perfect ass, and let's not even discuss the way his package was everything a woman could dream of. But now, his shoulders are a bit bigger, his abs are more defined, his legs thick, and his cock looks even better than he did before. "You keep looking at me like that." He walks to me, my core getting wet. "We won't leave this room."

"I'm just…" I blink to make myself stop drooling over him. "I was just…" I turn and walk to the bathroom, hoping he isn't going to follow me, but I can see him in the mirror as I walk over to the shower, opening the glass door, and turning the black knobs. "We shouldn't have done that." I fold my arms over my chest and I really wish we were dressed and not doing this naked. "We did not just do this."

"But we did," he reminds me, smirking at me. "We even did it in this room."

"We can't do this anymore." I swallow the lump in my throat.

"Why not?" he asks, and I throw my hands up in the air.

"I'm dating someone," I lie to him. I mean, technically, Charles and I are kind of dating. Even though I told him I wasn't ready to date anyone now.

"Yeah, you are," he proclaims. "Me." He points at himself, and I roll my eyes.

"Not just you," I tell him, hoping he gets pissed enough that he will storm out but instead he laughs even louder.

"No, you aren't." He shakes his head, not one ounce of jealousy in his words, which annoys me.

"How do you know?" I ask, cocking my hip to the side. I look at myself in the mirror and see he gave me a hickey right next to my hip bone, and another one right on top of my pelvis.

"Because if you were." He comes over to me and I want to take a step back, but my body is a hussy and instead I put my shoulder back, putting my tits out there more for him. He puts his hands on my hips. "You wouldn't have kissed me, let alone slept with me." He bends and takes one of the nipples into his mouth.

"You were literally engaged two weeks ago," I remind him, looking at him and all he does is shrug, like it wasn't a big deal.

"But I'm not now," he confirms, kissing my collarbone.

"But..." I push him away from me because if he's touching me, everything in my head goes blurry. "But—"

He walks back to me, grabbing my face in his hands. "Sofia," he says my name, "when it comes to me and you." His thumbs rub my cheeks. "There is nothing that can compare to it." I look into his eyes. "What I had with Helena was nothing, and I say this with the most respect that I can, it was nothing like what we had. What we have, it's something I can't even explain." I start to say something but he kisses my lips to stop me. "Stop fighting this, Sofia, and listen to my words. What I gave to you, I never gave to anyone else. I thought I loved her, thought it was it, but I was wrong and that is on me. Whatever the reason, I was meant to always be with you. You were always mine." He kisses me softly. "Now, do you want me to make you breakfast?"

"No," I snap out.

"Okay, good," he says softly, "I'll go get something started." He turns to walk out of the bathroom. "Do you want me to bring the food to your bed?"

"No," I reply, avoiding even looking at him as I get in the shower. Putting my head back, I let the warm water wash over me. "You done fucked up," I mumble to myself as I wash away the smell of sex off me. "You just had to jump his bones."

I rinse off, getting out of the shower, and grabbing a

robe. Instead of going downstairs like I want to, I stay in the bathroom, putting on my makeup and doing my hair.

"You're avoiding me." I hear Matthew from the door of the bathroom. I look over and see that he's dressed in the outfit he wore last night. He holds a mug of coffee in one hand. "Figured that I would bring you your coffee instead of letting it get cold." He hands me the coffee.

"Thank you," I tell him softly, grabbing the cup. He holds the cup with me.

"I'm going to go," he says, and my stomach sinks, not wanting him to go but knowing that it's for the best. He leans in, and I let him kiss me, the kiss lingering. "I'll call you later."

"Okay," I reply softly, my lips still tingling from his kiss.

"You going to answer my call?" he asks with a smirk.

"No." I chuckle and he bends to give me one more kiss before he leaves.

"Later, Sofia!" he yells right before he walks out of the house, closing the door behind him. I avoid looking at myself in the mirror, instead going into the closet and grabbing a pair of navy pants. Sliding them over my hips and tying them before I walk over to pick a sheer white shirt with a champagne silk camisole under it, two long sashes at the collar tie in a loose knot. I slip into nude shoes before walking out of the house and driving to work.

I jog up the front steps of the office, pulling open the door before putting my sunglasses on the top of my head. "Morning," I call from the front door. Clarabella and Presley walk out of the kitchen with coffees in their hands. "Hey," I say to them as I start to walk down to my office, passing Shelby's office. She looks up as I smile and wave, seeing Clarabella and Presley behind me.

I walk into my office, tossing my bag on the chair. "You got laid." I look over my shoulder to see Clarabella looking at me with a twinkle in her eyes.

"What?" I choke, shocked, my heart speeding up as I try to play dumb. "No." I avoid looking at her as I walk behind my desk. "How can you tell?"

"You literally came in here skipping," Presley notes, rolling her lips and bringing her cup to her mouth.

I gasp out in shock. "No, I wasn't!" I shake my head at the same time.

"Was it the guy from the app?" Shelby pushes into my office and I just look at them, not saying a word.

"Oh my God, who was it?" Presley asks.

"You might as well just tell us who it was so we can get on with this day," Shelby states. "Once this one gets a sniff at something, she doesn't let up." She motions with her head toward Clarabella.

I sit down in the chair behind my desk, putting my hand on top of it and folding my hands together. "Fine," I come clean, "Matthew."

His name is not even fully out of my mouth before the questions start coming in rapid fire.

"Shut your mouth," Presley blurts, her mouth open.

"You did not," Shelby says, her eyes looking at me like they will come out of her sockets.

"How good was it?" Clarabella asks as she pulls the

chair from in front of my desk to the side, sitting.

"It was fine," I downplay it, not wanting to do this but knowing I've let the cat out of the bag.

"It was fine?" Clarabella says, shocked. "Then you aren't doing it right. Jesus, I remember the second time I hooked up with Luke, it was even better than the first, and that was explosive."

"Ugh," I say, throwing up my hands. "Fine, it was amazing. It was so much better than it was the last time. I don't know what it was, but it was like I was looking for him since leaving him." I look at them. "Does that even make sense?"

"You had sex with people after him?" Presley asks, and I scoff.

"Well, obviously, I had to get him out of my system." My legs start to go up and down. "But I think it was after the second guy that I was like, maybe I need to connect with someone before banging them."

"How did that work out for you?" Presley asks, and I glare at her.

"I just banged a guy who I said I would never talk to again, and I think I saw fireworks." I lean back in the chair. "It was a fifteen out of ten."

"So now what?" Shelby asks the same question I was asking myself the whole time since I woke up.

"Now, nothing. Now, hopefully, this is out of our system and we move on," I declare and the three of them laugh.

"I'm putting down bets that he shows up again," Clarabella announces, getting up, "and the sex is even better than it was last night and this morning."

"How did you know they had sex this morning?" Presley asks as she gets up.

"Who doesn't get up and have morning sex?" Clarabella scoffs at them, and now it's my turn to roll my lips when they just avoid looking at her.

"You girls need to take care of your men more." She shakes her head. "My man skips to work every single day."

"Every day?" Shelby says, folding her arms over her chest.

"If it's not sex, at least a blow job," Clarabella declares.

"Luke is not allowed to talk to Bennett, ever," Presley says as the two of them walk out of the office, arguing about what is a good number of times to have sex in a week.

I don't even listen to them. Instead, I glance over at the window, looking out at the sun in the sky, when my phone beeps from my purse. I get up and walk over to take it out.

Matthew: I'll see you tonight.

I put the phone down, not bothering to answer him. "No, you won't," I say out loud at the same time that my head calls me a liar.

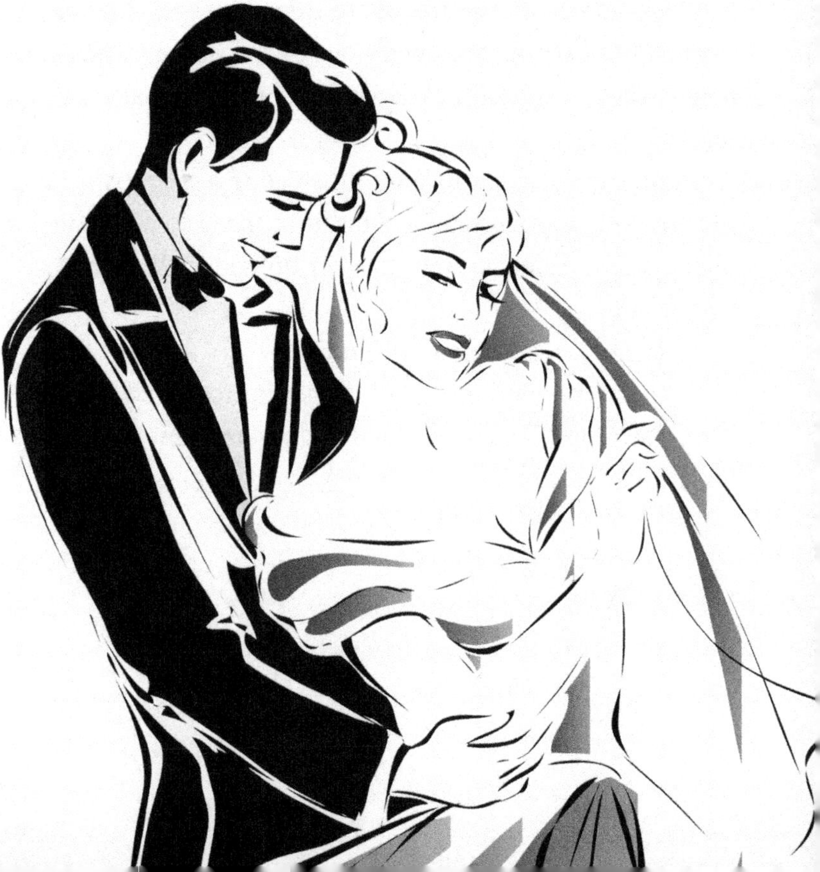

Twenty-Six

Matthew

I walk out of practice with my phone in one hand and my protein shake in the other, shaking it up and down. I pull open my text messages. The last text I sent Sofia is still unanswered but says delivered. I smile, knowing this was what she was going to do. I don't even know why I'm so surprised right now.

I knew this morning when she didn't come downstairs to get her coffee that she was putting space between us. I knew when I kissed her goodbye that she would not answer me. Last night was one of the greatest nights of my life. Fuck, being with her again. It was as if my soul was closed off for the last two years and I was finally alive. Which is crazy, but I now see I was just going through the motions of what I thought my life should be instead of actually living my life.

Instead of texting her again, I opt to call her. The phone rings four times before it heads to voice mail.

"You've reached Sofia Barnes. Please leave me a message, and I'll get back to you as soon as I can."

"Hey, baby," I say softly, knowing it's going to piss her off. "It's me, call me back. Miss you." I hang up and head home.

As soon as I get home, I make my way out to the back of the house, going straight for the gym. I spend a couple of hours in there doing my workout, and the phone doesn't ring the whole time. I mean, it rings but it's not who I want it to be. Christopher calls me, my mother even calls me, but nothing from Sofia.

Walking into the house, I go straight to the kitchen and grab one of the prepared meals I have in the fridge. I put it in the microwave for a couple of minutes before standing and eating it straight out of the container. I quickly shower, and when I get out, I wear jeans and a white polo shirt before jogging out to my car. I dial Sofia again, but it goes straight to voice mail this time. She's ignored me all day, and I don't bother leaving her a message this time.

I drive by her workplace first, seeing her car isn't there and all of the lights are off. Turning around, I head straight to her house. I pull up to her house and see a truck in her driveway next to her car.

I park on the street, looking at the truck twice before walking up the steps to her house. I ring the doorbell, turning to look over at the truck again. My hands go to my hips as my stomach gets tight.

I hear the door unlock, turning to see Sofia open the door. She is still dressed in her work clothes, looking just as beautiful as ever. The smile on my face quickly fades when she comes out of the house and closes the door behind her. The feeling I had in my stomach gets even stronger. "What are you doing here?" Her voice is almost a whisper as she looks at me with a frantic look on her face, then turns to look at the closed door.

I watch her and I swear I feel like I'm going to throw up all over the place. "Is someone inside?" I ask as my heart sinks in my chest. My breathing starts to come in pants as I wait for her to answer.

She's about to tell me something when the door opens behind her and, I swear to God, I'm getting ready to throat punch whoever is in her house. The door opens, and I see Casey step out. I recognize him from the picture my uncle Matthew showed me. He's wearing dress pants with a dress shirt with sleeves rolled up at the arms. He stares at me with a glare. "Oh my God," Sofia mumbles from beside me, and I look over to see her closing her eyes and shaking her head.

"Who are you?" he asks, his voice calm and monotone. He puts his hands in his pants pockets.

"I'm Matthew," I tell him, even though we did meet once a long, long time ago.

"Why are you here?" His eyes never leave mine as he takes me in.

"I'm here to see Sofia." I look down at her and smile

at her as she looks like she's ready to freak out.

"Why?" he asks, and I have to think about how to say this without sticking my foot in my mouth.

"Okay," Sofia finally cuts in, "that's enough of the interrogation." She looks at her grandfather and then looks over at me. "We were just going to have dinner." She looks at her grandfather. "Do you want to join us?" she asks, and the nerves that were all over my body are now gone.

"No," Casey snaps.

At the same time, I say, "Sure."

Sofia walks away from me to stand in front of Casey. "Be nice," she tells her grandfather, then turns back to look at me.

I follow her lead and stand in front of her. "Hi," I say softly and then bend to kiss her on her lips.

"Did you just kiss me in front of my grandfather?" Sofia hisses, now almost yelling.

I roll my lips and look over to Casey, who is now glaring at me even harder than he was before. His hands are out of his pockets and folded in front of him.

"Yeah," I finally say, "I guess I did."

"Can you not?" Sofia says and I put my hand on her shoulder. She looks at said hand. "We were just going to eat."

"There isn't enough food," Casey states, and I just smile.

"No worries, I'm not that hungry," I lie to him.

Sofia huffs and walks away from me, my arm falling beside me. She steps into the house, stopping beside

Casey. "Why would you lie about the food?" Sofia folds her arms over her chest. "You think he's not going to see the twenty-seven plates of food Grandma sent for me?"

She shakes her head and walks into the house, leaving Casey and me staring at each other. Each of us sizing up the other before Sofia storms back to us and pulls Casey by his arm away from the door so I can walk in. I step into the house, and Casey takes one more look at me before he walks back into the house, leaving me with just Sofia.

"You never called me," I tell her, and she just shakes her head.

"You would think one would get the message." I can't help but chuckle as I wrap an arm around her waist, pulling her to me.

"Oh, I got the message loud and clear," I inform her and her eyes soften when I lower my mouth to hers. "Now, let's go before your grandfather plans my murder."

Sofia throws her head back and laughs. "That happened the minute you kissed me in front of him," she states, turning to walk into the house but my hand slips into hers. "You are pushing it." She side-eyes me as we round into the kitchen and I see the plates she was talking about. Casey is standing in the middle of the kitchen, facing us, his phone in his hand. He's typing like crazy and looks up at us.

His eyes go from us to our hands. "Oh, good, you stayed," he says sarcastically. "Great."

"Come and get something to eat." She pulls me to the kitchen and hands me a plate.

"Thank you," I reply, grabbing the plate as I pile food onto it. I'm so nervous I have no idea what I'm putting on it, only I need to keep my hands busy.

When Sofia sees me look at her, she points over at the stools. "Go sit." I nod at her and walk over to the seats and look back at her.

"Where are you sitting?" I ask, knowing I am going to stake my claim as my uncle Matthew says, and the minute I think that, I know I'm going down a one-way street the wrong way.

"At the end," she says and I pull out the stool next to the end. She comes over and places her plate down next to me, followed by Casey, who pulls out the seat facing us.

"What do you do, Matthew?" he asks, and I remember my uncle telling me about him, so I know he knows exactly what I do.

"I play hockey," I reply, cutting a piece of chicken fried steak.

"How did you and Sofia meet?" he asks, and again, I know he knows.

"We dated a couple of years ago."

"Oh, that's right," he says like a light bulb just went off in his head, but I know better. "And you dumped her."

"We broke up." I swallow down the bile. "Yes."

"Pops," Sofia says between clenched teeth, "can we not do this?"

"Fine," he grunts, and sadly, I know he's not finished with me. "So how did you two get back to talking?"

I want to groan and hit my head on the island in front

of me, but I made my bed and now I have to lie in it, even if I don't want to. I'm about to lay it all out for him. "We met in town," Sofia interjects, "ran into each other one night."

I look over at her, and she just looks at her grandfather. "Next question."

"Are you two dating?" he asks.

I pfft out, "Absolutely."

At the same time, Sofia says, "Not really."

"That's interesting," he says, smirking at me, as I turn to glare at Sofia, who doesn't look back at me.

"So you spent the night," Casey states, right before he slides a piece of chicken fried steak into his mouth.

I look at him, never once looking away, because then I would be guilty of something. "Oh my God," Sofia retorts, "you did not just ask him that."

"Did he or did he not come here last night and leave this morning?" Casey tilts his head to the side.

"Pops," Sofia hisses out, "you said you would mind your business."

"Listen, it's not my fault you have a Ring camera." He holds up his hands. "And I get reports of who comes and goes." He smiles at Sofia and then turns his eyes to me.

I look over at Sofia and smirk. "I did," I tell him. "She's here, so I'm going to be spending time wherever she is."

"Is that so?" He leans back in his chair.

"It is." I mimic his move, trying not to let him see how fucking nervous I am. "How long will you be in town?"

"I'm not sure yet," he evades. "Haven't decided."

Sofia laughs at him. "He's leaving after dinner."

"That's too bad," I tell him, and he just stares at me.

"And why is that?" He sits up straight, his finger tapping the counter in front of him.

"My family is coming down on Saturday for my hockey game, and Sofia will be coming to meet them." I put my arm on her chair. "If you were here, I would love for you to meet them."

He looks at me, the two of us almost as if we are playing chess. Except I don't know how to play chess, but something says he does, and he usually wins. "Count us in," he declares, looking at Sofia. "I'll be back Saturday with the parents." He pushes away from the island. "I'll call you later," he tells Sofia and kisses her cheek, nodding at me. "See you Saturday."

He turns to walk out of the house, and only when the door slams shut does Sofia turn her glare to me. "Now you've done it."

"Done what?" I ask, feigning innocence. "I just invited him to a game."

She shakes her head. "You have no idea what you just did." She closes her eyes. "He's going to bring my parents."

"Good," I reply, cutting another piece of meat. "Our parents can finally meet."

"This is a nightmare," she huffs. "It's going to be a nightmare."

I laugh. "What's the worst that can happen?" Even with the words out of my mouth, I know I don't even want to answer that question. All I know is that push came to shove and I had to show her I meant business.

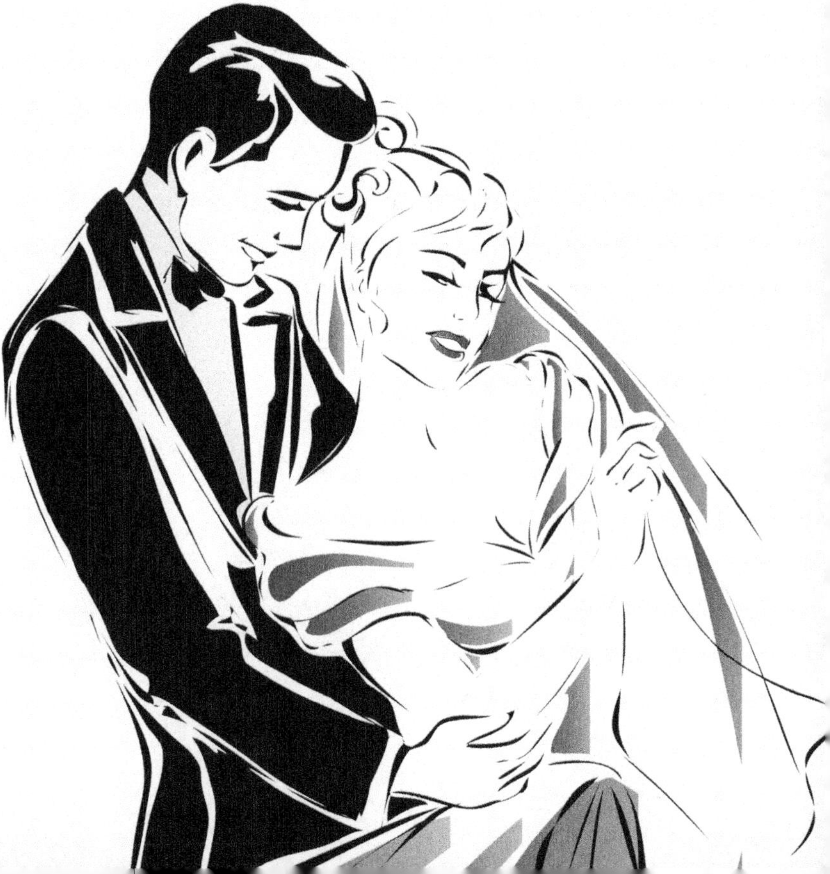

Twenty-Seven

Sofia

"You have a delivery," Addison says, walking into my office. I look up from my computer screen and see she is carrying a crystal vase of flowers and a square white box in the other hand. "They smell wonderful," she notes, putting the vase at the corner of my desk, the smell of roses fills the office. "And this is for you." She hands me the box. "I wonder who they are from?" She winks at me.

"Yes, I wonder," Clarabella says, walking into my office. "What does the card say?"

"I have no idea," I reply, looking at the white box in my hand with a big light blue satin bow. I pull the sash as it falls away from the box. Opening the box, the white card is on top of the tissue paper.

My name is written in the middle of the card, and I know that writing. Taking the card out, I read what he had written to me.

I loved you before. I love you now. I will love you always.

M.

My heart speeds up, my stomach gets tight, there is a mix of emotions I'm going through, and it feels like I'm on a merry-go-round that has yet to stop but is going full speed around. "Um," I deflect, not sure I can repeat what is on the card without my voice quivering. I don't even bother looking up at them when I hold the card out.

I don't know who takes it until I hear the gasp. "Oh my," Addison says, and I blink away the tears in my eyes. I see her hand it to Clarabella, who looks down at the card, her eyes going as big as saucers as she turns back to look at me.

"What's in the box?" she asks, and my hands tremble as I pull the tissue flap open on one side and then on the other.

A frame sits in the middle of the box with three picture slots. **Before, Now, After** are the headings under the three picture slots. I am not the one gasping when I look down at the first picture in the box. It was taken on our first night out four years ago. Matthew is looking at the camera with his hat on backward smiling, and my face is turned to his side in profile and is filled with such a big smile that my eyes crinkle at the sides.

My eyes go immediately to the next picture taken

late last night after we finished cleaning up my kitchen and putting away the food my grandmother sent. He was telling me about how nervous he was with my grandfather and also telling me he's going to put white hockey tape on top of the Ring camera. He had me laughing so hard, I had tears in my eyes. He pulled me to him and kissed my lips before he whipped out his phone. I had no idea how the picture even came out because as soon as he took it, he put the phone down, and then picked me up and took me upstairs where we took a bubble bath together.

"Is that?" Clarabella asks, leaning over. "Pictures?"

"It is." I swallow down the lump, looking at the empty slot for the third picture.

I pick up the frame and turn it to her. "Whoa," she says, "is that—"

"It's nothing," I say, trying to grab it back from her and tuck it back in the white box.

"Is that?" she asks as she looks from one picture to the next.

"Yeah, it's the same picture, just a couple of years apart," I confirm, trying not to dwell on it, while also trying not to freak out that he still had the picture of us lying around that he could have found it.

"How is it that you have the same look in both pictures?" Clarabella laughs while she asks the question.

"I do not!" I shriek. "I certainly do not." I look over at Addison, who has a scared look, probably because I sound like a crazy lunatic right now.

Clarabella is unfazed by my tone and all she does is look at me and burst out laughing even more. "Yes, you do." She hands me back the frame. "It's there in both pictures. It's love, and it's written all over your face."

I put my hand to my chest in shock, as if she had just told me the tooth fairy wasn't real the morning after I lost a tooth and came up empty-handed. "I don't love him." The words taste wrong as soon as I say them, and I hate it. "I like him." My eyebrows shoot up. "A bit."

"You're lying." Clarabella points a finger at me. I look down at the frame, and I can't even try to tell her that she's full of it. If I didn't know myself and I looked at these pictures, I would probably—most likely—think the same thing.

"I can't love him." I say the words. My voice is almost a whisper as it dawns on me that I went and fucking fell in love with him. "This is me getting him out of my system." I look at Clarabella, who just nods her head at me without telling me *sure it is.*

"That is what this is." I look over at Addison, who smiles at me almost like, *you poor thing.* I get up, the chair flying back. "I'm not in love with him," I tell them both, wrapping up the frame in the white box. "This is…" I try to think of the words to say. "Nothing." I look at both of them as I put the cover on the box and walk around my desk. My body is filled with endless nerves. I grab my purse, picking it up, "I'm," I say, looking at them, "I'll see you both tomorrow. Good night."

"It's ten a.m.," Addison states and Clarabella just claps her hands together as she bursts out laughing.

"Call me if you need anything," I tell Addison and storm out, pissed at myself for letting this get to me again.

"Unbelievable," I mumble as I toss my purse on the seat beside me and then put the white box on top of it.

I don't even know how long it takes me to get home, but I park in the garage when I do. I leave the box and my purse in the car before walking into the house. The phone pings in my hand, and I see it's from Matthew

Matthew: Did you like the gift?

"No," I tell myself, "no, I did not." My fingers are on the keypad, ready to answer him.

Me: What gift? In meetings back-to-back. Have three bride meetings today, will only finish really late. I'll call you when I'm done.

I press send before I walk straight upstairs to my bedroom. The covers are still all messed up from this morning when we had sex as soon as my alarm started ringing. I kick off my heels and undress before I strip the bed and wash the sheets. My phone rings a couple of times, and every time, it's Matthew. The sun goes down, and I make sure all the blinds are closed around the house. I sit in the middle of my bed with the television on, but the sound as low as can be. The phone on the night side table with unanswered texts from Matthew.

Matthew: Do you want to come here after work?

Matthew: Swung by the office to drop off something to eat. Where are you?

Matthew: Can you call me?

I ignore the phone calls. I ignore the text messages. I ignore it all. Lying in bed, I watch the hours tick by when I hear my phone ringing at midnight, right before the knock on my door. "Fuck," I mouth without saying anything.

"Sofia," he says my name as I sneak down the stairs, trying not to make a sound. "If you don't open the door," he warns, his voice clear as day, "I'm calling your grandfather and telling him I can't find you." I close my eyes, wondering if he would really do that. "I don't have his number, but I'm sure I can get a hold of someone." I finally step down the last step. "Maybe if I speak into the Ring camera," he says, and I shake my head, knowing he's not going to go away. "Open the door, Sofia."

I unlock the door and slowly open the door. "Fuck," Matthew hisses. "Thank God you're okay." He walks in and grabs me around my waist, burying his face in my neck. "I was so worried." He puts me down, and I stare at him. "Were you here all night long?" he asks.

"Yes," I reply softly.

"Why the silence?" He asks the question, his voice as soft as mine.

"Because I didn't feel like talking to you," I answer him honestly.

He looks into my eyes, searching for something. "Care to tell me why?"

"No." I shake my head at the same time I say the word.

"What's going on?" His eyes never leave mine.

I take a deep breath. "I don't want to do this anymore," I speak the words I've been repeating to myself all night. Ignoring how the pain in my chest is even stronger now that I'm actually saying them to him and not just in my head.

He folds his arms over his chest. "Define this?"

I throw up my hands. "Me, you, the sex." I swallow the lump that has crawled up from my stomach to my throat. "All of it." He shakes his head. "You can't just shake your head," I snap. "I slept with you to get you out of my system." Saying the words I hope will hurt him enough that he just lets me be. That he just goes, and we can be done with whatever this is.

"How is that working out for you?" His question confuses me. "How is getting me out of your system working for you?" He puts his hands on his hips. "Because I'll tell you right now." The sting of tears threatens to come, so I blink them away. "I thought I loved you before." He shakes his head. "Like I knew I loved you when I was an immature idiot." He takes a step closer to me, closing the distance between us. "But now." His face goes from a smirk to a full-blown smile. "Now that I've been with and without you, I can safely say I love you more." I want to tell him to stop talking, but nothing comes out of me. "It just cemented everything."

"Ugh, oh my God, Matthew." I finally get the courage to say something, and I'm thankful it's not coming out with me sobbing. "You can't just say things like that."

"Why not?" The age-old question.

"Because I said so." I look at him, and all he does is laugh at me.

"Can we go to bed yet?" he asks softly. "I've been driving around town the last four hours. I'm exhausted." Why does that make my heart skip a beat? Why does everything he says make my heart flutter? Why? Oh, I know why, because I love it.

"I'm going to bed in my bed and you are going to your bed." I point at him.

He just looks at me. "Then go pack a bag." He points at the stairs and in the direction of my bedroom.

"I don't want to pack a bag." I almost stomp my foot, and he just shrugs.

"Okay, fine." He turns and I somehow think he's leaving, which makes me internally freak out even more. Instead of leaving, he shuts the door and then turns to walk to the stairs.

"I'm not leaving."

"Why?" I don't even know why I'm asking him this but I can't help myself.

He comes back and stands in front of me, his hand coming out to cup my cheek. His thumb rubs my cheekbone back and forth. My breaths are coming in short pants as I wait for him to speak. The words finally come out in a soft breath. "Because you're here."

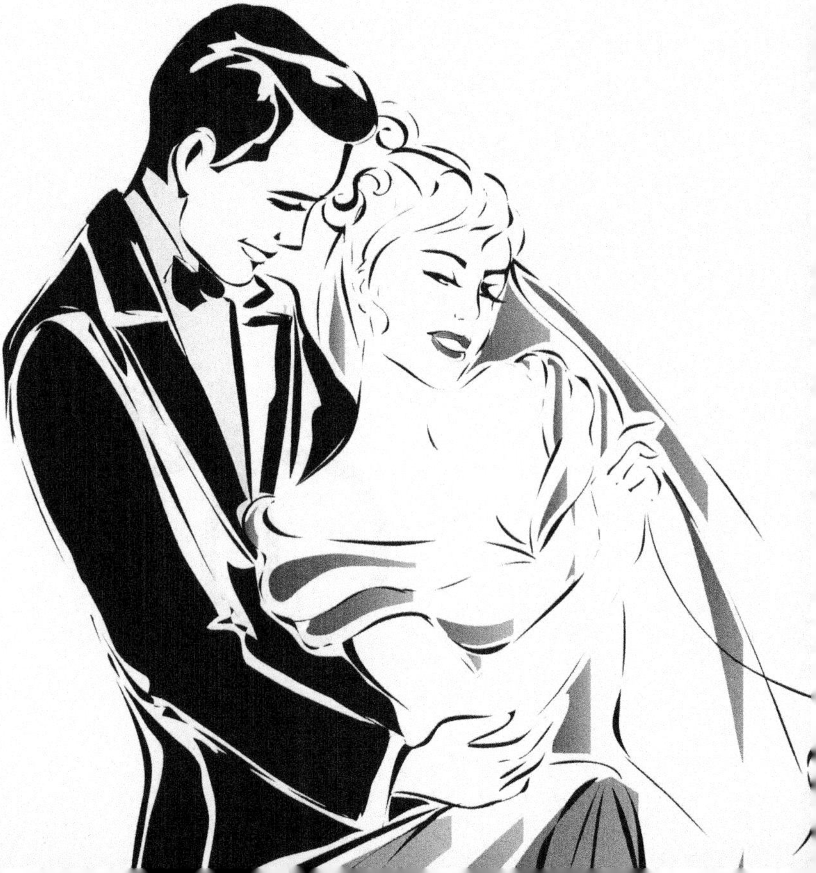

Twenty-Eight

Matthew

I stand in front of her, my hand coming up to cup her cheek, because I need to touch her after driving around for the last four hours looking for her. Searching in every single parking lot I passed by to look for her car, afraid she finally ran away from me. Afraid she would never let me see her again. I can't even put into words how desperate I was. Having her face in my hand, I can't help but breathe a sigh of relief. She has tried to push me away every single day since I forced myself back into her life. But she needs to finally hear it, needs to feel it, needs to know it. "Because you're here." My voice is as strong as it can be without it cracking.

I see her eyes blink a million times a minute, so I

know she's fighting it back. Know she doesn't want to give in. "Sofia." Her name is on my lips all the time now. "We can go as slow as you want." I don't let my eyes roam from hers. "But at the end of the day, Sofia." I swallow the lump and fear down. Fear that she won't give in to what she wants. Fear she won't forgive me for throwing her away. Fear I'm going to have to spend the rest of my life without her, no matter how much I push her. "All I want is to be by your side."

She licks her lips, not pushing me away. "Why?" Her voice is so low, I know this is going to be my only shot.

"Because I'm not a stupid kid anymore." I want to kiss her so badly, but she needs to know, needs to understand how I can't live life without her. "Because I know what my life is without you." I take a deep inhale, not willing to see it, not willing to live it. "And I know what my life is with you." The strength she had to hold back the tears is a losing battle, and just like me, she lets go of a single tear, except I'm here to brush away her tear. "And clear as day, I would pick you every time." I lick my lips, my mouth going so dry I don't know how I continue, but I do, with my heart beating so fast in my chest it's putting additional pressure on my heart. "I fucked up, a colossal fuckup." I try to smile, but the pain in my chest from when I lost her comes front and center again. "The way we came together again is not ideal." I smirk for a second. "But I have to think we would have crossed paths again." The agony of it not happening is too much to bear. "I have to believe this because there is no one for me but you." I trail off.

"You had Helena." She puts her hand on my wrist that is still holding her face.

"I did and I wish that I hadn't." I shake my head. "I can see now that what I felt for her was nothing." My voice quivers. "I didn't give her me." I wipe another tear away from her cheek. "I didn't give her parts of me." Her lips quiver at the same time mine do. "Because that part of me was always yours." I stare into her eyes. "Tell me you hear me, Sofia." I put my forehead to hers. "Tell me what you feel for me isn't anything. As much as I can't and don't want to, I'll let you be. I'll love you from afar. I'll live my life knowing I will never love anyone but you." I wait a second before the plea comes out. "Tell me."

"I'm afraid," she finally admits. "I'm so afraid."

"I failed you once, Sofia, by not being what you needed. By not being the man who you deserved. You have to know. You have to know that I would never do that again. It kills me inside knowing I was the man who was supposed to protect you. I was the man who was supposed to do everything to make sure you felt no pain, but I was, in fact, the one who inflicted the pain on you." My hand shakes now as I hold her face.

"Don't hurt me again," she pleads, the words slicing through my heart one word at a time.

"I promise you; I'll spend the rest of my life making up for it." She stares into my eyes this time. The turmoil that we both feel is etched on our faces.

I wait for her to say something, anything, waiting as if my life sentence is being delivered. "I hear you," she says. I don't let her say another word, I lower my lips to hers, the taste of our tears on our lips as I kiss her like it's the first time all over again. My tongue slides into her mouth as I wrap my arm around her waist, while the other one gets buried in her hair. She moves her head to one side and I pick her up. Her arms wrap around my neck at the same time her legs wrap around my hips.

I walk over to the stairs going to her bedroom. Every single light is off in the house, but I make it to her bedroom like I've been in this house a million times before. Once I walk into her room, she peels herself out of my arms, her hand going to my cheek. "I love you." The words come out breathlessly. "I fought it," she admits, and I hate that I can't see her eyes. "Said it would never happen. I was wrong." She kisses my neck, her hand squeezing my T-shirt in her fingers, pulling it up and over my head. "I didn't think this would ever happen again," she says, looking down. "I wished for it for so long that I thought it would never happen."

"It was always meant to be," I assure her as she opens the sash of her robe. Slipping it over her shoulders and down to her feet, she stands in front of me wearing a white camisole with matching panties.

She walks beside me, slipping her hand in mine, and she kisses my shoulder and pulls me with her to the bed. "It was always meant to be you," she declares to me, sitting on the bed, pulling my arm down so I sit next to her. Her hands go to my face. "It was always you." My heart soars in my chest. "It's always going to be you."

"You bet your ass it will be," I vow, right before I

claim her mouth. Wrapping my arm around her waist, I lower her back to the bed. There in the middle of her darkened room, I make love to her.

I slide into her at the same time she arches her back off the bed. "I love you," I say as my forehead rests on hers.

Her hands come up to hold my face as she pants. "I love you," she says, my tongue sliding back into her mouth as I try not to pound into her. "Harder." She lets go of my lips and I slam into her. "Yes," she whispers, wrapping her legs and arms around me. My face buried in her neck, I slam into her over and over again. She thrusts her hips up to meet mine and squeezes my cock so hard I don't move in her. "Matthew." My name is on her lips, as she jumps over the ledge, and I'm not far behind her with her name on my lips as well. I collapse on top of her, her limbs going weak around me, falling to the side.

"Do you want to take a shower with me?" I kiss her neck, pulling her closer and closer to me.

"Okay," she agrees and then wraps herself around me again. I walk to the bathroom, turning on the bathroom light.

I finally see her face and notice her eyes are red. "Why were you crying?"

"Who says I was crying?" she huffs as I place her ass on the counter before turning and starting the shower. She turns to look at herself in the mirror and then gasps. "I was feeling sorry for myself." She gets down and tries to fix her hair.

"You wouldn't have had to feel sorry for yourself if you would have answered my texts or phone calls," I tell her, bending to kiss her neck.

She cocks her head to the side. "I wouldn't have had to feel sorry for myself if you just—" I don't even wait for her to say anything. I just press my lips to hers. "Yeah, that's what I thought," she says once I let go of her lips.

"You going to re-meet my family?" I ask, bending and kissing her neck.

"Yes," she says breathlessly, looking up at me. "I think I have to. My parents are coming down with my grandparents."

"This would be a perfect time to ask your father for your hand in marriage," I suggest, watching her face as she glares at me.

"That would be the opposite of a perfect time to ask for anything," she declares and pushes me away from her.

I can't help but laugh. "Well, my parents are coming into town tomorrow morning so I said we would meet them for lunch." Her mouth opens and then closes. "They can come here, or we can go to my house."

"I don't..." she says, and I put up my hand.

"She never lived in my house," I assure her. "But it's on the market, and from what my mom said, it looks like it's sold."

"You're selling your house?" she asks, shocked.

"I'm selling my house. We're moving in with each other," I inform her, "and we aren't getting a fucking Ring camera."

She laughs at the last part. "We're moving in with each other?"

"Yes." I nod my head.

"You could just move in here," she says, and I fold my arms over my chest.

"Who bought this house?" I ask, knowing full well who bought the house. She doesn't say anything. "Exactly, so we are going to be looking for a house. I'm going to buy said house, and then we are moving in with each other." Her eyebrows go up. "And then we are going to get married and have babies."

"Why can't we both buy the house?" she asks, and I roll my eyes and then laugh.

"Because I take care of you from this point on." Her eyes go into slits. "Whatever you need, I'm going to be the one taking care of you."

"And if I say no?" she asks.

"Do you love me?" I ask, and she rolls her eyes at me. "Do you not want to go to bed with each other every night?" I don't wait for her to answer. "Because I want to go to bed with you every night I'm home. I want a house with you where we combine all our shit. Where we put up frames. Where you yell at me for leaving my socks beside the basket and not in it." I smirk at her. "I want to know that you are in our bed when I'm on the road. Now, is that too much to ask?"

She looks at me, this woman I let go of all those years ago. The woman who has owned my whole heart since I met her. Here, in the middle of her bathroom, in the middle of the night, she agrees with me. "Fine," she huffs, walking toward the shower, "let's move in together."

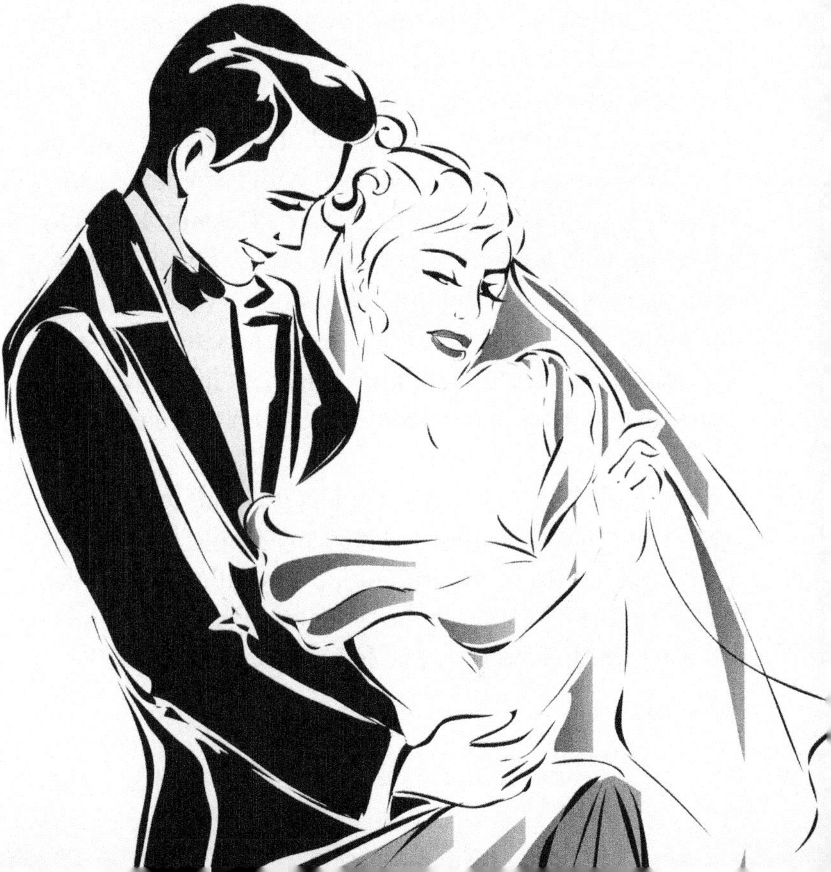

Twenty-Nine

Sofia

"What do you think about this?" I say, stepping out of the walk-in closet. Matthew turns his attention from the phone in his hand to me. He is lying on top of the bed dressed in blue jeans and a white T-shirt with a baseball hat on his head.

He smiles while he looks at me. "You look amazing. Like always."

"But does this say I really love your son?" I ask. Turning to look at the long mirror, I see myself in my white jeans with a long-sleeve cashmere sweater folded at the neck. "And I'll make him happy."

He chuckles as he gets off the bed and approaches me, putting his hands on my hips. "The smile on my face says everything," he says, and my heart skips a beat. Ever since I opened the door to him at midnight, his words have hit me right in the middle of my heart. His words have filled the void in my soul I didn't know was there. A void I denied ever having. A void only his love could fill.

"I just want them to like me," I admit to him, "again." I try to make a joke out of it.

"They are going to love you, as they always have," he assures me, and I try not to think about how they felt about Helena, if they liked her or not. Were they sad about it? I have so many questions and that just fuels the anxiety to another level.

The doorbell rings and he winks at me. "Showtime," he says, grabbing my hand in his and walking out of the bedroom together. The doorbell rings again and he huffs as he walks to the door.

He grabs the handle and unlocks it. "You want to cool your horses?" he says, pulling open the door, expecting it to be his parents but instead it's not.

"Why are you even answering the door?" my grandfather Casey says. "This is not your door."

"Um," Matthew stutters.

"Oh, would you knock it off?" my grandmother Olivia says, pushing him to the side. "Hello, Matthew," she greets, walking in the door and going to him to kiss him on the cheek. "You look different."

"Um." That's all Matthew can say.

"What are you doing here?" I ask them as I make my way to the front door.

"Your grandfather," my grandmother states, putting

her purse down on the table, "was like a bat out of hell getting here."

"What are you doing here?" I look over to the door and see my father standing there scowling. "Answering the door like you own the place."

"Dad," I gasp out loud and shake my head, "he does live here."

"What?" my father and grandfather both gasp out.

"Um, I don't think so," my father counters, putting his hands on his hips.

"Would you go away?" my mother says, walking into the door. "Matthew, we are so happy to see you again."

"Again," my father pffts out. "Not that happy."

"Mr. Barnes," Matthew says, going over to my father, extending his hand, "great to see you again."

My father just looks at the hand and then looks at him. "Reed Barnes, if you know what is good for you." My mother glares at him. "You will remember this is your daughter's house and he is…" She trails off.

"The one she goes to bed with every night," my grandmother pipes up, and I close my eyes to stop the embarrassment from filling my face, but I suddenly feel the heat rise to my cheeks.

"Now, you two"—her voice gets tight—"you better be on your best behavior." I look over at her and she is glaring at my father and grandfather. "Or else."

I don't have a chance to say anything else because I hear the sound of doors closing. One, two, three, four, five, six, seven, eight—all like clockwork. "What the—" My father looks over his shoulder.

"My family," Matthew says, and I put my hand to my stomach to make the nerves go away. Matthew sees it and comes over to me. He grabs my face in his hands. "They are going to love you." He kisses my lips.

My grandmother and mother smile at Matthew while my father pffts again. "Of course they are going to love her. What is not to love?"

"Hello." I hear a man's voice and look over to the front door, seeing Matthew's dad. "You must be Sofia's dad." He walks to my father and holds out his hand. I am not going to lie, I stand here with bated breath, wondering if my father is going to pull something but he extends his hand to Viktor.

"Nice to meet you," he mumbles, "this is my father." He looks over to my grandfather. "Casey."

Viktor extends his hand to my grandfather. "Pleasure," he says to him. "These are my brothers-in-law Matthew, Max, and Evan."

"Gentlemen," his uncle Matthew says, extending his hand, "great to meet you."

"Hello." My grandmother walks to the front door. "I'm Olivia, please ignore my husband and son, they seem to have forgotten their manners." She forces a smile at them. "Come in."

I slip my hand in Matthew's as I wait for them to walk in. "Sofia," Viktor says, coming over and giving me a big hug, "so nice to see you again." Very different from how my family treated Matthew, which will be discussed when we aren't in front of so many people.

I drop Matthew's hand to hug him, and he moves

aside as Matthew's mother comes to me. "Hi," she says and she looks like she's blinking away tears, "you are beautiful as always." She takes me in her arms and hugs me. "Do you remember Karrie, who is married to Matthew senior?"

"Did you just call him senior?" Max says, laughing and shaking his head. "That's a new one. I think we should put that on your business card." Matthew glares over at him.

"Allison is married to Max, and Zara is married to Evan." I nod at the woman, and by the time the introductions are done with all the women, I'm ready for a nice stiff drink.

"Shall we go into…" I start to say and then look at the number of people in my home. "I want to say kitchen but I don't think it's big enough for all of us."

"Oh, please," Allison says, "we are used to too many people and small spaces." She looks around the house. "You have a lovely home."

"Did you guys know they are living together?" my father asks, and my eyes go big. I silently look around, hoping the ground opens up and swallows me whole.

"What?" his uncle Matthew gasps. "You can't live with her." He looks over at Matthew. "You have to marry her." He shakes his head. "Did we not teach you anything?" he mumbles.

"Oh, here we go," I hear Zoe say, then she looks over at my mother and grandmother. "I apologize for anything that my brother, husband, or brother-in-law says."

"Same," my mother says to her.

"I guess this settles it," my grandfather says, standing next to Uncle Matthew, "you can't live with each other."

"That settles nothing." Matthew puts his hands on his hips and looks over at my grandfather and his uncle. "I'm buying us a house, and we are moving into it, married or not married."

"Buying a house?" my father questions. "She has a house, this one."

"But it's not our house." I stand next to Matthew, a united front. "So we are getting our house and—"

"And," his uncle Matthew says, "getting married."

"What is it with you and getting married?" Zara asks him. "It's the twentieth century."

"Shall we move to the kitchen?" my mother suggests. "I brought some sweets," she says, then looks at my father. "Can you go get them?"

"My mother is the owner of STE Sweets," I say and the women all gasp.

"I'm obsessed with the lemon cranberry scones," Zoe declares.

"Well, you're in luck. I brought extra," my mother says and then looks over at the guys. "Why are we all standing here watching?" She looks at my father and then my grandfather.

"Do you want me to tell Charlotte how we behaved today?" my grandmother Olivia threatens them. "Perhaps we can FaceTime her on that shiny new iPad you got her." They look at each other before turning to walk out of the house.

"Go help." Zoe points at the men. "And be nice."

"I'll be back," Matthew says, kissing my lips and he walks out.

"I'm going to go and get things going in the kitchen," my mother and grandmother inform us.

"If it's okay," Zoe says, "can we have a moment?" She looks at me.

My mother and grandmother both look at me, not sure what to do or say. "Of course," I finally say nervously, wanting to vomit all over the place. "Let's go in the office." I point over to the closed door right in front of us, opening it, and stepping into it.

"This is so pretty," Zoe compliments, stepping in, and I close the door behind us. "Can we sit?" she asks, pointing over at the big white plush love seat.

"Of course." I nod, walking over to the couch and sitting down. My hand on my leg trembles just a bit. "I'm sorry if I stutter or I'm nervous."

Zoe sits next to me and reaches out her hand to take mine in hers. "If anyone should be nervous, it's me," she says. "I just wanted to clear the air a bit. I know how you must be feeling with the whole…" She uses her hand to go in a circle, not sure what to say.

"The whole him being engaged to Helena and being their wedding planner," I say the words for her and she puts her head back and groans, making me laugh.

"I thought I was going to be okay doing this," she says softly, looking down at our hands. "I knew the minute he said he was getting married, it was the wrong thing for him to do." My heart pounds in my chest. "I mean, he didn't even propose to her, who does that?" She looks at me and I can see she is trying not to cry. "I love my son, I really do, but I had no words."

"It's okay," I say softly, "I get it."

"No, I don't think that you do," she replies softly. "I think it was always you, Sofia. I think after you guys went your separate ways because of another stupid thing he did." She shakes her head. "He didn't think he could love like that again, so he just chose what he did. What I'm trying to say is, I think he's only ever loved you, and now that you're back, I have a feeling it's for good." She smiles. "I know we can be a lot, trust me I know, but I just want to say how happy we are for you two."

"Wow," I say, blinking away my own tears. "I can't tell you what that means to me. I was nervous, so nervous, today because, well, he was just engaged, and I didn't know if you would be accepting of it."

"I'm not going to say anything I shouldn't, but let's just say, it wasn't a good fit all the way around." She smirks, just like her son. "This," she says, pointing at me, "is the perfect fit."

I'm about to say something to her when the door opens, and Matthew sticks his head in. "What?" The smile on his face goes away when he sees me trying not to cry. "What in the world? Why are you making my girl cry?" He walks in, or maybe he's pushed in by Viktor, who comes in.

"What are you doing in here?" he asks, not reading the room. The smile on his face also leaves as soon as he sees the two of us crying. "What is going on? Why is she crying?"

"I am not crying," I sniffle.

"Nothing," Zoe says. "I was just trying to tell her, you know, that we're happy she's back."

"And I was thanking her for being open-minded with me, especially since it's very soon after Helena." I look at Viktor, who looks over at his son.

"Look, I'd love to sit here and talk about this longer," Viktor says, "but Matthew senior and Casey are literally having a pissing contest, and I'm just hoping no one whips out a private part."

"Of course he is." I lift my arms. "I'm sorry if he makes you feel uncomfortable. I'm the first grandchild."

"Oh, please," Viktor says, "we have no excuse for Matthew senior, he just is."

"Can you give us a minute?" Matthew says to his parents, who nod and walk out of the room.

"You have one minute," I tell him, "and then I have to go and take care of my grandfather."

"Are you really okay?" he asks, putting his arms around my waist and bringing me closer to him.

"Yes," I say, smiling up at him. "I really am okay. What I'm not okay with is the way my grandfather and father treated you. That is not okay."

"I don't care as long as you are with me at the end of the day. They can do what they want to me."

"No." I shake my head. "This is not okay," I tell him, and I'm about to tell him more when the door swings open. "Showtime," I mumble.

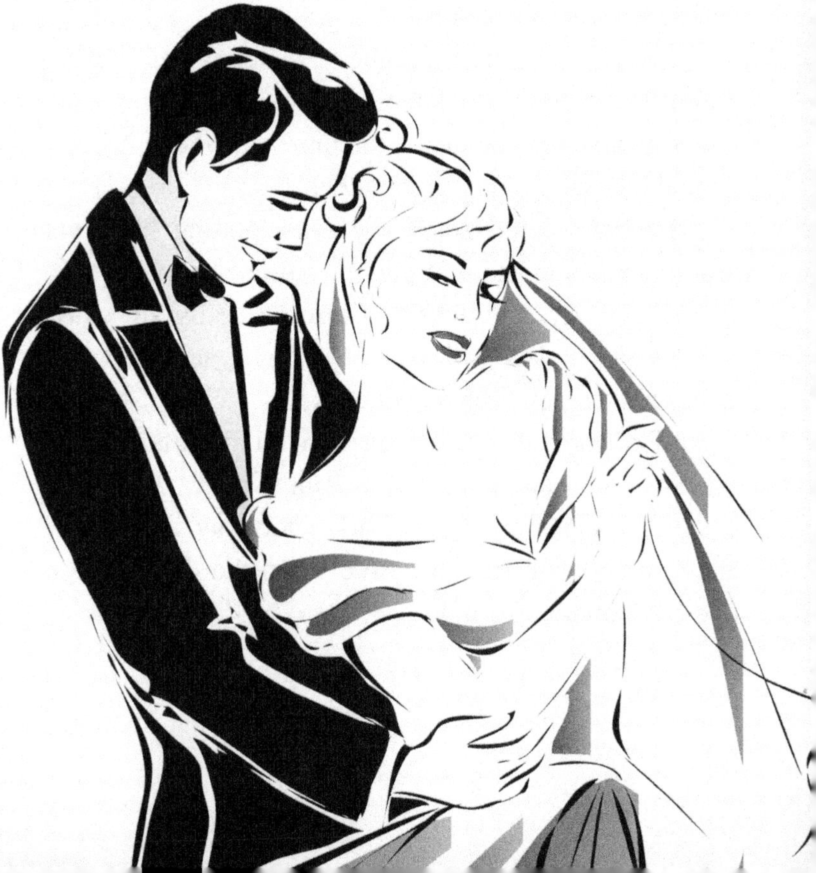

Thirty

Matthew

"What is going on in here?" Casey walks into the office. "Why is she crying?" He takes one look at Sofia, then looks at me, glaring.

"Do you want to know why I'm crying?" Sofia asks, her voice tight. "I'll tell you why." Her voice goes higher. "Actually, this should be done in front of everyone," she says, storming out of the room.

"Sofia," I call, following her out as she makes her way to the kitchen where everyone is either standing or sitting.

"I have an announcement to make," she states loudly.

"Oh my God, she's pregnant," Uncle Matthew says and I just shake my head.

"She is not pregnant," I say before everyone freaks, "not that I would care." I look at her and she gives me a *not right now* look.

"I just want to say thank you to Matthew's family for being so welcoming to me." I look over at them, smiling. "And then you have my family." She glares at her father and her grandfather. "You two." She points at them. "You have not been so kind or welcoming at all." Her father says something and she holds up her hand. "Now, I don't know how you want to hear this, but I want you to listen. He is my choice." She points at me.

"Thanks, baby," I say happily, but she whips her head toward me.

"Not now." I roll my lips, holding up my hands. "He is my choice, and I am his. Which means that I'm going to do life with him. I'm going to move in with him. I'm going to share my life with him. My good days and my bad days. I'm going to have babies with him." She looks back at Uncle Matthew. "Not now, but eventually. I am doing all of this, and if you don't respect that, then you don't respect me, and if you don't respect me, then I won't have it in my life." Hazel gasps. "So you have a choice to make. You can be in my life, and by that, it means you will be nice to him and treat him with the same kindness and respect his family treats me with, or you can be out of my life, which means that come holidays, we aren't going to be there."

"Now hold on a minute," Reed starts, "it's just that—"

"It's nothing, Reed," Hazel hisses at him. "Did you listen to a word that she said?"

"We had no choice. She said she had an announcement to make," Reed says, earning himself a glare from Hazel. "Fine." He holds up his hand. "We'll be respectful." He looks at her. "Happy?"

"It's a start," Sofia says.

"I would like to say something." I hold up my hand and see my father and my uncles just shaking their heads, telling me it's not a good idea, but I'm only going to get one shot at this. "I'm sorry for what I did to Sofia," I apologize, looking at her and putting my arm around her and pulling her to me. "And like I told her, I will spend forever making her not regret giving me another chance." She slips her arm around my waist. "And I hope that you all give me another chance to prove myself to you and to her."

"You do not have to do that," Olivia says. "Sofia is the only one you need to prove that to, and if she has chosen to have you in her life, we have to believe that she knows what she's doing." She glares over to her husband. "That should be enough for us." Her eyebrows go up. "Right?"

He glares back at her. "Before you agree to anything," my uncle Matthew says, and I want to groan, "you should tell them what you are about to do."

"What he's about to do or what he just did?" Max asks, standing next to Matthew, his eyes on Casey, who just stares at them, and it looks like he's smirking.

He doesn't back down like most people who try to go head-to-head with my uncles. "Interesting." That is the only thing Casey says.

"I think it's safe to say we both have our sources."

My uncle Matthew puts his hands in his pockets. "Better they hear it from you, don't you think?"

"What is going on?" Sofia whispers as she looks over at her grandfather, who avoids looking at her. The guilt is now written on his face and I can't even imagine what it is that he did. Whatever it is, it must be bad.

"Casey Barnes," Olivia says, her teeth clenched together, "what did you do?"

"I didn't do anything," he deflects, turning to my uncle Matthew, "yet. But I've decided to buy a hockey team." I don't even have time to process what is going on until I hear my uncle Matthew.

"Oh my God," I hear Hazel say at the same time I feel the air drain out of the room.

"Not just any hockey team," my uncle Max declares, "none other than Matty's team." He points at me.

The blood must drain from my face because I'm shocked "What?" I say almost in a whisper. As soon as the shock fades, which is seconds later, it turns to anger. Pissed, I'm so pissed now.

"You bought his hockey team?" Sofia asks, looking at her grandfather, her own face going pale.

"It's not his team," Casey states, "he plays for the team. I own it."

"I have a contract," I finally say, and my father comes to stand beside me.

"Trust me, I know," Casey assures me, "for another year, and then we'll see, I guess."

"Fine," I say, letting out a huge breath and feeling so defeated I just want to storm out of here.

"If that is what you want, I can always play overseas." I stare at him while I say this. "Norway has a great team. Finland also. Paris. Europe is a great place to play. I know a couple of people who play there, and that is what I'll do if I have to."

"If he goes," Sofia announces, "I go with him." Her voice is so low, I'm not sure anyone can hear her. "You do that and I'll leave and go with him. And then you'll never see us."

"Now wait a minute," Reed says and I look over to see Hazel getting up and walking over to grab a tissue as she wipes away the tears. "Let's not get ahead of ourselves."

"Casey Barnes," Olivia demands, "you are not buying that team. You cancel that right now."

"He can't." My uncle Matthew laughs, clapping his hands. "Not only did he buy the team, he bought it for way over asking price." He shakes his head. "It's not even that great of a team." My uncle looks at me. "I mean, you're the best on the team, but if you wanted to buy a hockey team, you should have called me. You ran a check on me three weeks ago, surely you had my number. You knew exactly what I did and who I did it for. You must have known I owned not only the New York team but we are also looking to branch out to the West Coast." Casey now just looks at my uncle, his eyebrows going up. "You aren't the only one who does the computer stuff."

"Stefano Markos," Casey says of my cousin, "I knew he would catch the trail."

"What is all this?" my father asks and I look over at him. "My son made a mistake. A mistake a kid makes and he knows he's made a mistake. He's admitted he made a mistake and now you want to come in here and what, ruin him?" His voice goes tight at the end.

"No," Reed says quickly, trying to sugarcoat things, "of course not."

"That isn't what we are hearing," he says. "People fuck up, trust me, I know. I was one of them. But in life it's about getting the chance to make your wrongs right." He looks at me. "You aren't going anywhere, you hear me? Nowhere."

"I've heard enough," Sofia declares. "Excuse me." She walks toward the stairs and goes up them.

She walks into her room, and I look over at her father and her grandfather. "Are you happy now?" I look at the two men who are just standing there. Reed looks like he's in shock, Casey looks like he's about to wring someone's neck, most likely mine. "I never wanted it to be like this," I tell them. "I love her with everything I have, but I'm not going to stand here and let you hurt her. I'll take her away from it all before I let that happen." I look over at my father. "I'm going to go and make sure she's okay."

I'm about to walk up the stairs when I see her walking back down the stairs with a bag in her hand. "Where is she going?" My mother gets up to go to her. "Sofia."

She doesn't say anything to anyone, she just walks to the door, grabs her purse, and then comes back and puts down the key on the counter. "Here is the key to the house." She looks at her father and then her grandfather. "I don't need it anymore."

She then walks to me with the biggest tears in her eyes, and all I can do is hold my arms out to her. "Thank you for coming and meeting me." She turns to talk to my side of the family. "I'm sorry about all this, I hope you guys won't hold this against me," she says as she wipes tears away from her eyes. "Can we go?"

"Anywhere," I tell her. "We can go anywhere."

"Okay, stop," Casey snaps, his voice going loud. "Why don't we all take a second?"

"No," Sofia states, "you had a second. You had more than a second."

"You have to see I was only doing it for you," Casey tells her. "I would do anything for you."

"No, you wouldn't," Sofia counters stubbornly, "because if you would, you wouldn't have tried to go behind everyone's back and try to ruin his career."

"I can't ruin his career," Casey says, "I can't even skate."

"You better do better than that." Olivia folds her arms over her chest.

"Okay, fine." He holds up his hands. "I'm sorry."

"For?" Sofia asks and I know she's getting her way. She did this whole thing to trick him. "I'm sorry for being a donkey? I'm sorry for acting like a crazy person in front of strangers? I'm sorry for buying a hockey team, even if you have no idea what the rules are?"

"Pfft," Casey retorts, "I know the rules."

Sofia stands straight. "How many innings?"

"Periods," my uncle mumbles to him, trying to help him. "Three."

"Three," Casey says, "and they are called periods. But yes, all that. I promise I will try for real to get to know him and I promise I won't interfere with his contract."

"And the house we buy?" Sofia counters.

"Say no." My uncle puts his hand in front of his mouth.

"We could all go see the house together," my mom suggests. "I have four listings tomorrow."

"I leave in the afternoon," I say and then look over at Casey. "But if you want, we can look at some today." I kiss Sofia's head. "I meant what I said, I'll do whatever makes her happy. I know you make her happy, so I'll work with you."

"Can we all agree to call a truce?" Reed says, letting out a huge sigh.

"We can all agree," Casey replies, looking at my uncle Matthew. "Got to say." He smirks. "It was good sparring with you. You should come down to the farm. I can teach you how to shoot."

"You should come by my hockey arena. I can teach you to skate," my uncle fires back, laughing. "Bought a hockey team." He shakes his head. "Good move."

"I need a drink," Olivia states. "Let's have some sweet tea."

"Oh, I like tea," my aunt Zara says.

The girls all get up and I see the men are all talking to each other. "Well." I look down at Sofia. "Nice play with the bag, is it empty?"

She looks up at me and I see her smirk. "Of course it is, you thought I could pack a bag in three minutes?"

I throw my head back and laugh. "You were always mine," I tell her, "and now I'm taking you." I kiss her lips and wrap my arms around her.

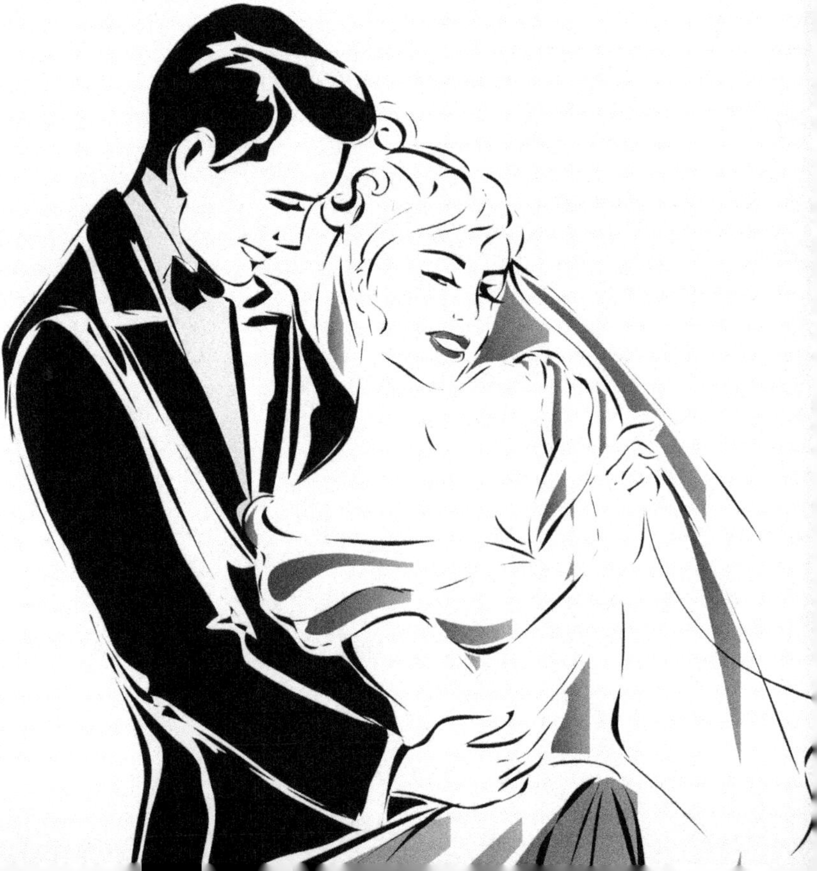

Epilogue One

Matthew

Nine Months Later

"You really think this is a good idea?" Sofia asks as I walk out of the bathroom. Running my hands through my wet hair, I look over to her standing in front of the full-length mirror. She is wearing blue shorts and a white tank top. Her skin looks like the sun just kissed it and I know the tan is from spending the last four days riding her horse.

"Absolutely not." I shake my head. "There is not one thing I think is good about my family, and by my family I mean the whole circus, meeting your family." I walk toward her as I bend down and kiss her lips. "When did you think I thought this was a good idea?" I then kiss her bare shoulder as she just looks at me in the mirror. "I think I even shook my head while you were talking about this at Christmastime." From the time we had the showdown with her family, we've never been apart, well, except for when I've been on the road.

"I was drunk," she huffs at me, "and nervous about meeting everyone. How was I supposed to know that Matthew senior would have called my grandfather? They were talking about the huge family vacation. Do you think it dawned on me that he would get so excited about our family reunion, he would think it was a good idea to be included?" I can't help but laugh at her as she glares at me.

"I told you those two together was not a good idea, and then you throw in my uncle Max and it's a recipe for disaster." I put my hands on her hips, standing behind her. "You had to have known. Fuck, everyone now owns a horse. I can't even picture them riding a horse. My father sent me a horse's picture the other day, asking me if it was a good breed. It's like Autotrader but for horses."

The doorbell rings and we both look at each other. I kiss her once more on the neck before walking out and to the front door. The top half of the door is all glass, something we are going to have to change for the next time. Yesterday, I walked out in my boxers and her cousin was looking into the window. Today, it's my father's turn. "It's my father," I say over my shoulder toward the bedroom area.

I unlock the door, something apparently they don't

do here because, well, they know everyone, and besides, who is going to break into your house? "Hi," I greet when I open the door and my father steps in, hugging me with one hand before kissing my head, just like he did when I was a kid.

"Hey," he replies, looking around, "is the coast clear?"

"She's in the bedroom." My voice is low as I look to make sure she isn't nearby. "Is everything okay?"

"Everything is set up," he confirms and then smiles over my shoulder. "Hi," he says, and I look over to see Sofia walking into the room. She comes over and gives my dad a hug and a kiss on the cheek.

"You ready?" he asks, and she nods her head.

"As ready as I'll ever be, I guess," she grumbles as she grabs her phone and puts it in her pocket. We walk out into the glorious sunny day, her hand slipping into mine. "This is going to be so much fun," she says sarcastically and even my father laughs.

"Where is Zoe?" Sofia asks.

"She was with your mother and aunts this morning. They were showing the girls how to bake something, but then I think I heard there was some sweet tea involved." He shrugs. "So no one eat those cookies."

We all laugh as I open the back door of the truck for Sofia to get into it. I step in and kiss her before I close the door and hop into the front passenger side. My foot moves up and down with nerves, today is a big day in more ways than I can put into words. When we are close to her grandparents' farm, I spot what seems to be over a hundred cars. "Holy shit," Sofia squeaks from the back.

I glance at what she is looking at and see that my uncles Matthew and Max are riding horses with Casey and Reed. "Why aren't they using a saddle?" she asks and my father laughs.

"It's not manly enough." My father looks back at her. "When your father got on the horse by grabbing onto its mane, well, Matthew tried and almost kicked himself in the face. Max fell on his ass. It took over ten minutes to finally get on the horse."

My father stops the car next to the four men and I press the button to open the window. "Hey," I say, giving them the chin up. "What are you doing?"

"We're barebacking," Max states, and I cringe.

"Never say that again." I shake my head.

"You know, your balls are going to be in your throat." My father leans over me to tell them.

"We are fine," Matthew says, wincing, "go away."

My father pulls over and parks the truck. I get out and look over to see the four of them trotting somewhere in the distance, and I wonder if they have everything set. "What's wrong with you?" Sofia asks as she comes over to stand next to me. I look at her. "You look like you are going to throw up and then someone is going to kick you in the balls."

"It's the other way around," my father jokes, slapping my shoulder, "first you kick him in the balls and then he throws up."

"I'm fine," I lie to her. I'm not fine. I'm the opposite of fine. I feel like I'm going to throw up, and I am not sure how much longer I can hold off without either vomiting or spilling the secret.

"We need to get you some smelling salts," my father mumbles to me as he walks ahead of me toward her grandparents' house. I've been here before on a Sunday, and if I thought my family Sunday dinners were loud and crazy, I have to give it to Sofia's family. Everyone is here, every single time. Kids run around in the distance, the older kids riding horses and racing. The adults sit around, scattered throughout the big backyard at the round wooden tables. Her grandparents sit at one, just looking out at everything they've got.

When I walk into the yard, it's the same, except this time the people are double as I look over and see my aunts sitting with Sofia's aunts, the whole table of women laughing at something. My uncle Evan and Justin stand behind them as they just shake their heads.

"Go say hello to Charlotte and Billy." My father nudges me toward the table where Billy and Charlotte sit, but this time they are with my grandparents.

"There they are," my grandfather Cooper says, getting up and walking over to us. He opens his arms for me, and I give him a hug. "You get more beautiful every time," he declares, looking over at Sofia and hugging her as well.

"Takes after my wife," Billy states, getting up followed by Charlotte and my grandmother.

Sofia goes over to her grandfather and hugs him, then kisses her grandmother. "Hi." She smiles at my grandmother and hugs her. "Are you having a good time?" she asks and my grandmother laughs.

"We were sitting down, explaining the family tree to them," she says. "It's a lot of people."

I look around and slip my hand in Sofia's. "Let's go for a walk," I suggest, and she just smiles up at me.

"Have fun," our grandparents say at the same time and then laugh.

"What's going on with the aunts?" I ask over my shoulder.

"They got into the special sweet tea that Billy saves for the men," Charlotte explains.

"You should have been here twenty minutes ago. They were all rolling on the lawn," my grandmother says, laughing.

"Should we say hello to everyone?" Sofia asks. We look over and see my cousins with my aunts, and they are taking sips of a glass and passing it around. "I say no."

I just laugh. "Can you take me to the creek?" I ask and she smiles at me.

"You are obsessed with that creek," she remarks, and I'm not really obsessed with it.

"I'm obsessed with the way your eyes light up when you are near it," I fill her in as we walk past the barn, "and the way you smile so contently that you let out a little sigh." She smiles over at me.

We walk through the trees, the sound of twigs snapping under our feet as we walk through the dense trees. The sun is kept out and you can hear every single bird chirping in the distance. "Isn't it peaceful," Sofia observes and all I can do is nod my head.

"What in the world?" Sofia says as she stops walking. I look up and see there are trees that have twinkle lights wrapped around them. "What is this?" She moves her feet slowly as she makes it to the clearing and sees a lot of twinkle lights are all over the trees.

I stand in the middle of the clearing as she turns in a circle and takes in all the lights. "Do you think they did this for your family?" she asks as she turns to face me.

The minute her eyes meet mine, I bend to one knee. "Sofia," I say, and she gasps and puts both hands over her mouth.

"What is going on?" She takes a step back.

All I can do is smile at her. "From the moment I laid eyes on you." I tilt my head to the side. "I knew two seconds later I had to know who you were." She laughs at that little joke.

"Matthew." She says my name between tears and a beaming smile.

"Marry me." I close my eyes. "After all the ways I practiced asking you this, the only two words I can remember are those two." I shake my head. "When I was getting ready to propose to you, I went to my father and told him. He came with me to ask your father for your hand in marriage."

"Oh my," she says, her laughter filling the forest.

"Yeah, well, he said no." I shake my head, thinking of when he snapped out no, but then Hazel came into the room, and he changed his mind. "Luckily for him, I was going to do it no matter what he said." I take out the black box from my pocket. "When it was time to pick your ring, well, everyone showed up. There was some back-and-forth and it was a nightmare, but all I wanted was to tell you when I got home. All I wanted to do was slip it on your hand and ask you to be mine forever. All I ever want is for you to be mine." I smile up at her. "Sofia, you have made my dreams come true by giving me another chance. You have shown me what true love really means. You have shown me what it feels like to be loved unconditionally. I want to have babies with you. I want to ride horses with you. I want to hold your hand when you are happy and raise you up when you are sad. I want it all, Sofia, and I want it with no one but you." I open the box and she gasps. "So what do you say, Sofia? Will you marry me and make me the happiest man in the world?"

She doesn't answer because she's too busy charging at me and wrapping her arms around my neck. The ring box flies out of my hand as I make sure she doesn't fall to the side, but in doing so I watch the ring literally fly through the air. "Oh my God!" Sofia shrieks.

"The ring!" she yells, and I hear voices now.

"He had one job," I hear Reed say from the forest.

"She charged him." I hear my father now. "Was he supposed to let her fall?" I shake my head and look over at the box and the ring that is right next to it.

"He found it, you see," my father states.

"This was supposed to be just the two of us," I tell her, and all she does is smile at me.

"I wouldn't want it any other way," she replies, holding my face and kissing my lips.

"Should we go and congratulate them now?" I hear my uncle Max say.

"She didn't say yes yet," Casey growls. "She can still say no."

"She isn't going to say no," my uncle Matthew pffts out. "She's kissing him."

"I'm not saying no!" Sofia now yells over her shoulder. "I will never, ever say no."

"Is that a fact?" I ask, and I just smirk. "So if I said, let's get married today?"

"He did not," Reed groans. "Did he just—"

"Matthew," she says, and I hold up my hand.

"What if I said I took care of everything and all you have to do is choose the dress?" I look at her, seeing the shock in her eyes.

"How—how did you do all this?" she asks, and I hear laughing.

"How do you think he did?" She looks over my shoulder and there they are, the women who have made all this happen: Shelby, Clarabella, Presley, and Addison.

"So what do you say?" I ask again. "Want to get married?"

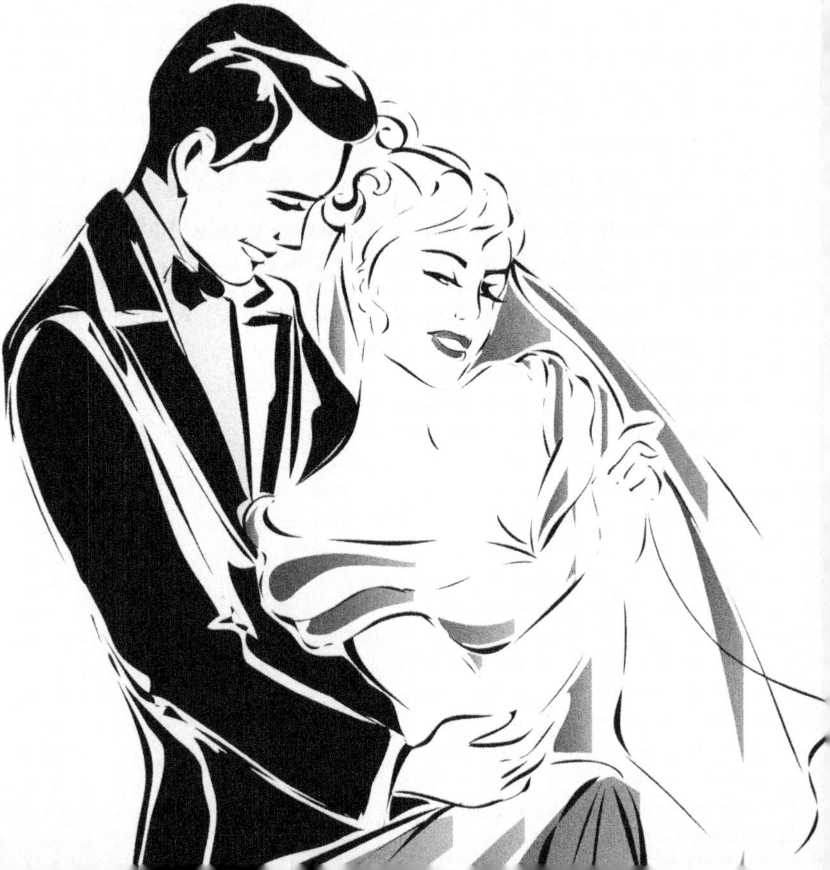

Epilogue Two

Sofia

I'm in too much shock to say anything. I look over to the girls standing at the side. "You didn't think we would miss this, did you?" Clarabella asks, shaking her head.

"We would have killed him if he did this without us," Presley declares, smiling.

"So are we doing this?" Shelby smirks at me. "Are we getting married?" She tilts her head to the side. "Today?"

I don't know what comes over me. I don't know if it's the heat or the fact both our families are together or the fact that all I want is to be his wife. "Yes."

The girls all cheer on the side and the line of men all groan. "Okay, people." Shelby claps her hands. "We have things to do."

I look over and see my grandfather put his hands on his hips. "I thought we did everything we had to do?"

"You." Clarabella comes to me. "Congratulations, but this is no time to celebrate." She puts her hand around my arm. "It's time to get you dressed and drunk."

"Um," Matthew says, "does she need the ring?" He holds up the ring he crawled around for right after I tackled him.

"She does," Addison confirms, smiling at him. "Go put it on her." She claps her hands so happily. In the last nine months Addison has excelled more than I can ever say. She has surpassed just answering phones. Little does she know, next month, Shelby is taking a little step back and she is going to be given her first ever client, and I couldn't be happier for her.

"Sofia," Matthew says, picking up my hand. "Will you marry me?"

"We don't have time for this," Presley states. "She already said yes, just slip it on her. The girls are waiting."

"Well, we are trying to sober them up but most of them are really excited," Clarabella explains. "Your grandmother is losing her mind with all the dresses Zara was able to get. She even bowed down to her and then fell." My grandfather takes a step forward. "She's fine." Then she mumbles, "Nothing a little makeup can't hide.

"We have her," Clarabella says, looking at Addison who just nods her head. "You two." She points at Shelby and Presley. "Gather the men."

"Gather the men," Uncle Matthew says. "What the fuck does that mean?"

"I think it means if you try to run, she's going to," Max tries to say without laughing but can't stop, "lasso you."

"Dibs," my grandfather calls, folding his hands over his chest as Uncle Matthew glares at him.

Clarabella grabs my hand and pulls me toward a golf cart I didn't even see. "Get in."

"Where are we going?" I ask them, and they just smirk at me. I look down at the square diamond ring on my finger and I can't help the tears that form.

"Oh my God," I say when I see where we are headed. "Great-grandpa Kaine's barn." I see my pink tractor outside, with cans at the back of it with a huge Just Married sign.

The barn was falling down when we moved here but was redone a couple of years ago. It was made three times as big as it was before, and it was used to house all the farm equipment. "Fun fact," I share, getting out of the golf cart, "I was conceived in this barn."

"Well, it's full circle now," Clarabella says. "Do you want to see the reception space, or do you want to go and do the dresses?"

I take a deep breath. "Please, I trust you guys with my life," I declare. "Take me to the dresses."

"Yay!" Addison cheers, clapping again. "I'm so excited, we all have bets," she says as they take me to the side of the barn that is used for office spaces. The minute we get close enough, I hear the laughter and squealing.

"She's here!" I hear my mother shout out and then the door opens. "Did she say yes?" She fumbles out her words.

"I said yes." I hold up my hand and then my grandmother stumbles out followed by Zoe, who blinks so fast all she can do is laugh. "When does this buzz go away?" she asks my grandmother, who just howls with laughter.

"How much did you drink?" I ask when I get close enough.

"Just a smidgen," my mother replies, holding up five fingers.

"It's going to be fine." Clarabella must see the frantic look I have on my face. "The only ones who need to be sober for this are Presley and Shelby."

"What?" Addison gasps.

"They have the men who are going to be putting the finishing touches on the ceremony space," Clarabella informs Addison. "All we have to do is make sure no one's boobs are falling out and all private areas aren't showing."

"Can we pick a dress?" Zara says, sticking her head out of the office.

"Yes, let's," I agree, walking in and stopping in my tracks. What was an office is now filled with twenty mirrors all around the four walls, with tables of makeup in front of them and antique chairs. In the middle of the room are small round tables with benches so people can sit. "This is…" I look up at the elegant chandelier hanging there.

"This is nothing," Addison states, pointing at the door. "You should see in there."

"Now," Clarabella says, "we got everyone's measurements and we thought it would be nice to do a soft lilac-colored dress for the wedding party." I put my hands to my mouth because just three months ago I said that is what I wanted. "Zara pulled out all the stops."

I don't even have a chance to say anything more because my cousins come crashing in, along with his. "Well, needless to say, she got dresses for every person in a variety of colors." We walk into the room, and I swear it's like going to a bridal shop, except it's in my barn.

"But for you," Zara says, coming over, "for you, your mother and grandmother made the call." She walks over to me. "But if you don't like it, I have a backup plan."

"Of course you do," I say and then look over to the rack where my dress hangs. It's the most beautiful dress I've ever seen in my life. My hands pick up one of the delicate sleeves, going over the little embroidered flowers. They are all over the dress, little flowers and leaves everywhere with a skin-colored slip right under the whole dress.

The back is all open. "If you don't like it," my mother says, "there is another one."

"No." I shake my head. "This is perfect." I smile at her, and I don't have anything else to say because I'm taken and put down in a chair, while the makeup people are doing my face and someone comes to do my hair. I can't even tell you how many people are in the room, but it looks like there are about a hundred women.

"You look beautiful," Zoe compliments, drinking a

cup of coffee. "He's so happy," she says. "Thank you for loving him like you do." She uses her thumb to wipe away the tears.

I'm about to say something when I hear a commotion coming from outside and then what sounds like four shots fired. "What is going on?"

Addison rushes in panting. "Everything is fine," she assures me, trying to push her hair to the side. "The men were thinking of maybe saluting you guys by shooting off guns and one sort of misfired." She forces a smile on her face. "No one is hurt."

I laugh at her at the same time someone knocks at the door. "Can I come in?" a male voice says as he sticks his head in. "I come with gifts," he says, and I stand and look at Stefano, who is Matthew's cousin.

He's six foot four with black hair and green eyes. He's wearing tan pants with a white shirt and a tan vest, and I have to wonder if he's part of the bridal party. I don't even have a chance to say anything when I hear Addison next to me gasp.

Stefano's eyes go from me and then to Addison. "Oh my God," I hear Addison say as she puts her hand to her mouth. "It's you."

The color on Stefano's face drains and he looks like he's seen a ghost. "You," he says in a whisper. My head goes back and forth to him and then to her. No one else in the room realizes what is going on. I'm about to ask them if they know each other when I hear Avery shriek.

"Momma, Momma," she says, looking up at her, "I get to wear a princess dress." She turns around in a circle on one foot stumbling while she looks at me and it's then my mouth hits the floor.

"Oh my God," Stefano says, putting his hand to his mouth.

"Stefano." I hear someone call him, and turning I see a woman coming into the room. "Baby, where did you go?" she says, slipping her hand through his. "Who do we have here?"

THE END

Dearest Love,

Oh my God. Who saw that coming?
I can tell you that I did not.
Addison has come face-to-face with her baby daddy.
It was a moment she's always dreamed of.
What she didn't dream of is coming face-to-face with him and his girlfriend.
What is he going to say when he finds out he's a dad?
What is she going to do when they have to co-parent?
Will he end up marrying his girlfriend?
Will she plan his wedding for them?
Only time will tell.

XOXO
Love, NM

Printed in Dunstable, United Kingdom

68738531R00188